The
yuletide Brides

A Collection of Four Holiday Novellas

GLYNNIS CAMPBELL

THE YULETIDE BRIDES
Compilation copyright © 2020 by Glynnis Campbell
A Yuletide Kiss © 2017 by Glynnis Campbell
A Rivenloch Christmas © 2018 by Glynnis Campbell
The Handfasting © 2015 by Glynnis Campbell
The Stowaway © 2019 by Glynnis Campbell

Cover design by Richard Campbell
Formatting by Author E.M.S.

Glynnis Campbell – Publisher
P.O. Box 341144
Arleta, California 91331

ISBN-13: 978-1-63480-143-0
Contact: glynnis@glynnis.net

Published in the United States of America

Yuletide Brides...

*A very special collection of four holiday novellas set
in the world of historical Scotland, spanning the centuries
with yuletide cheer and heartwarming romance.
Stories to snuggle up with on a cold winter's night!*

A YULETIDE KISS
(A Warrior Maids of Rivenloch novella)
A half-Viking shieldmaiden has until Yuletide to choose
a bridegroom...or one will be chosen for her.

A RIVENLOCH CHRISTMAS
(A Warrior Daughters of Rivenloch tale)
A medieval clan reunion turns into a desperate search
for three missing lasses as impetuous and daring
as their warrior mothers.

THE HANDFASTING
(A Knights of de Ware novella)
A French knight betrothed to a Highland heiress falls in love
with his spirited bride, then realizes he's been tricked into
wedding the wrong sister.

THE STOWAWAY
(A California Legends novella)
A notorious Scottish rake, scuttled aboard a ship bound
for America, has to rely on a spirited young botanist
to restore his good name.

OTHER BOOKS BY
GLYNNIS CAMPBELL

THE WARRIOR MAIDS OF RIVENLOCH
The Shipwreck (novella)
A Yuletide Kiss (short story)
Lady Danger
Captive Heart
Knight's Prize

THE WARRIOR DAUGHTERS OF RIVENLOCH
The Storming (novella)
A Rivenloch Christmas (short story)
Bride of Fire
Bride of Ice
Bride of Mist

THE KNIGHTS OF DE WARE
The Handfasting (novella)
My Champion
My Warrior
My Hero

MEDIEVAL OUTLAWS
The Reiver (novella)
Danger's Kiss
Passion's Exile
Desire's Ransom

THE SCOTTISH LASSES
The Outcast (novella)
MacFarland's Lass
MacAdam's Lass
MacKenzie's Lass

THE CALIFORNIA LEGENDS
The Stowaway (novella)
Native Gold
Native Wolf
Native Hawk

CONTENTS

A Yuletide Kiss

A Warrior Maids of Rivenloch Prequel Novella

A half-Viking shieldmaiden has until Yuletide to choose a bridegroom...or one will be chosen for her.

A YULETIDE KISS

LATE NINTH CENTURY PICTLAND

On his eleventh pass across the upstairs room of the alehouse, Brude MeqqUvan cursed softly and pounded the side of his fist against the plaster wall. The impact rattled the cup of ale on the table beside him. He caught it before it could spill. Then he took a bracing swig of the bitter brew and set it back down.

This was all a mistake.

He should never have listened to his brothers.

It was Taran who had wrung the drunken confession from him last night in the first place.

Then Drest had convinced him of the merits of never going into battle unprepared.

And before Brude even had time to consider the wisdom of their proposition, Galan had made the arrangements this morn. He'd stopped at this questionable establishment to drop silver into the palm of the alewife, telling her he needed the best harlot she had for the deed.

Now, behind a closed door and still fully dressed, Brude

paced the oak planks, more anxious about the woman he was about to face than any warrior he'd ever battled.

He ran uneasy knuckles over his black-bearded chin, eyeing the bed with mistrust.

It was too short for him. His feet were going to hang off the end.

He scowled at the frame. He wondered if it was sturdy enough. He took hold of one of the four wooden posts and gave it a jiggle. It seemed well-built. But then he wasn't sure how energetic things might become.

The brown wool coverlet was threadbare. He supposed it didn't matter. He wasn't going to spend the night. Once the task was accomplished, he'd continue on to the keep at Rivenloch. And there he would meet the heiress he was to marry.

Like the ale, the thought of marriage left a bitter taste in his mouth. A wife seemed like an unwelcome burden for a warrior like him. The idea of a mewling, helpless lass standing in the way of his ambitions held no appeal.

He narrowed his eyes at the bed linens peeping out from beneath the coverlet. He hoped the pallet didn't harbor fleas.

Then he let out a heavy breath. He supposed his brothers were right. He would be wise to prepare for his husbandly duty. Before facing his betrothed, he should test his weapon— at least once.

He smirked in self-mockery.

The truth was, despite being seasoned in battle, Brude was yet untried in bed.

He was sure the soldiers he'd defeated over a lifetime of waging war would be astonished to know that.

Brude the Brutal was the most feared warrior in Pictland. His name was whispered to children to make them behave, bellowed in battle to frighten the enemy. It was the stuff of nightmares. Fierce and merciless, Brude fought with a vengeance born of wild barbarian blood.

Surely it should come as no surprise then that no woman had ever dared come close enough to speak to him, clasp his hand, or press her lips to his, much less come to his bed.

He supposed he could have forced himself on a woman somewhere along the way. But that seemed unmanly, like killing a child in battle. What victory was there in conquering a foe so obviously inferior?

He could have paid for the services of a harlot before now. But his mind and his body had always been preoccupied with more important things. He was too busy waging war, administering justice, and learning to lead the clan—which would be his responsibility when his father left this world—to think about trysting.

Indeed, if not for the need to unite the two kingdoms of MeqqUvan and Rivenloch, Brude might never have married. Hel, if not for his upcoming nuptials, he might well have gone to his grave a virgin.

After all, he reasoned, tussling between the covers with a maid couldn't possibly be as thrilling as crossing swords with a champion. No woman in soft sendal could compare to a skilled warrior in chainmail. Nothing could match the fire that surged in his blood when he vanquished a worthy opponent. And no maid's kiss could be as sweet as the taste of victory in war.

Something suddenly bumped the door, and Brude's heart leaped into his throat. His sword was halfway drawn before he remembered this was not the battlefield.

The laughter outside indicated a couple passing by. He sheathed his sword and sank onto the bed on unsteady legs.

"Shite."

What was wrong with him? His heart was racing. His breath was shallow. Sweat slicked his brow. His jaw was clamped as tightly as a clamshell. He was more nervous, waiting for the harlot, than he'd ever been in combat.

What if the wench was old and withered? What if she had the pox? What if she laughed at his inexperience?

Or more likely, what if, once she laid eyes on him, she ran from the room, shrieking in fright?

Brude had never shied away from battle. But now he gazed morosely at the closed window, wondering if it was too late to throw open the shutters, drop onto the snow below, and escape into the winter morn.

Kimbery pulled the edges of her gray woolen hood across her face to hide the plumes of her warm breath on the cold air. She'd managed to slip the pursuit of her da's men, a pack of broad-shouldered Vikings who'd landed on her shores two decades ago and never left.

The Northmen had been heroes to a four-year-old lass with no father. They'd quickly adopted her—a half-Viking child of rape—as their own. But now that Kimbery was a grown woman, their ubiquitous presence was smothering.

It wouldn't be long before they discovered her tracks in the snow. She couldn't stay in the woods. Though her fury was fiery enough at the moment to keep her from feeling the biting frost, she had to find a way to escape—permanently.

She supposed the situation was her own fault. She simply hadn't believed her parents capable of such a calculating and coldhearted scheme.

When they'd said they expected Kimbery to find a husband before Yuletide, she'd taken it as a friendly suggestion.

Never had she imagined it was a threat.

Her mother, Avril, the head of the clan of Rivenloch, had decided it was time for twenty-five-year-old Kimbery to start a family.

Kimbery didn't see what the hurry was.

She realized, of course, that even though she had younger

brothers and sisters with babes of their own, the line of succession went through the firstborn women of the clan. Ultimately, it would be Kimbery's daughter who carried on the Rivenloch title.

But Kimbery figured she had plenty of time. After all, her parents were healthy and would rule for decades to come. Kimbery had many childbearing years left.

Besides, it wasn't like she could find a suitable husband at Rivenloch. She'd grown up as a shieldmaiden, sparring beside most of the eligible men. They were brothers-in-arms to her. She couldn't imagine kissing them, let alone wedding and bedding them.

Did her mother think Kimbery could just conjure a groom at will?

She supposed that shouldn't be surprising. After all, her mother's husband had literally washed up on the beach, like some gift from Aegir, the sea god.

But not everyone was as lucky in love as Avril and Brandr, her shipwrecked Viking, the man Kimbery had called Da from the very beginning.

And now, just this morn, the day before Yuletide, Kimbery's parents had given her a very unwelcome gift. Avril had announced that, since Kimbery had failed to procure a husband in the allotted time, they'd sent for one.

Kimbery had naturally flown into a rage, demanding they send him back.

Brandr had said it was too late, that the betrothal had been arranged and that her husband was already on his way.

She was shocked by their callousness. For over twenty years, she'd been allowed to live freely here as the daughter of the laird. She'd slept in a Rivenloch bed, supped at a Rivenloch table, fought with the Rivenloch forces. How could her parents oust her from her idyllic life and into a marriage she didn't want?

They couldn't, she decided. Kimbery was nothing if not headstrong. She refused to be backed into a corner. Let her bridegroom come then. She'd make his life so unbearable, he'd beg to be released from the betrothal.

Then her da had revealed the name of her husband-to-be, and the blood had drained from her face.

He was the most feared villain in Pictland. A dark, massive warrior with barbarian blood, he was considered more beast than man. One glare from his black eyes could chill bones. One curse from his twisted lips could damn a person's soul to Hel.

It was said he'd butchered a fearsome giant with his great blade, singlehandedly slaughtered an entire company of Romans, and slain a rabid wolf with his bare hands.

How could her own parents have chosen such a monster to be her husband?

Avril had made light of Kimbery's alarm. Brandr had insisted the rumors were unfounded. They seemed utterly oblivious to the danger they were putting her in.

Desperate to escape a horrific fate, Kimbery decided she would have to take drastic measures.

It wasn't yet Yuletide, she'd argued. There was still one day left for her to find a husband.

Of course, Avril and Brandr had laughed at that. Kimbery hadn't found a suitable groom in twenty-five years. What made her imagine she could find one in one day?

But the truth was she had no intention of finding a suitable groom. Or any groom, for that matter. She only told them that to buy time.

Meanwhile, with no real plan except to run away before her monstrous husband-to-be could arrive, Kimbery threw on her cloak, grabbed her dagger, and stole out of the keep into the forest.

Her parents must have expected her to flee. Not long after she began slogging through the snow, Kimbery had spied six of her da's best men following her. And now they had picked up her trail.

"Shite."

How could she lose them? Where could she go?

She bit the corner of her lip.

This far from Rivenloch, there was only one place close enough to seek refuge. About a mile up ahead, if she cut through the forest, stood a roadside alehouse. It was a place of ill repute. Aebbe Cambeul, the alewife there, employed a few maids of questionable virtue. She was known to supply men with more than ale.

It was the last place the Vikings would think to look for the respectable laird's daughter.

All Kimbery had to do was throw them off her scent.

She scoured the ground until she found a hefty rock and tested its weight in her palm. Then, waiting until the men were facing away, she hurled the rock as hard as she could in the direction she'd just come.

While they rushed to investigate the sound, she slipped silently onward through the trees, careful to cover her tracks.

By the time she emerged on the road, it was snowing again. Despite the icy air, she was breathless and sweaty from the exertion of running.

The disreputable thatched alehouse looked remarkably inviting. The golden glow of firelight leaked through the cracks in the shuttered windows of the lower level. And above the upper floor, thick white smoke curled from the chimney into the gray sky.

Kimbery hesitated. If anyone in the alehouse recognized her, they'd report her to her da's men. But chances were, on the day before Yule, the only people inside were travelers, strangers who had no idea who she was.

With a hasty glance over her shoulder, she hurried forward. Pulling her hood closer around her face to conceal the one feature that would surely give her away—her white-blonde hair—she pushed through the door.

Trying to remain as inconspicuous as possible, she quickly perused the room. A russet-haired youth warmed his hands by the peat fire. Three big, black-bearded men swapped stories at a table, guzzling ale and laughing loudly. Aebbe the alewife served buttered bread to a young couple with a babe in swaddling. Meanwhile, Modwenna, one of Aebbe's harlots, minced up the stairs.

Kimbery figured she'd follow Modwenna and hide in one of the upstairs chambers until she was sure her da's men hadn't spotted her.

She'd begun edging casually toward the steps and climbed three stairs when Aebbe suddenly called out, "Here, lass! Where are you going?"

Fearful the alewife would expose her identity, Kimbery scurried up five more steps.

The alehouse door opened with an abrupt bang under the power of a Viking arm. The sound distracted the alewife long enough for Kimbery to finish taking the stairs and slip out of sight.

Damn! How had the Northmen gotten here so soon?

There were four chambers along the upstairs hallway. Modwenna the harlot was rapping on the door to the third room. Hiding her face, Kimbery knocked at the first door. Nobody answered. When she tried the latch, it was locked.

From downstairs, she could hear the boom of demanding Viking voices. Modwenna frowned at the noise, then shrugged at Kimbery and lifted her hand to knock on the third door again.

Kimbery swiftly moved to the second chamber, pounding on the door. To her dismay, again there was no reply, and the door wouldn't open.

Now Modwenna was staring at her, puzzled. Just as the harlot lifted her hand to knock a third time, Kimbery heard heavy footfalls on the steps below. The Vikings were coming upstairs.

The harlot's knuckles were still touching the third chamber door when it was suddenly snatched open.

Thinking fast, Kimbery shoved the harlot aside and slipped through the crack of the door, barreling into the chamber and its occupant. She turned long enough to slam and latch the door.

"What the devil?" someone growled behind her.

"Shh!" she hissed, pressing her ear to the door and holding up a hand to silence the occupant.

They were coming. She recognized Axlan's bold voice, demanding to know where the laird's daughter was.

She could also hear a soft reply, probably Modwenna, telling them some wench had pushed her. But Kimbery was sure the harlot hadn't recognized her.

Behind her, the occupant of the room grumbled, "Is that my brother at the door?"

"Hush!" she bade him again.

"If it is, I'll speak to him," he stated, ignoring her command, "because if you're not here of your own accord..."

Exasperated, she turned to him with a scowl.

Her angry oath instantly dissolved on her tongue.

Before her was the most magnificent creature she'd ever seen. He was gigantic, more wide-shouldered and broad-chested than Axlan, her da's best warrior. Beneath the epaulets of his leather hauberk, she could see solid, well-muscled arms that strained the fabric of his brown woolen shirt. His thick hair and beard were as black as midnight. His mouth was grim. His jaw was resolute. His brows were furrowed, and beneath them, his eyes were as deep, dark, and unforgiving as the midnight sky.

Perfect, she thought. If anyone could protect her against a pack of Vikings, it was this beast.

When Brude finally mustered the courage to answer the knock at his chamber door, he was relieved. Whatever conflict was going on, it was a welcome distraction and a more familiar battleground.

But the way the harlot had burst in, as if chased by demons, made him think his brothers had forced the woman to do their bidding. And that he couldn't allow.

Then, when she turned and he saw her delicate features—her fair and beautiful face, framed by the soft gray of her hood, her wide and innocent blue eyes, her tender pink lips—he knew this had been a mistake.

Now that she'd laid eyes on him, she would surely run in horror from the room.

But she didn't.

In fact, after she'd given him a cursory glance from head to toe, as if she were sizing him up for a coat of chainmail, she gave him a fearless nod of approval.

For an instant he was stunned.

Then a loud banging against the door made her curse in surprise.

He clapped a hand to the hilt of his sword.

But before he could draw steel, the lass threw herself at him.

She was stronger than she looked. His shoulder blades hit the wall with a thud as she knocked him backward, clinging to his hauberk. He raised his hands defensively, not wishing to do her harm.

When another pounding broke the latch on the door, he expected his brothers to come charging in.

His first instinct was to protect the woman.

But he was prevented when she seized the back of his neck

and pulled his head down to hers, pressing her lips against him in a forceful and demanding kiss.

At first, he was too shocked to move. Her mouth felt soft and foreign, inviting and compelling. For an instant, nothing else seemed to matter.

But the commotion of the intruders crowding into the doorway finally won his attention. As he pulled away and peered over her hood, he saw several blond giants mixed in with his brothers. Vikings. Perhaps they wanted the beauty for themselves.

He glanced down at her hooded face, which she was keeping carefully concealed from the others. She looked up at him with beseeching blue eyes, wordlessly begging him not to give her to them.

At that moment, his brother Taran growled at the Vikings, "How dare you interrupt a man at his bed sport."

"Bed sport? *Bed* sport!" one of the Vikings exclaimed. "That is no harlot!"

Galan argued, "Indeed? Well, she took our coin readily enough!"

The lovely blue-eyed maid suddenly hissed a whisper at Brude, "Kiss me!"

A second blond warrior crossed his arms over his chest. "If she's a harlot, I'll eat my helm."

"If she *isn't* a harlot," Galan said, standing nose-to-nose with the Viking, *"I'll* eat your helm, and I'll take my coin back."

The lass in his arms skewered Brude with a poisonous glare and bit out words in a harsh whisper. "Kiss. Me."

She wasn't the first woman to look at him with such viciousness. He was used to hateful leers. The few women who weren't terrified of him despised him.

What he wasn't prepared for was the sharp point of the woman's dagger pressing against his ballocks.

Needing no more convincing, he lowered his head and gave her what she demanded. She withdrew the dagger.

Somewhere, distantly, as he reveled in the sensual pleasure of her kiss, he heard the Vikings deciding they'd made a mistake, that she couldn't possibly be the woman they sought after all.

But Brude scarcely noticed when they closed the door. Nothing could distract him from the intriguing sensation of the woman's yielding mouth, the fresh fragrance of her skin, the warm caress of her gentle breath on his face.

Kimbery meant to end the kiss as soon as she heard the door close.

She just never heard it close.

Instead, a hot and sultry wind rushed through her ears, swirling around her head, blocking out all other sound, blowing through her soul with devastating force.

The kiss went on and on—gentle, searching, sweet. The warmth of his flesh thawed her winter-chilled face. The masculine rasp of his beard against her skin excited her. The unexpected suppleness of his lips made her ache with tenderness. It felt like she'd waited all her life for this.

Her head spun.

Her breath quickened.

Her heart melted.

Then the dagger dropped from her limp fingers and hit the floor.

The sound split them apart faster than an axe.

She staggered back, blinking as if awakening from a dream.

The man looked just as astounded. There were still stern creases in his forehead, but the dark fire in his eyes had softened to smoldering coals. His jaw, unyielding before, was now relaxed, and his mouth—his delicious, warm, supple mouth—was open in wonder.

14

Flustered, she averted her gaze.

He bent down slowly, intending to retrieve her dagger.

Panicked that he might confiscate it, she dove for the weapon and rose, brandishing it before her.

Backed against the wall, he had nowhere to go.

She licked her lips. Now what was she going to do?

For a long while they only stared at each other. Finally, he narrowed his gaze at her, drilling into her with his night-black eyes.

"You're not a harlot, are you?" he asked.

She stared back at him, working out the best reply.

If she said nay, he'd call the Vikings back and turn her over to them.

If she said aye, he might be more willing to assist in her escape. Of course, saying aye also came with the risk of certain entitlements he might expect.

On the other hand, how much could he do while she held a dagger on him?

"Aye, of course I am," she said, challenging him with a lift of her chin.

"You're here of your own free will?"

"Aye."

"And you were paid?"

"That's right," she said. At least, she thought that was right. That was how it was usually done, she assumed. A harlot would be paid before she... Kimbery gulped.

"Then why are you holding a dagger on me?" he asked.

That was a good question. She racked her brain for an answer until her gaze landed on his blade. Arching her brow, she asked, "Why are *you* still wearing your sword?"

Brude supposed that was a reasonable enough question, though none of this encounter seemed to be what he'd expected.

What was the woman hiding?

Why had that retinue of Northmen stormed the door?

And what kind of harlot brought a dagger to a tryst?

Since he knew better than to startle an armed woman, he unbuckled his sword belt with care. She had to realize, however, that surrendering his blade made him no less dangerous. He could snap her slender neck in one hand.

Still, she showed no fear of him, which was rather disarming in itself. How curious it was to be alone with a woman who wasn't reviled by his size or intimidated by his scowl.

He wound the leather belt around his sheathed sword and propped it in the corner.

When he turned back, showing her his empty hands, she bit her lip, looking uneasy. Her fingers flexed around the hilt of the dagger. She was obviously not so willing to relinquish her own weapon.

"Do you think they're gone?" she asked.

He nodded. He'd heard the pounding of their steps down the stairs. At least, he *thought* he'd heard it. After that world-shattering kiss, it might have been the pounding of his heart.

There was a sudden sharp rap on the door, and she gasped, turning toward the sound with weapon raised.

Through the door, he heard a muffled female voice. "Let me in."

"Shite," the dagger-wielding lass muttered. "Modwenna."

After a moment, there was another knock, and the woman outside spoke again. "I don't know who you are, Miss, but you've got the wrong chamber."

Brude frowned. What the devil was going on?

The lass turned back to him. She narrowed her silver-blue eyes, quickly assessing him again from head to toe. Then she motioned him forward with her dagger. "You answer the door. Tell her to leave."

He growled. He didn't much like a wee wench with a dagger ordering him about. But he did want to find out what was afoot.

Keeping an eye on the lass and moving slowly so she wouldn't stab him by accident, he crossed the room. She pulled her hood closer around her face. When he cracked open the door, she moved to hide behind it.

The short, brown-haired maid at the door opened her mouth to say something and froze. She stood with her mouth agape as her eyes moved slowly upward from the middle of his chest to meet his gaze, then went round with horror.

"I...I...I..." She gulped. "Nay. Nay, my mistake." She blinked and scuttled backwards, calling into the room, "He's...he's all yours, Miss."

Brude smirked. That was more like it. *That* was the reaction his dark and stormy countenance usually got from women.

As the frightened wench scurried down the hall, he closed the door.

When he turned back, the blue-eyed lass in his chamber was smiling. *Smiling.* That never happened.

"Good," she said. "Now no one will trouble us for a while."

He hoped she was right. He might be new to this, but he was fairly certain it was preferable to have privacy for such things.

"What about your dagger?" he asked, nodding to the weapon still in her grip.

She looked uncertain. But in the end, she placed it on the table, beside his cup of ale. "May I?" She picked up the cup.

He nodded. Galan had bought Brude that ale to steady his nerves. But the harlot probably needed it more than he did.

She gave him a brief salute with the cup. When she tipped back the ale, her hood fell away, exposing the most beautiful, silky, pale blonde hair he'd ever seen. The maid must have Viking blood. Her long tresses, which flowed softly past her cheek and disappeared beneath her cloak, were caught at the sides of her brow in a few tiny braids. He had the sudden, absurd urge to fondle one of those braids, though he knew his clumsy fingers would probably tangle the delicate thing.

Then his heart sank as he realized this was never going to work. The lass was obviously far too fragile for the likes of him. She was no bigger than a kitten. He would crush her.

Just as he was mentally lamenting his brutishness and her frailty, she finished off the ale, set down the cup, and let out a loud belch.

He couldn't help but snicker in surprise.

She immediately covered her mouth in embarrassment, which made him chuckle more.

Then she leveled him with an irritated glare and gave him a spiteful shove, to little effect.

His laughter grew. Had the wee kitten actually shoved him?

She shoved him again, a little harder.

He looked at her, incredulous. Nobody shoved Brude the Brutal. It was the height of foolishness, like poking a wolf.

With a bemused grin, before she could make that mistake again, he captured the kitten's paws.

To Kimbery's consternation, her shove had scarcely budged the big oaf. And now he'd trapped her wrists. What had been only annoying a moment ago seemed suddenly threatening.

Her first instinct was to fight him. Snap her wrists down. Kick him hard between the legs. Smash her elbow into his chin. That was what Kimbery the Shieldmaiden would do.

But at the moment, he didn't know she was a shieldmaiden. To him, she was a harlot. And a harlot would do no such thing. Until she could be certain her da's men were far away, she had to keep up the ruse of being the wench he'd hired.

So she bit back her warrior urges and tried to imagine how

Modwenna would behave. With any luck, she'd figure out how to keep the man in a congenial mood while she worked out the next part of her escape.

Despite his shackle-firm grip, his eyes were dancing, which made him look a bit less menacing. He really was quite handsome—in a fierce and feral way—especially when he was smiling like that.

She lowered her gaze to his mouth and was instantly reminded of their kiss—their warm, lingering, languorous kiss. She wasn't sure what he'd done to her with that kiss, but she'd grown weak from it, almost as if he'd drunk every last drop of her will.

As she continued to gaze at him, his smile gradually faded, and his eyes lowered to her lips. His thumbs idly brushed the tender inside skin of her wrists, hypnotizing her with their caress.

She gulped. She dared not reveal the truth by resisting him. Yet she felt dangerously vulnerable, as if he dangled her at the edge of a very high cliff.

"May I kiss you again?" he breathed.

Her breath caught in her throat. She was hardly in a position to refuse him. He'd paid for her services after all. And to turn him down would rouse suspicion.

It was only a kiss, she reasoned. And there was something tender and endearing about a man who had her at his mercy asking permission for a kiss. She supposed one kiss would do no harm. She nodded.

His sigh touched her face like a balmy, welcome breeze. As he slanted his head, his beard tickled her cheek. When his lips met hers, the contact was faltering, uncertain.

She answered tentatively at first as well, keeping her wits about her, staying aloof, determined to maintain the upper hand.

It worked for a moment.

Then he began to move his lips over hers, tasting her, savoring her carefully, as if he were nibbling a handful of juicy, ripe blackberries.

His kiss was so curiously compelling that she was drawn to respond. Lightly, like a butterfly harvesting nectar, she began to sample his delicious mouth.

He released her wrists then, but only to capture her jaw. Cradling her head like a precious jewel between trembling hands, he explored her further—touching his tongue to the corners of her mouth, biting and sucking on her bottom lip.

She let him continue, telling herself she had to maintain the deception. But even she wasn't sure she believed that.

With a low, sensuous growl, he deepened the kiss. Again and again he brushed his eager lips over her yielding flesh. Finally, as if he were starving, he opened his mouth wide, feasting upon her.

Despite her best intentions, his fast-growing desperation set fire to her desires. Her blood steamed. Her breath quickened. Soon her nails gouged into the leather of his hauberk. She fed upon him with an unnatural, insatiable hunger, wanting and needing more.

He gave her more. When she parted her lips with a gasp, he slipped his tongue between them to taste her more fully. The instant his tongue touched hers, searing current raced through her veins, igniting her passion. Her head buzzed with sizzling energy. Every nerve came to life. While she gasped out in wordless longing, their tongues danced and battled and mated.

Beyond thought, she floated in a euphoric haze. Her hands moved with a will of their own, drifting up his chest, encircling his neck, drawing him closer. Beneath her cool fingers, his flesh was hot and inviting.

A quiet moan came unbidden from her lips. The sound of it, foreign to her ears, spurred her on to new levels of arousal.

He groaned in response. The savage rumble of his voice sent

a shiver up her spine, curving around her ears to awaken a primal hunger within her.

Brimming with mindless urgency, she clawed at him, snarling her fingers in his hair, unsure what she intended, but too overwrought to cease. Every inch of her longed to touch every inch of him. She smashed her bosom against his chest, relishing the hardness of his leather hauberk against her straining breasts.

And then his hands trailed down her back, making her arch in response, until they rested indecently low on her buttocks.

She thought she could be no more aroused.

She was wrong.

He coaxed her hips slowly forward with the pressure of his fingers until their bodies collided.

She gasped at the sensation of his iron-hard length against the aching bud of need between her legs.

Never had Brude felt anything so divine. He sucked a sharp breath of desire between his teeth as the woman ground her pliant body against the swelling in his trousers.

Whatever he was doing must have pleased her, for she clung to him with breathless passion, as if she never wished to part.

His brothers had said it would be like this—that the harlot would know what to do and that he need only follow his instincts. It seemed they were right. But now his instincts told him to remove all obstructions between them.

Impatient, yet unwilling to spend more than an instant away from her, he pulled away just long enough to unbuckle his hauberk. Then, still kissing her as frequently as possible, he tugged his hauberk free and cast it onto the floor.

Her eyes were glazed with longing as she followed his example, unpinning her cloak and throwing it onto the bed.

His breath caught. Her deep azure apron brought the blue

of her eyes to life. And the white linen kirtle underneath it perfectly draped her feminine curves, whetting his appetite for more.

Unfortunately, he knew very little about removing a woman's garments. He hesitated over the strands of amber and blue glass beads suspended between the twin silver brooches of her apron, unsure whether to unpin the brooches or simply slip it off her shoulders.

Thankfully, he didn't have to decide. As he gazed at her with hunger smoldering in his eyes, she let out a soft cry of need and unpinned the brooches herself.

Meanwhile, he swallowed hard and rummaged under his long woolen shirt, struggling with the belt holding up his trousers.

She shimmied out of her blue apron, casting it atop her discarded cloak.

He loosened the drawstring of his linen undergarments and pulled them down with his trousers, kicking them off.

Bending down, she pulled off her leather boots and the woolen stockings beneath.

He did likewise, stopping to bestow upon her a kiss full of feverish yearning.

She pulled away, licking her lips. Then she labored over the pin of her kirtle, wincing in dismay as she pierced her neck with the sharp point.

He frowned and unpinned it for her, peeling back the edge of her kirtle to kiss the tiny wound just below her throat.

Meanwhile, her fingers wrenched at his shirt as if she wished to tear it from his body.

Her eagerness pleased him. And yet he feared—unable to temper his need and stone-hard with desire—that he might hurt her.

The lass, frustrated by her ineffectual attempts at removing his shirt, turned back to her own clothing. She slipped the kirtle from her shoulders, pulled off the long sleeves, and dragged it down to her waist.

The sight of her bare breasts—so fair, so innocent, so perfect—drove his hunger to new heights. And when she tugged the dress down over her hips, letting it pool at her feet, his mouth went dry with lust.

She was beautiful—pale and delicate, yet with sleek strength. Tendrils of her moonlight-colored hair flowed down over her shoulders and teased at her breasts, concealing and then revealing the rosy peaks. The gentle curve of her waist was as graceful as a longboat. And lower, her lovely thatch of flax-gold curls looked curiously inviting.

He knew he should say something. He should say how much he wanted her. He should tell her she was beautiful. He should ask her permission to touch her.

But he couldn't seem to form words as he continued to feast his eyes on her angelic body and felt a devilish fire rise in his.

With a groan of lust, he removed his linen shirt, the last obstacle between them.

He'd imagined it was impossible for his desire to grow.

He was wrong. This time when they came together in a kiss, the ecstasy of her pillowy breasts colliding with his chest and her warm abdomen pressing against his raging arousal left him drunk with longing.

Driven by impulse alone, he caressed the silk-smooth globes of her buttocks and lifted her up, turning to brace her against the plaster wall. She cried out in passion, squeezing her eyes shut and digging her fingers into his shoulders.

If he wasn't quite certain how to proceed, he knew she'd guide him. In another moment, she'd sheathe his blade within her willing womb and grant him sweet relief.

Then, just as he was about to storm the gates of her heavenly fortress, she pushed at his shoulders and twisted aside.

"Nay!" she cried out on a gasp. "Nay! Stop!"

He heard her plea as if from a distance, and he was sorely tempted to ignore it.

But he was no beast.

It took all his will to comply, and his body cursed him as he pulled away and let her slide down the wall.

But the instant she staggered away, he snarled in rage and frustration and punched the wall, cracking the plaster this time.

He glanced over his shoulder, sure his outburst would scare her away.

It didn't.

"Go on!" he snapped. "Leave!"

"Nay! I can explain."

He shook his bruised knuckles. He needed no explanation. It was obvious she didn't wish to couple with him. He didn't want to hear the sordid details.

"There's no need," he grunted. "But I trust you'll return the coin my brother paid."

Kimbery heard the bitterness in his voice, and it saddened her.

"This is my fault," she admitted. "I should never have..." She sighed and sat on the bed, clutching her discarded kirtle modestly in front of her.

What she'd done was as reckless as mounting a wild horse. She should never have let him kiss her again. She definitely shouldn't have taken off her clothes.

But she hadn't wanted to stop. The pretense had rapidly taken on a life of its own. Lost in a fog of rapture, she'd wanted nothing more than to mate with this hulking, hungry, ferocious beast.

And until the moment she finally begged him to stop, she couldn't remember why that would *not* be a good idea. He obviously wanted her. And she definitely wanted him. Every inch of her burned with yearning, from her breasts, grazing with delicious friction against his chest, to the place between her thighs, throbbing in white-hot demand.

Only at the instant that he pinned her against the wall, preparing to lay siege to her body, did she finally remember just who she was.

She wasn't a common harlot, free to couple with whomever she wished.

She was Kimbery, daughter of Avril and Brandr, keeper of the title of Rivenloch, shieldmaiden and future laird of the clan. It was her responsibility to marry and give birth to the next generation of great warriors. She couldn't be trysting with every handsome stranger who passed by.

She'd had to force the words from her lips, for she knew they would bring an end to her joy. And she knew by the tension in his jaw that it cost all his self-control to stop. But he had stopped. And for that she was grateful. It saved her having to use her warrior skills to thwart him.

The fact that he'd punched the wall hadn't surprised her. She'd been raised with hot-tempered Vikings. She'd even put her own fist through a wall once or twice herself.

But now she had to explain, even if he didn't want to hear it. She started again. "I should never have misled you."

His chuckle was devoid of humor. He reached down to retrieve his shirt, using it to conceal his loins as he turned back to her. He was such a magnificent creature, she had a hard time focusing on what she meant to say next. And for one mad moment, she envisioned the next generation of great warriors she could make with such a man.

His scowl was colored with disappointment, anger, and something else—a sort of sad inevitability that said he should have expected as much.

She didn't mean to tell him everything. She only meant to say what was necessary so she could make a clean escape.

But when she saw the tiny glimmer of hurt in his eyes, she found she cared what he thought of her. She didn't want him to think that she didn't desire him. Nor did she want him to believe she'd intentionally seduced him, only to abandon him. And because she was born with more than her share of pride, she especially didn't want him to think she was leaving because she was afraid of him.

So she confessed.

"I'm not really a harlot. I'm..." She wouldn't tell him her name. That was too risky. But there was no reason to conceal the rest. "I'm a runaway bride. Those men you saw, they mean to drag me back and force me to marry a...a cruel and vicious man, a man with a violent temper and an iron fist." She stiffened her jaw. "But I won't do it. I won't let them sacrifice my maidenhood and leave me at the mercy of a monster, just because they need an heir to..." She stopped before she could blurt out too much.

"You're not a harlot?"

She furrowed her brows. Was that all he had heard? "Nay."

"You're a runaway bride?"

"Aye."

"And you're a virgin."

Her frown deepened. She didn't see how that was really his concern, especially since they weren't going to pursue any bed sport. Nonetheless, she answered him. "Aye."

The last thing she expected was for him to burst out laughing.

Disconcerted, she clutched her kirtle tighter. "It's not funny."

"Oh, aye, it is," he assured her, his black eyes dancing with humor.

He unfurled his long shirt and slipped it back on over his head.

If Kimbery stole one last pining glimpse, she couldn't be blamed. His was a splendid body. She thought she'd never again see a man so gloriously endowed.

26

Brude should have realized the woman was not a harlot. She was too lovely and fresh-faced to be a seasoned prostitute, no matter how seductive she seemed. What amusement Galan would get out of the fact that he'd somehow managed to match his untried brother with an untried maiden.

Of course, he understood now why she'd stopped him. A woman's maidenhood was not to be taken lightly. She was right to preserve it for the man she meant to wed.

To be honest, he was still impressed that she wasn't fleeing in fear. And since she was being candid with him, he was moved to be just as frank with her. Perhaps she would see the humor of it as well.

"We're quite a pair, you and I," he confessed in a murmur, sitting beside her on the bed. "You see, we're *both* virgins."

Astonished by his admission, she lowered her hands to her lap, inadvertently exposing her breasts—her lovely, tempting breasts. He ached, just looking at them.

His smoky gaze must have given him away. She lifted the kirtle back up and proceeded to try to slip back into it without exposing more skin.

Meanwhile, he tried to avert his eyes.

Neither of them was very successful.

"Since I'm soon to be wed," he continued, "my brothers thought it was time I was initiated. They didn't want me to be untried in battle when I bed my bride."

That coaxed a smirk out of her. "And you ended up with me?" She thought that over and had to admit, "That *is* funny."

"The blind leading the blind."

She smiled. Then her smile faded. "Oh. *Oh!*" Her kirtle in place, she stood and reached for her apron. "I should fetch Modwenna back then. After all, you've paid good coin and—"

He caught her wrist. "Don't bother. She won't come. I believe she fled in terror."

"What? Why?"

It made him smile that she even had to ask that. It wasn't that Brude was ugly. Or evil. He was just...imposing. With his large size, his dark features, and his black scowl, women found him menacing. *Most* women.

But if this woman didn't think so, he wasn't about to argue with her. So he shrugged.

She sat back down beside him. "So then how do you plan to...get your battle experience?"

"I guess I'll have to rely on my instincts." Then, with an openness that surprised him, he confessed, "Mostly I don't want to hurt my bride."

She nodded, then looked at her hands in her lap. "It's thoughtful of you, wanting to be a good husband."

Brude could see she was thinking about her own predicament. He plucked his linen under-trousers from the floor and began to put them on.

"What will you do?" he asked gently. It wasn't necessary to explain what he meant.

She swallowed, and for one moment, he glimpsed her uncertainty. Then she straightened proudly and said, "I'm not going to marry a monster. That's for certain. They cannot make me."

Brude would disagree. That pack of Vikings looked more than capable of making the wee lass do whatever they wished. He pulled his under-trousers over his hips and tied them, then reached for his woolen trews.

"You can't hide here forever," he pointed out.

Kimbery almost wished she *could* hide here forever.

But she wasn't thinking straight. She needed to get dressed and shake off the vestiges of desire that lingered with the alluring warrior so close. She could feel his warmth, smell the intoxicating scent of spice and smoke and leather that clung to him. The fires of lust were slow to die. She had to douse them quickly and plan her next move.

She put her apron on over her kirtle and picked up the silver brooches with their connecting beads.

"I wish I didn't have to wed," she said. It was the first time she'd admitted it aloud. It was a relief to be able to confide in a stranger. "I don't really want a husband."

"Why not?" he said, shoving his legs, one at a time, into his trousers.

She paused, thinking it over. "I was raised to be a shieldmaiden."

He cast a cursory glance at her, arching a dubious brow.

"I'm stronger than I look," she informed him as she pinned on the first brooch. "I was born with a shield on my arm and a blade in my hand. What do I know about keeping a house? Or pleasing a husband? Or bringing up children?"

Her fingers faltered on the second brooch as the truth hit her. She was afraid. It wasn't independence or stubbornness or even the prospect of wedding a notorious villain that had made her run away. It was fear of marriage itself.

"To be honest," he said, threading his belt through the loops of his trousers, "I don't want a wife either."

"Really?" Her brows went up. "Why not?"

"I'm a warrior as well. What need do I have of a companion? Give me a blade of strong steel and a wrong to right, and I'm content."

"Exactly!" she chimed in, adding dreamily, "There's nothing like the weight of a well-made sword or the battle cry of a well-trained army."

"The thunder of a charge," he mused.

"The clash of steel on steel."

"The boldness that fires the blood."

"The satisfaction of dodging a deadly blow."

"And *delivering* a deadly blow."

"Aye! And the taste of victory…" She sighed.

"It's as sweet as honey."

"Aye."

He understood her. Completely. Why did no one else?

The warrior drew his brows together and shook his head. "My proficiency lies on the battlefield, not in the bedchamber."

Kimbery would argue that. He might be inexperienced, but she had very much enjoyed his proficiency in the bedchamber.

Still, she knew what he meant. "Why must everyone marry?"

"Precisely."

"I mean, it's not like there aren't enough bairns being made."

"Right." He buckled his belt.

"And maybe some of us aren't meant to be…"

"Domesticated?"

"Aye!"

The dark giant knew exactly what she meant. Why couldn't her parents understand?

She sank back down onto the bed. "It's a shame we can't just run away together, you and I."

He chuckled. "Two errant warriors-in-arms?"

She chuckled back. "Aye."

His smile was wistful. "I suspect we're both too honorable for that."

She wasn't so sure. For one impulsive moment, she considered confiscating his weapon and absconding with him at sword point.

But he was right. In the end, a warrior's honor was everything. Besides, he had three big, burly brothers waiting below. She didn't think they'd allow her to abduct him without a fight. And then there was his bride. He obviously cared about her, even if he didn't particularly want a wife.

Like Kimbery, when it came to marriage, it seemed he was only afraid of his own inadequacy.

"If it eases your mind," she ventured as he began to don his hauberk, "I think your bride will be pleased." She was appalled when her voice cracked over the words. "She's a very lucky lass."

He gave her a doubtful glance. "That's generous of you to say. But that hasn't been my experience with lasses so far."

Surely he was jesting. Kimbery couldn't imagine a woman *not* wanting this divine warrior in her bed.

Feeling suddenly very melancholy and hopeless and sorry for herself, she ducked away—hiding the foolish tears gathering in her eyes—to search for her boots.

Somehow he sensed her despair. Buckling his sword belt over his hauberk, he softly vowed, "Listen. If you need a champion against this foul beast, my lady, I will gladly fight for you."

That made her feel even more like sobbing. But she was a shieldmaiden, not a child. So she turned to him with forced smugness. "Thank you for the offer, but I fight my own battles."

She could see she wasn't fooling him. There was pity in his eyes. But since there was nothing to be done for it, she choked back her tears and made quick work of her stockings and boots.

He did the same.

Her cloak was still on the bed. She idly stroked the hood. She didn't want to leave. But she couldn't stay here. And it was best she travel while the day was young. She draped the cloak over her shoulder.

"Do you think my da's men are gone?" she asked.

"I'll take a look."

Arming herself with her dagger, she followed him as he went to the door. No one was in the passageway.

She stayed close behind him as he cautiously descended the stairs. Of course, as soon as he appeared, his ribald brothers started teasing him mercilessly about his haste in accomplishing the deed. Feeling suddenly and fiercely protective of this man who felt like her kindred spirit, she drew her dagger and prepared to confront them.

He halted abruptly on the steps, but she elbowed her way past him, determined to defend his honor.

Then she too stopped on the stairs, and her heart sank. The Vikings hadn't left after all. They were swigging ale with his brothers. By the looks of them, the whole lot had been drinking ceaselessly since they'd arrived.

"To Kimbery of Rivenloch!" Axlan raised his cup in a drunken salute, and the others followed.

She gasped. Bloody Hel. So much for her anonymity. What would she do now? No matter the odds, she wasn't about to surrender to her da's men. She refused to let them drag her home to become a barbarian's bride.

She steeled her spine. Relying on her wits and her warrior instincts, she used the only leverage she had left.

As much as it pained her to betray him, she turned on the stairs to face the warrior. She pressed the point of her dagger against the vein pulsing in his throat, effectively taking him hostage. With her free hand, she reached for his sword, intending to disarm him.

But his hand clapped over hers with lightning speed before she could draw the blade. When she glanced up, a black storm was brewing in his eyes.

"You," he bit out.

She blinked. What he meant by that, she didn't know. After all, he was a stranger here. He probably had no idea who she was.

He was probably just angry that she'd turned on him.

Maybe when he heard her plan, he'd realize that she was

only bluffing in order to make her escape. Maybe then he would play along.

She called out to his brothers. "Let me go, let me leave the alehouse, and I won't hurt him."

She expected gasps of horror and disbelief. Instead, his brothers laughed, which vexed and confused her.

"Hurt him?" one of them scoffed. "Oh, I'm sure Brude can take care of himself."

Kimbery's breath caught.

Brude.

Brude?

She froze. It felt as if the whole world froze with her. Her thoughts, however, continued to swirl around her like a wild snowstorm.

It couldn't be. Surely it was only a coincidence.

Brude was a common enough name.

Besides, the Brude she was meant to marry was mean, despicable, barbaric. And he wasn't due to arrive until the morrow.

Yet even as she assured herself of these things, deep inside, she sensed the truth.

This *was* Brude.

Brude the Brutal.

Her betrothed. Hel, he'd even admitted he was about to be wed.

If there was any shred of doubt in her mind, it vanished when she turned her gaze slowly up to his and glimpsed the cold and silent fury in his eyes.

Instantly, every ugly word she'd uttered to him about her evil betrothed came rushing into her head. What had she called him? A monster?

She gulped. Then she made a deadly mistake. For one perilous instant, she let down her guard. Her voice was a rough whisper. "I didn't mean..."

Before she could even finish, he swatted her dagger hand away, took a step back, and drew his sword, setting it under her chin.

She'd hardly had time to gasp when he skewered her with a glare, grinding the words between his teeth. "You were running away. You meant to cheat me of my bride."

The men downstairs let out a collective "ooh" of disapproval.

Her first reaction was guilt. He was right. She *had* been running away from him.

But then she realized he wasn't exactly blameless. She straightened in outrage and knocked his blade aside with her dagger. "*You* meant to cheat on your bride with a harlot."

The men "oohed" again, louder.

Brude narrowed his eyes. She could see she'd hit her mark. But there was no way he was going to let a maid best him in battle.

Brude's pride wouldn't allow him to let her win, even if she was right. Not while his brothers and that pack of Northmen were looking on, judging the man who was to wed the laird of Rivenloch.

Damn! Of all the women who could have come to his chamber, how could he have ended up with his own bride-to-be?

While he was wondering that, the little minx lunged forward with her dagger, and he almost didn't leap back in time.

Wrenched back into the moment, he swept his blade forward, intending to whack her with the flat of it.

But she ducked with unexpected speed. His sword whooshed over the top of her head, striking the wall and breaking loose a chip of plaster.

She thrust forward with her dagger then, under his guard.

Thankfully, his leather hauberk prevented her from doing much damage.

Bringing his blade back, he raised it vertically, intending to use the pommel to give her a light but punishing rap on the back of her head.

Again, she dodged out of the way. The sprite was so small and fast, he couldn't catch her.

He assumed her Viking kin would come to her rescue. Then his brothers would naturally join in. An ugly melee would result. But the oafs only sat with their cups of ale, alternately whooping and gasping over every thrust and dodge.

Kimbery came at him like a wasp, her dagger biting at his legs.

He managed to hold her off with his sword, though just barely.

When he least expected it, she sprang up with her weapon, nicking the side of his neck.

Before the dagger could slice off his ear, he yanked his head away.

She chose that moment to barrel forward, knocking him off balance. He landed with a thud on his arse. But to her horror and his brothers' chagrin, she tripped and fell as well, with her face in his groin.

He grunted, folded in half from the impact.

With a mortified cry, she scrambled backward down the steps as fast as she could.

They found their weapons at the same time. He lifted his sword. She lifted her dagger.

She was obviously outmatched. Not only was his blade longer, but he had the superior reach and an upstairs advantage.

Yet, as he moved his way down the stairs, countering her dagger strikes, the stubborn wench continued to stand her ground, tossing her snowy blonde locks and glaring at him with her icy blue eyes. Her teeth were bared, and her breast heaved.

She really was magnificent. Apparently, his brothers thought so as well. They were hooting and whistling as if this were the best entertainment they'd ever seen.

But suddenly Brude couldn't remember why he was fighting her. There were other things he'd much rather be doing with the hot-blooded shieldmaiden, especially now that he knew she belonged to him by rights. And the sooner he put an end to this nonsense, the sooner he could start doing those other things.

In the midst of that thought, she surged toward him with a loud battle cry, and as her dagger swept near his face, he seized her wrist. Dropping his sword and letting it clatter down the steps, he used his free hand to pry the weapon from her fingers. Then he stabbed her dagger forcefully into the wall, sinking it deep, where it could do no harm.

For a moment, at a stalemate, they stared at each other, panting.

Whose idea it was, he would never know. But somehow they collided in a violent, passionate, earthshaking kiss.

He was vaguely aware of the cheers and laughter coming from the men downstairs. But his mind was on more pressing things.

Their mouths battled with bruising force. Like hungry hounds, they gorged on each other with mindless rapture. With their lips still locked, he lifted her. She clung to him, moaning softly as he turned and mounted the rest of the stairs.

He kicked the door open, cradling her in his arms as he continued to feast on her delicious flesh, moving from her tender lips to her flushed cheek to her throbbing throat. He nuzzled her ear, and she gasped and threw her head back, driving her claws into his neck.

He paused only to lay her out on the bed. Gazing at her beautiful, womanly body, he felt temptation usurp his loins, hardening him and filling him with keen desire. He could wait no longer. He unbuckled his armor, casting it aside. He wrenched his shirt so violently from his shoulders that it tore. He kicked off his boots and pulled off his trousers.

She was only one step behind him. And her eagerness—tugging off her own boots, tossing off her apron, and slipping out of her kirtle—was even more intoxicating than the vision of her naked body.

The sight of him—glorious, bare, unashamed—filled Kimbery with awe and intense craving. And now that she knew he was her betrothed, that they belonged together, that he wanted her as much as she wanted him, there was nothing to stop her from satisfying that urge. She longed to join with him—now—to become one with the man who was to be her husband.

Still, as dark and menacing and proud as he looked—his fists clenched, his eyes smoldering, looming like a conquering warrior over her—he mastered his needs enough to croak out, "May I, my bride?"

She rose on her elbows and nearly sobbed out in reply. "Oh, aye!"

He came to her with great care, tempering his passions for fear of hurting her. Hovering over her, he wove his fingers through hers. With cautious tenderness, he kissed her brow, her eyelids, her cheek. His beard grazed her flesh as he dared to venture lower.

She arched up as his tongue brushed lightly down her throat and across her bosom. And when he covered her breast with his mouth, suckling softly, she drew a breath between her clenched teeth at the divine sensation, squeezing his fingers between her own.

He released one hand to let his fingers explore her. The callused tips glided over her collar bone, along her breast, over her ribs, and lower.

She held her breath in anticipation, knowing his path would

eventually lead to the place where she felt the most powerful ache. And when his fingers finally slipped into that burning crevice, she cried out with joy.

He immediately withdrew his hand. "Did I hurt you?"

"Nay!" She almost laughed at that. But then she glimpsed genuine concern in his eyes. How anyone could call him brutal, she didn't know. "Nay," she repeated. Then she lowered her eyes. He was rigid with need. "May I, my husband?"

He gulped, then nodded.

She barely touched him, and yet his nostrils flared, and his jaw tensed as if her touch was flame. "Did I hurt you?"

He shook his head and moved his hand over hers, urging her to hold him in her palm. He was as hard as iron, yet as soft as velvet. And when she moved her fingers around him, a groan welled up from deep in his throat, from a primitive place that beckoned to her as surely as a wolf calling to its mate.

She wanted him.

She wanted him now.

With artless grace, she wrapped her legs around him, arching toward him, begging wordlessly to be besieged.

His brow glistened with a lusty glow, and yet he hesitated, afraid he might do her injury.

Finally, fearless with yearning and impatient with his restraint, Kimbery rose to him, impaling herself upon his fleshly blade.

The small pinch of pain was nothing compared to the ecstasy of feeling him inside her. She melted like snow against the flame of his body. And his erotic shudder as she sheathed him sent a thrill of power through her that was more intoxicating and empowering than winning a battle.

When he began to move within her, she met him, stroke for stroke. What they lacked in experience, they made up for in instinct. Like well-matched champions, they warred together. He glided with feverish intensity over her throbbing core. She rapidly lost her capacity for thought.

They mated with mindless abandon, honing passion to a finer and finer point, until he stiffened and she felt a sudden release. Like a spear soaring through the air, simultaneously weightless and powerful, she sailed and hit her mark with lethal force, crying out in wonder and shivering from the impact.

Later, Brude's brothers would tease him, saying the folk in the next village had heard his glorious bellow. But at the moment, all he knew was that his cry of victory didn't express half the triumph he felt ringing in every bone of his body.

He'd been wrong. Making love was much better than waging war. Grappling with a woman was far more rewarding than fighting a foe. Feeling the shudder of her release was more satisfying than breaking an enemy sword. And the explosion of his own climax was more exhilarating than defeating the Roman army.

She'd laid waste to him, drained him of every bit of his strength. He'd surrendered to her. But she'd surrendered to him as well.

They gasped together in breathless exhaustion. Their skin was slick with sweat. Their eyes smoked with spent desire.

Finally, lest he smother the poor lass, he carefully rolled off of her and collapsed back on the pallet.

She wasted no time, snuggling up against him again. She claimed his chest with her arm and wrapped a possessive leg over his hips. And as they lay entwined—his body splayed across the covers, her lithe limbs tangled with his—he thought he'd never felt so complete or so at peace.

For a long time, the only sound in the room was the soughing of their breath, and after a while, he wondered if she might have drifted off to sleep.

Then she drowsily murmured, "You're not so brutal."

He grinned. "Don't tell my enemies."

Her low chuckle warmed his chest.

He wrapped one of her tiny braids around his finger and tugged her closer to kiss her. He thought he could get used to having this sweet shieldmaiden in his bed.

She nestled in the crook of his arm and let out a dreamy sigh. "I wish we could stay here all Yuletide."

"I would, but I fear I have a runaway bride to chase down."

She gave him a playful swat on the chest, and he caught her hand, weaving his fingers through hers.

"Damn," she muttered.

"What?"

"I dread going downstairs. There's nothing as infuriating as a pack of smug Vikings."

"Unless it's my gloating MeqqUvan brothers."

Kimbery gave him a sympathetic smile. Mostly, she wasn't looking forward to facing her parents. They'd clearly see this as their conquest. They'd won. They were marrying off their stubborn daughter to the man of their choice.

Then she drew her brows together.

She blinked.

Something wasn't right. This had all happened too easily. It couldn't have been mere coincidence that they'd met at the alehouse. It was all too suspect.

After a moment, she sat up with a gasp of realization.

Brude rose up on an elbow. "What is it?"

"They knew all along."

"Who?"

"My da's men. Your brothers. This is not by chance."

The more she thought about it, the more obvious it became. It was absurd that the Vikings she'd known for twenty years hadn't recognized her on sight when they burst into the room, even with her face hidden. They'd been tracking her. If nothing else, they would have known her by her cloak.

And if they'd somehow *not* recognized her and believed they had the wrong woman, wouldn't they have left at once to continue their frantic search?

Instead, they'd remained at the alehouse, drinking with Brude's brothers.

"They're downstairs, toasting their success," she realized. "My parents plotted this whole thing. They knew I would run away. They sent the Vikings after me to make sure I'd come here."

"But how could they know I'd be..." Brude began. Then he sat up beside her. "My brothers. Galan insisted we stop at this particular alehouse."

"See?" She closed her eyes to angry slits. "Bloody conniving knaves. They were *all* part of it."

"But what about the harlot my brothers hired?"

"That didn't matter," she explained. "They knew all they had to do was to get us to meet, that I'd fall in love with you at first sight."

"What?" He was staring at her as if she were mad.

She hated to admit it, but it was true. Her parents had picked the perfect man. He was strong and capable, passionate and caring, gentle and honorable. They knew she'd never be able to resist him.

"Oh, Brude, be serious. Who *wouldn't* fall instantly in love with you?"

He was gazing at her now as if she were a goddess. It made her glow inside.

That adoring glance led to a kiss, which led to another, and soon they were writhing in the delightful throes of passion once again.

The second coupling was even better than the first. In fact, Kimbery had a feeling that if they continued with such pleasurable bed sport, it wouldn't be long before they made a whole army of wee warriors for Rivenloch.

But even in the afterglow of lovemaking, they both knew they couldn't linger in this paradise. With the short days of winter, it would grow dark soon. And Kimbery didn't want to miss Yuletide.

She got up from the bed and gathered her clothing. "I suppose we're going to have to tuck our tails between our legs and face the gloating rogues downstairs."

He was watching her from the bed with his arms laced behind his head, displaying muscles that left her breathless. Then he gave her a sly grin that made his black eyes sparkle with mischief. "I've got a better idea."

For one mad moment, she thought he meant to seduce her...again.

Then he sat forward with a warrior's eagerness. "Are you up for revenge?"

She liked the sound of that. "Always."

And so it was that the scheming pair of betrothed warriors-in-arms outwitted their traitor kin. They stole out of the window, dropped onto the snow, and made their own way back to Rivenloch, leaving their befuddled conspirators to wonder what had become of them.

When Kimbery and Brude MeqqUvan strode, arm in arm, through the gates of Rivenloch, it was in their own time and on their own terms. They were greeted by Avril and Brandr, who graciously resisted the urge to crow over their matchmaking success.

The bride and groom were handfasted the next morn, much to the chagrin of the late-arriving and shamefaced Vikings and MeqqUvan brothers.

Their marriage bed was decked with sprigs of mistletoe for love and fertility, and the Yule log burned bright into the night to bless their union.

And that very night, the magic of the Yuletide season rained down upon Kimbery the Shieldmaiden and Brude the Brutal, for the next heir of Rivenloch was born exactly nine months later.

More books from the Warrior Maids of Rivenloch series:
The Shipwreck (novella)
Lady Danger
Captive Heart
Knight's Prize

A Rivenloch Christmas

A Wee Holiday Tale
The Warrior Daughters of Rivenloch

*A medieval clan reunion turns into a desperate search
for three missing lasses as impetuous and daring
as their warrior mothers.*

Deirdre

Deirdre blamed the mistletoe. If her incorrigible husband hadn't scattered the wicked plant all over Rivenloch in the spirit of his Norman Noël, none of what happened would have happened.

It wasn't as if they'd never had Christmas at the castle before. Deirdre's Viking father had built a chapel in the courtyard for her Christian mother so she could celebrate her holy days. When Deirdre's mother passed away, the clan continued to mark Christmas in her memory—with a few sprigs of holly, a sizable feast, and a word or two of thanksgiving. But that was all.

This year, however, Deirdre's husband Pagan had decided that wasn't enough. When Deirdre's two sisters, Helena and Miriel, announced they were bringing their families to Rivenloch to spend the holiday season together for the first time in three years, Pagan had insisted on decking the castle halls in full Christmas splendor.

47

Deirdre couldn't tell him nay. She'd never been able to resist her husband. Especially when he gazed at her with such childlike enthusiasm. So she indulged him, even though she knew her practical sisters would never appreciate his efforts.

True to form, warlike Helena muttered that the festive boughs of holly were hiding all the glorious shields of defeated enemies hung on the walls.

Thrifty Miriel confided that the beeswax candles lighting every inch of the great hall seemed a great waste of coin.

The sisters' father, Laird Gellir, grumbled into his white beard, irked by anything at odds with his Viking Jul.

Her sisters' husbands, however, were quite impressed. Like Pagan, they had Norman blood in their veins. The décor likely reminded Colin and Rand of home.

But it was their collective children's wide-eyed wonder at the colorful mummers Pagan had hired to reenact the birth of Jesus that convinced Deirdre she'd been right to let him bring Christmas to Rivenloch.

An enormous log, large enough to burn for twelve days, was hauled in from the forest and placed on the fire.

The entire clan crowded into the hall for a giant feast—the first of twelve, featuring roast boar with all the trimmings.

Wassail flowed freely.

Carolers and a consort filled the hall with song.

That was when the cursed mistletoe began to wreak havoc in the household.

Pagan had hung it in every corner.

Above every doorway.

And from every beam of Rivenloch's great hall.

The irksome sprigs were everywhere.

And when Deirdre innocently asked what the mistletoe was for, Pagan had been only too glad to show her.

Of course, when they arrived, Colin and Rand had to demonstrate its use to their wives as well.

Thus began the trouble…

Currently, Deirdre watched the mummers from the foot of the corner stairs of the great hall. She had to smile at the way her four children were gazing at the spectacle in slack-jawed amazement.

She absently rubbed a hand across her belly. Nothing showed yet. But soon there would be a fifth to add to their brood. She planned to tell Pagan tonight, after the performance.

Of course, the announcement of one's fifth child wasn't terribly surprising or newsworthy. Still, she knew Pagan would be pleased. He was a doting father who took great pride in their growing army of warrior lads and lasses.

Her gaze again slipped sideways to observe her children— Hallie, Gellir, Brand, and Julian. There was her devoted husband now, crouched between the two lasses. He was pointing out the bright star painted on a screen behind the players.

Sometime after the mummers' Mary and Joseph had secured lodging at a stable, and before the three kings arrived with gifts, Pagan left the children. He sidled up to Deirdre, wrapping an arm around her waist.

She sighed in pleasure and snuggled closer. Even after all this time, she never tired of his affection.

Then he cleared his throat.

She glanced at him.

He was giving her *that* look. The smoky, sparkling, gray-green gaze that always made her heart beat faster.

The knave. He knew very well what that look did to her. And when his eyes lifted to indicate the branch of mistletoe dangling from the archway, it didn't matter that they'd been wed for seven years. Her heart fluttered like a windblown pennon.

Thankfully, he pulled her into the shadows of the stairwell to claim the kiss she owed him. After all, *one* lavish spectacle in the great hall was enough.

Pagan tasted like sweet mulled wassail. Apple and cinnamon and ginger. She drank his desire with eager thirst.

He cradled her jaw with one battle-callused hand, sweeping the pad of his thumb across her cheek.

The fingers of his other hand traced the upper edge of her gown, toying with the silver Thor's hammer she always wore around her neck. Then they dipped dangerously low beneath the linen of her shift. He stroked the top of her breast with a feather-light touch.

When the rogue delved farther to graze her nipple, she gasped and pressed closer. Beneath his belt, against her abdomen, she could feel firm evidence that he had more in mind than just kissing.

She moaned with anticipation, weaving her fingers through his thick, freshly washed curls.

Curls that wound loosely around her knuckles like a fond caress.

Curls as warm and golden as the blaze burning on the fire.

Curls he'd passed on to two of their children and...

She let out a sigh of regret.

A tiny frown settled between her brows as she pulled away.

"Ah, Pagan, we can't," she whispered. "The children."

"What children?" he murmured, easing forward for another kiss.

But Deirdre, as the eldest daughter, had always been the responsible one. That was why her father had entrusted her with the lairdship of Rivenloch. As much as she longed to continue their play, she placed a restraining palm on Pagan's chest.

"We can't just leave them..." she trailed off. Leave them what?

"Leave them what?" Pagan said, echoing her thoughts with a sly grin. "Completely enthralled by the Christmas play? Happy as a litter of pups? Safe in the company of the entire clan?"

He was right, of course. The children were safe. They'd

never miss their parents. In fact, everyone in the hall was so well entertained, Pagan and Deirdre probably wouldn't be missed by a soul.

She answered his smile. Lord, he was irresistible. Especially when his eyes smoldered like that.

He tilted his head to trail kisses down the side of her neck. Delicious shivers coursed through her. Like sword iron in a hot crucible, her knees melted beneath her.

After that, she had no willpower whatsoever.

Somehow she managed to stagger up the stairs to their chamber.

When he closed the door behind them, Deirdre wasted no time. Breathing heavily, she backed toward the bed and slipped the dark blue velvet kirtle from her shoulders.

He advanced, sliding her sleeves ever lower to nibble at her exposed flesh.

Meanwhile, she seized his leather belt, unbuckling it with practiced haste and casting it aside. It slithered across the oak floor like Eden's tempting serpent.

He swept the gold mesh coif from her hair, and her long tresses tumbled over her bare shoulders.

Hungry to taste his warm flesh, Deirdre wrenched his indigo surcoat down. It lodged across his broad shoulders. She went for her dagger, intent on slicing through the laces.

But Pagan seized her wrist and halted her with a sensual chuckle. "Patience, wench. You know, they untie."

She didn't want to wait that long. Then again, she didn't want to have to explain the severed laces to their guests. She dropped the blade.

With a wicked twinkle in his eyes, Pagan slowly spread the laces and drew the surcoat over his head. He tossed the garment onto the chest at the foot of the bed. Then he hooked his thumbs expectantly in the waist of his trews, perusing her from head to toe.

"Well, m'lady?" he asked. "I believe it's your turn."

She unbuckled her own belt and dropped it to the floor. She kicked off her soft leather shoes. Finally, with her eyes fixed on her husband's cocky mouth—the mouth she wanted to feel over every inch of her skin—she lifted the kirtle off over her head.

Pagan's nostrils flared. He wasted no time, leaning back against the plaster wall to pull off his boots and stockings. He untied and yanked down his trews. His undershirt unfurled halfway to his knees. But there was no mistaking the state of his arousal when he freed the beast beneath the linen.

Deirdre gave him a knowing smile. She perched on the edge of the bed, peeling back her stockings, inch by inch, to expose her long legs.

His gaze darkened. He groaned in appreciation. Hauling his undershirt over his head, he pushed off the wall, anxious to join her.

She made quick work of her shift. The cloud of linen had barely floated to the floor when Pagan collided with her in a hot, demanding embrace.

With fevered gasps and in a tangle of limbs, they clambered onto the bed.

After enduring a chaste week full of holiday preparations, their hunger erupted in a gluttonous rush.

With the desperation of a starving waif, Deirdre fed on Pagan's supple shoulder, his corded neck, his succulent mouth.

While Pagan's hands boldly claimed her body, he pelted her face with kisses as soft as snowflakes. He stroked her with practiced skill, knowing all her most vulnerable places.

The spot behind her knee.

The tender inside of her thigh.

The sensitive space beneath her ear.

Then he clasped his fingers through hers and turned until his weight pinned her to the bed.

At one time, she would have fought him. When she'd first met Pagan, she believed that making love was akin to waging battle. One warrior always emerged the victor, one the vanquished.

But now she knew better. If love was war, it was a war fought between equals, full of surrender and triumph all at once. Pagan might have the upper hand now. But she would conquer him before the night was over. Deirdre might feel victorious in the throes of passion. But he would master her in the end.

Lovemaking was an amazing, exhilarating, glorious alliance that never failed to awe and inspire her. She would never tire of it.

While he held her hands captive, his tongue made lazy designs down her throat. Delight shivered through her every nerve. He grazed her collarbone, moving her Thor's hammer aside with his teeth. Then he teased along the top of her bosom until she arched up, willing him to do more.

"So impatient," he teased in a whisper.

She growled in response.

Then he released one of her hands and retrieved something from beneath the pillow on the bed.

With a mischievous grin, he showed her what it was.

He'd hidden a sprig of mistletoe under her pillow.

"Knave," she scolded.

He swept the tiny plant along her eyebrows, kissing each eyelid in turn. Then he traced the bridge of her nose. When she wrinkled it in protest, he soothed the tickle with a kiss. He brushed her lips with the white berries and lowered his mouth to bestow a kiss there.

With her free hand, she seized the back of his neck and drew him closer to deepen the kiss. He obliged her for only a moment before removing her hand and chiding her with a shake of the mistletoe.

"We have time," he murmured. "I'm certain the three kings haven't even arrived yet."

In truth, she'd forgotten all about the mummers. And Christmas. And their guests. She was only eager to engage her husband...who seemed intent on making her wait.

She held her breath as he circled her breast with the mistletoe, spiraling closer and closer to the aching center. Finally, with a low groan of pleasure, he cast the plant aside and lowered his mouth to enclose her.

Every nerve awakened like bright lightning illuminating a dark sky. Her hands tightened into fists. Her eyes closed in sensual joy. The divine throbbing of her nipple echoed deep in her womb, intensifying into an urgent need.

He moved to suckle at her other breast. Desire struck her like another bolt of lightning, shooting current through her body to the swelling bud between her thighs. She squeezed his hand in hers, trying to convey the power of her lust for him.

While she squirmed in impatience, with the back of his knuckles, he smoothed the hollow of her abdomen and flirted with the curve of her hip. He trailed wet kisses along her arm and lapped at the inside of her elbow. He opened their joined hands and pressed a devoted kiss into her palm.

Finally, she could endure no more delay.

Patting across the pallet with her free hand, she found and closed her fingers around the discarded sprig of mistletoe. She wrested loose her trapped hand and pushed against Pagan's chest, forcing him up off of her. Then she slipped the mistletoe between their bodies, brazenly setting it atop the nest of curls where she most wanted a kiss.

His face blossomed in a devilish grin. Emerald flames leaped in his eyes.

What followed was a sensuous blur of wanton delight.

He feasted upon her.

She feasted upon him.

At last, they joined in unadulterated bliss.

And when they ultimately exploded together, it was in a searing blaze of fireworks to rival those they'd witnessed years ago during the famous siege of Rivenloch.

The mistletoe was crushed in their coupling.

Christmas was forgotten.

And in the soothing music of their subsiding passion and slowing breath, they drifted into a slumber that was long, deep, complacent.

Hours later, before she even opened her eyes, Deirdre smiled, feeling the heat of Pagan's backside against her belly. She snuggled closer, basking in the recollection of their lovemaking.

Then her brow creased. She'd forgotten to tell him about the babe.

"Pagan," she sleepily murmured.

He didn't respond.

She ruffled his hair.

Still he didn't respond.

When she finally pried open her eyelids, the glow of rare winter sunlight was already seeping through the shutters.

She gasped in panic and blinked against the light. Bloody hell. Where had the night gone?

"Pagan," she whispered urgently, shaking him.

The children...their guests...the clan...

She may have enjoyed a night of wanton, well-deserved pleasure. But it had been at the price of abandoning her duties as laird. She cursed under her breath, sweeping a dried mistletoe twig from the sheets.

Lucifer's ballocks. How could she have been so careless?

PAGAN

agan thought Deirdre should bear at least part of the blame for what happened. After all, if she weren't so damned stunning and desirable and tempting, he wouldn't have spirited her away to their bedchamber in the first place.

Still half-asleep, he felt Deirdre jostling him.

But he didn't want to wake up.

If he woke up, he'd have to leave the bliss of his wife's bed. He'd have to walk away from her silky skin. The compelling fragrance of her hair. The warmth of the long, lithe limbs wrapped around him. And he wasn't ready to do that yet.

As much as he'd wanted to celebrate Christmas at Rivenloch, to share the traditions of his Norman Noël with his half-Scots children, at the moment all he could think about was the irresistible angel tucked under the bed linens with him.

After their delicious night together, he wanted to spend all day here with his beautiful wife.

Of course, he knew that was out of the question. Deirdre was laird, and he was the host of the festivities.

But surely they could linger here just a bit longer. Indeed, if his delectable wife continued to press those soft, supple breasts against his back like that, he wouldn't be fit to appear before company anyway.

Already he was rousing to the thought of coupling with her this morn.

He stretched, feigning a yawn. Then he turned to her with a cunning grin.

A knock at the door dashed his lusty mood.

"Shite!" Deirdre hissed, echoing Pagan's exact sentiments.

Pagan would have ignored the knock.

But Deirdre took her duties as laird seriously. So she scrambled out from under the coverlet.

He yielded with a sigh, falling back in disappointment on the mattress. But when she snatched the sheets off the bed to cover herself, leaving him nude, he frowned.

"Hey!"

She ignored his protest and headed for the door, giving him barely enough time to dive off the far side of the bed for cover. He was forced to cower behind the pallet in naked displeasure.

Peering over the top of the bed, he watched her haul open the door. She may have wrapped the sheets around her, but she'd left an enticing gap at the back, giving him a tempting glimpse of her sleek buttocks.

"What is it, Lucy?" Deirdre asked.

It was Deirdre's maidservant, Lucy Campbell. The wench had once been the castle flirt, until Pagan's best knight, Sir Rauve d'Honore, had won her heart. She was now Rauve's wife and a devoted nurse to their children.

Pagan only hoped she'd deliver her message and return to devoting herself to their children so he and Deirdre could get back to…

"Da! Da!"

That was Brand, four years old and full of fire. Pushing past his mother, he raced Pagan's way.

"Get up, Da!"

Pagan quickly seized a bolster from the bed to cover his nether regions just as the lad rounded the bed to jump onto his lap.

"Good morn, Brand," he groaned.

Five-year-old Gellir had more discretion. "Brand!" he reprimanded his little brother. "We're not to enter Ma and Da's bedchamber without permission."

"But 'tis Christmas," Brand argued.

From the doorway, Deirdre arched a brow.

That was Pagan's fault. He'd been using that excuse for the last fortnight for everything from letting the children stay up late to overindulging them with sweetmeats.

He sighed. "Come on in, Gellir. But only because 'tis Christmas."

When Gellir charged in as well, two-year-old Julian, trapped in Lucy's arms, screamed in protest and squirmed to get away.

Lucy sized up the situation with a slight widening of her eyes. "Perhaps we should return later, m'lady."

Pagan agreed. They should. But he knew his wife. And he knew better than to counter her authority when it came to the household.

"Nay," Deirdre said. "'Tis late. We should be up and about. We have guests."

She was right. They'd already stolen a night away from the clan. It was sheer greed on his part to want more. Yet who wouldn't want more when he was married to such a beautiful creature?

"Go on, lads," he said, giving his sons a swat on the rear. "We'll be down soon."

Once the children were gone and the door was closed, Pagan tossed the bolster onto the bed. He collected his discarded clothing and sat on the edge of the pallet. He'd just put one leg into his trews when, out of the corner of his eye, he saw Deirdre drop the sheets to the ground.

The sight of her perfectly sculpted body in all its naked glory made him stiffen at once. The breath caught in his chest.

But there was no point in false hope. He knew Deirdre's sense of honor was everything to her. The clan always came first.

So, willing his body to surrender, he continued pulling on his trews.

"Wait," Deirdre said, biting her lip in a rare moment of uncertainty.

He froze.

Then she let out a decisive sigh. Her eyelids dipped, and she sauntered toward him with sensual grace. "I suppose they can suffer without us for a little while longer."

There was no mistaking the sultry gleam in her clear blue eyes...nor the answering throb between his thighs.

"Are you sure?" he croaked. "I know how...the clan..."

She flashed a wicked, lopsided smile at him and shrugged. "'Tis Christmas."

RAND

Rand was sure this was all his fault. His lovely bride might have led him into temptation, convincing him to follow her into her secret hiding place at Rivenloch. But it was Rand who had fallen prey to distraction, all but forgetting the outside world.

When Miriel first slid the heavy chest away from the wall of the lower level storeroom, he narrowed his brows, puzzled. To his surprise, there was a large breach in the stone and a dark passage beyond.

He hunkered down to peer into the tunnel and whistled low. "Is this...?"

"Aye," she replied with a twinkling smile. "'Tis the passage-way that leads from the keep to the woods."

He nodded. He knew the clan legend well. His beloved Miriel had once used this secret tunnel to save Pagan's life. How brave she'd been—his meek, mild wife—fearlessly facing the dark and death to rescue her sister's husband.

"Go on," she urged. Her azure eyes gleamed as she nodded toward the tunnel. "Hurry."

He frowned. "In there?" The passage looked cold and damp and foreboding.

"Aye. 'Twon't take long."

He resisted the urge to ask her what wouldn't take long. She might look demure and delicate, but once Miriel had an idea in her head, there was no changing her mind.

She crossed her arms and arched a fine, dark brow at him. "Unless you're afraid."

He smirked. His sweet-faced wife could play him like a lute. "Hand me the torch."

She retrieved the torch from the wall sconce. He thrust it through the gap, revealing a widened earth tunnel that curved and disappeared around a corner.

The passage wasn't quite as dank as he expected when he stepped through the breach. He moved the brand to and fro, examining the walls. They were reasonably dry and free of vermin.

When he heard the scrape of the chest behind him, he wheeled in alarm, wondering for an instant if Miriel meant to close him up in the wall.

But she'd climbed into the passage beside him and was dragging the chest across the breach again.

He raised his brows. What did she intend?

When she turned toward him, he lifted the torch. What she intended was clear in her sultry blue eyes.

"Why, Lady Miriel," he accused with a grin, "here?"

She grazed his body with a lusty gaze that took his breath away. "Can you think of anywhere more private?"

She had a point. It was difficult enough, with four children under the age of eight, to find seclusion at home. But several days on the road had made intimacy nigh impossible. He longed to be with his wife.

Thanks to brilliant Miriel, they could finally be alone together in a place where even their clever children couldn't find them.

It wasn't that he didn't adore his children. Seven-year-old

Feiyan was like a shadow of Miriel with her fair skin, chestnut hair, and mild manner. Adam, their four-year-old, was Rand's pride and delight, and his younger brother Tian already showed promise as a scholar. Even the littlest, Alexander, made Rand smile with his antics.

But it seemed they were cleverer than most at seeking out their parents at the most inopportune times. For once, maybe he and Miriel could spend a few moments alone.

He studied the walls, looking for a place to plant the torch. Alas, there were no sconces in the tunnel.

In the flickering light, Miriel began undressing, sliding the scarlet kirtle from her shapely shoulders. Even that subtle gesture sent the blood rushing to Rand's loins.

He quickly scanned the dirt floor, looking for a place he could prop the brand, to no avail.

When she slipped the top of her kirtle down to her waist, revealing her small, firm breasts, he sucked a breath between his teeth at the tempting sight.

He gave a rueful chuckle, silently cursing his dilemma. If he dropped the torch, he'd no longer be able to see his breathtaking wife. But if he didn't, he wouldn't be able to avail himself of her charms.

The wicked lass chuckled at his frustration. "Have you not memorized my form?" she murmured. "Surely you can find me in the dark."

She shimmied out of the kirtle, letting it shiver to the ground. He gave up, tossing the brand aside.

A peat-black darkness fell instantly in the passage. For a moment, it felt as if the walls had closed in around him. But Miriel's hand immediately touched his chest, assuring him of her presence, and he drew her into his arms.

It was a curious and exciting sensation, making blind love to her. Deprived of sight, he found his other senses were heightened.

She smelled divine, as warm and comforting as mulled wine.

He sought her mouth with his, relishing the honey-sweet taste of her yielding lips.

She gasped and sighed and breathed softly against his ear. And when he let his hands and mouth explore all her curves and clefts, her purrs and moans made him shiver with need.

Best of all was the heavenly feel of her skin against his.

She clawed the clothing from him, and the desperate scrape of her nails made him catch his breath.

She pressed demanding fingers into the muscle of his shoulders, branding him with hot desire.

And when her tongue mated with his in an erotic tangle, he would have sworn the shadows lifted and that heavenly light filled the tunnel.

MIRIEL

Miriel had nothing to blame but her own self-ishness for what transpired. She should have stayed alert to the castle activity. She'd forgotten how isolated and peaceful it was here.

She'd made use of the tunnel on numerous occasions when she'd lived here with her sisters, though never for this sort of clandestine pursuit.

Here in the dark she wouldn't see Rand's elated face when she told him the glad tidings—that they were expecting their fifth child. But at least *this* time, she'd be the *first* to tell him.

She was determined that her meddlesome servant from the Orient wouldn't breathe a word of it to anyone before she had a chance to tell Rand. Odd, all-knowing Sung Li was prescient about these sorts of things, in the habit of informing everyone of Miriel's pregnancies, sometimes before even Miriel knew.

Not this time.

This time Sung Li wouldn't spoil the surprise.

Miriel's self-satisfied smile might be lost in the dark, but she had other ways to express her joy to her beloved husband.

Their tongues entwined, sweeping her up in a blinding whirl of desire. Thrilled by the challenge of finding her way around her husband's magnificent body by touch alone, Miriel realized she should have made use of the passageway earlier. The endless black was intriguing, their privacy assured.

His mouth left hers, seeking and finding her breast with expert skill, bathing her with tender care.

Her breath sharpened. She clenched her hands in his thick hair. The lazy circles he made with his tongue seemed to spiral down until she felt a coiled heat low in her belly.

She wanted him...now.

Snaking one hand down, she captured the steely confirmation of his arousal. He gasped against her bosom.

"What have I found here, husband?" she teased in a murmur. "Your dagger?"

His chuckle was full of fire. He answered her by wedging his fingers between her thighs, seeking and finding the treasure hidden there.

"And what is this, wife?" he whispered. "Some sweetmeat to nibble on?"

His words sent a rush of hot blood surging through her veins, warming her cheeks.

He gave her breast a farewell lick and then sank before her, kissing his way down her abdomen. When he reached the spot where all her sensation centered, he parted her gently, feasting on her flesh until her legs trembled beneath her.

She gripped his shoulders as she rode her yearning higher and higher, growing more breathless with each wave of lust. At the fine point of climax, she couldn't think, couldn't breathe. And then, she exploded in a burst of bright stars, as awe-inspiring as the paper rockets they'd once made together years before.

She would have collapsed to the ground had he not held her upright.

Once she caught her breath, she wriggled free of his hands and slid down until she knelt before him. She clasped his head between her hands and found his mouth with hers.

He tasted like her passion—warm and wet and mysterious.

She wrapped her arms around his neck, pressing the pillows of her breasts against his muscled chest.

Then she cupped his eager dagger and slowly lowered herself onto him.

He groaned in pleasure.

She echoed the sound.

He filled her perfectly. For a moment she only savored the feeling. But he was hungry for her and for his own long-awaited release.

So, clinging tightly to each other, they grappled as fiercely as they had on that night long ago when they'd engaged in deadly battle. But this time it was love that fueled their fight.

When Rand erupted in a victorious cry loud enough to wake the dead, a thrill of pleasure coursed through her as well.

The sound was quickly swallowed up by the earthen walls. Their weary breath made only the softest stirring on the air.

Miriel's mouth turned up in a smug smile as she rested her head against Rand's shoulder. Never in her wildest dreams had she considered the passageway she'd frequented so often in her youth would prove so useful now.

"'Tis the perfect hiding place, isn't it?" she whispered.

He agreed with a chuckle. "No one would ever suspect."

"And no one will ever find—"

The scrape of the trunk being dislodged and the light that stabbed suddenly into the tunnel made them separate and scramble for their clothes.

"Shite!" she hissed.

Clutching her kirtle awkwardly before her, she narrowed her eyes at the widening opening.

Sung Li was crouched there, staring in at them, completely unsurprised.

Miriel scowled back. How the wee old servant had managed to discover where Miriel was, not to mention singlehandedly sliding aside the heavy chest, was a mystery.

"What do you want?" Miriel snapped, vexed that she'd been interrupted, angrier that their trysting place had been found.

Before Sung Li could answer, their three sons—Adam, Tian, and Alexander—poked their heads in.

Bright four-year-old Adam, who had been studying with Sung Li, asked, "Ma, Da, what are you doing? Are you playing *Zhuōmícáng?*"

Sung Li had taught him the children's game of hide and seek from the Orient.

"Aye," Miriel quickly replied. "We were playing *Zhuōmícáng.* Da was hiding, and now I've found him."

Adam screwed up his forehead. "But why are you naked?"

Sung Li shooed the lads back and gave Miriel the impertinent, imperious frown to which Miriel had grown accustomed.

"Your daughter is missing," Sung Li informed her.

Miriel's heart fluttered. "Feiyan?"

Rand, who had no patience for Sung Li's vague declarations, hurried into his clothes, demanding, "What do you mean, missing?"

"You come," Sung Li instructed, turning away before Rand could bristle at a servant issuing orders.

Miriel's hands shook as she fastened her lacings. She was sure Feiyan was fine. The lass was a precocious seven-year-old, plagued by curiosity. She'd probably only wandered into a forgotten corner of Rivenloch...just as her parents had.

Nevertheless, Miriel made haste.

The lass could be anywhere.

It was wintertime. A storm might be coming.

And Rivenloch was a large estate surrounded by a dense wood where any manner of beast—or outlaw—could hide.

COLIN

Colin placed the blame for what happened squarely on his own head. It had been his idea to steal away from the keep this morn. He'd selfishly wanted time alone with his wife. He'd never imagined his simple wish would wreak such chaos.

He was admiring how the light shimmered upon his wife's tawny tresses when her sword came toward him in a downward slash. He raised his blade just in time to block the blow.

"Aha!" he crowed.

Undaunted, Helena tossed her head and braced to launch another attack, circling him like a wolf.

The buttery light of sunrise spilled across the fresh white snow as they sparred in Rivenloch's deserted tiltyard.

As always, Colin felt a curious combination of lust and wariness when he faced his wife in combat. Beautiful Helena's fiery glare might have been tempered by an eager, hungry grin. But he knew better than to trust that temper when she was in the heat of battle.

"Come, husband," she taunted, "we haven't got all morn."

He gave her a wry smile. He knew her tricks. She was trying

to make him careless. If she could urge him to incaution, she'd seize the upper hand.

"What's the hurry?" he asked, feigning nonchalance while he kept his sword at the ready.

"I'd hate for you to miss breakfast."

That made him snicker. Though no one would guess it from Helena's firm and shapely form, Colin's wife ate twice as much as a grown man. She was doubtless famished already this morn.

Sure enough, Helena attacked while he was in mid-laugh. But he was ready for her. As her blade thrust forward, he dodged aside.

Recovering quickly, she thrust again. He deflected the blow with a swipe of his shield. Snow sprayed across the field, glittering in the dawn's light.

Grinning like fools, they continued to face off, feinting and retreating, striking and blocking, whirling and leaping, slogging through the drifts until their steely chain mail was coated in powdery snow.

Helena's emerald eyes were bright with excitement. Her cheeks were flushed. Her breath made fine mist in the chill air. He hadn't seen her so happy in days. And that made *him* happy.

If there was one thing he knew about his wife, it was that she craved battle the way a caged falcon craves flight. Swordplay warmed her blood and made her feel alive. At home, she was accustomed to sparring with Colin every morn. But for the last sennight, there had been no time for even a brief tussle on the battlefield...or in the bedchamber, for that matter.

Of course, fulfilling her need for battle was Colin's less noble motive. He knew that nothing made Helena more amenable to his lusty advances than a good swordfight. He planned to take full advantage of that fact as soon as she tired of sparring.

The only hazard he faced after so many days of abstinence was distraction. Helena was a skilled and ruthless fighter. But sometimes that was hard to remember when he was gazing upon her wild golden locks. Her flashing eyes. Her challenging grin. And the way her chain mail draped her voluptuous breasts to perfection.

His inattention must have shown in his face, because she chose that instant to swing her blade around, hard enough to lop off his head. He raised his shield, warding off the blow just in time.

Unfortunately, surprise made his instincts take over. He immediately charged forward. His shield collided far too forcefully with her head, knocking her on her arse in the snow.

He staggered back with a grimace. God's blood. He hadn't meant to hit her that hard.

"Ah, Hel, I'm sorry," he began, preparing himself for a barrage of outraged cursing.

When none was forthcoming, he furrowed his brows. "Hel?"

Sitting in that undignified position, she stared blankly at the snow between her knees, stunned. She seemed lost in a distant world, unable to hear him. Without warning, her eyes rolled up, and she fell backward in a faint, landing with a soft plop in the snow.

"Hel!"

Colin's heart plunged into his gut. He dropped his weapons, cursing his careless strength. Then he dove forward onto his knees beside her to cradle her head.

"Hel, can you hear me?"

She wasn't moving.

"Hel? Helena."

Using his teeth, he tugged off one of his mailed gloves, dropping it beside him. With trembling fingers, he carefully brushed the stray hair from her face.

"Helena, wake up."

She was completely limp. He gave her a gentle shake.

"Come on, Hel."

There was no response. He patted her rosy cheeks, trying to get a response.

His heart was pounding now. He'd been knocked unconscious before and awakened. But he'd also seen men who didn't. Dear God, if he'd hurt his precious Helena, he'd never forgive himself. If he'd killed her...

His throat caught. Nay, he couldn't think of that.

Was she breathing?

He lowered his head, turning his ear to her parted lips.

That was his mistake.

The minx's wicked teeth suddenly clamped down on his earlobe, and his fear turned instantly to regret.

He bellowed in outrage and pain. Trapped and helpless in the viselike grip of her jaw, he wasn't even able to feel relief that she was alive.

She mumbled something he couldn't understand.

"What?" he gasped.

"I said," she bit out, still clinging tenaciously to his ear, "Do. You. Yield?"

A braver man would have simply endured the pain.

A pluckier man would have refused to surrender.

A prouder man would have sacrificed his ear and called it a wound of war.

But Colin was more clever than he was brave or plucky or proud. He chose his battles wisely. And he knew if he let her win *this* one...

"Aye," he squeaked out, "I yield."

When she released his ear with a smug chuckle, the honey warmth of her voice helped to soothe his pain. Still, when he drew his fingers across his tortured ear, he was surprised she hadn't drawn blood.

"That's your weakness, you know," she informed him with a cocky lift of her brow as she sat up, dusting the snow from her gloves.

Still cupping his sore ear, he sat back on his haunches with a wince. "My weakness?"

"Your soft heart."

"Indeed?" The corner of his lip tugged into a fleeting smile. Two could play at that game. "And what about *your* weakness?"

"*My* weakness?" she scoffed, hopping up to her feet and brushing the snow from her thighs. She stared smugly down at him. "And what would that be?"

He extended his hand for her assistance, and she took it, bracing herself to haul him to his feet.

Instead, he tugged back hard on her wrist, pulling her suddenly off-balance and forward into his lap with a clash of chain mail and a surprised squeak.

"Overconfidence," he whispered against her gasping mouth, just before he claimed it in a kiss.

ḢELENA

She might have been able to prevent the catastrophe, if only she hadn't lured Colin into the tiltyard. She'd known very well what she was doing. After all, Helena was no innocent. As sure as day led to night, sparring with her husband would lead to swiving him.

Of course, she'd *let* Colin pull her onto his lap. She wasn't fooled for an instant by his help-me-up ploy. She'd used that tactic herself countless times.

Still, she had no choice but to let him win. If she didn't, they would be fighting till noon. And she had other plans. The stable was only a few yards away, and it was as good a place as any for what she had in mind.

Afterward, she'd tell him the happy news. They would be blessed with their fifth child next year.

Colin would be ecstatic, of course. He and Pagan were engaged in a friendly competition for who could sire the most children. So far, they each had four.

Helena, on the other hand, had no interest in the numbers. She believed her sons and daughters—Hew, Grim, Jenefer, and Nichola—could knock the stuffing out of any of Pagan's children. And that was what mattered most to her.

But all thoughts of happy news and warrior children, indeed all rational thought, escaped her when Colin pressed demanding lips to hers. His breath melted her frost-chilled flesh. His tongue swirled like a warm snowstorm inside her mouth. And when he slipped his bare fingers into her damp hair, she locked her arms around his neck, deepening the kiss.

She might have stripped off her armor and made love to him right there in the snowy tiltyard, witnesses be damned. But she suddenly felt the sharp prick of Colin's dagger against her throat.

She gasped. Hell! She should have disarmed him. Perhaps she'd bitten his ear with a bit too much force. Perhaps he sought revenge.

"What do you want?" she whispered breathlessly.

Colin murmured against her mouth, "I'm taking you hostage."

Her lip curved into a one-sided grin. Colin never let her forget that when they'd first met, she'd abducted him and held him for ransom.

"Up," he commanded.

She held her hands up in surrender. Then she glanced down pointedly at his lap, where her backside was warming his loins. "Are you sure?"

"Wicked lass," he said, clucking his tongue. Then he prodded her with the dagger point. "I'm sure."

Slowly, carefully, lest she nick her neck on his blade, she eased up from his lap. He followed her, keeping his dagger at her throat, until they were both standing.

Smoldering mischief danced in his green gaze as it slowly caressed her body from head to toe.

"Now, m'lady," he drawled, "you're *my* hostage. What ransom shall I demand for a—"

Helena smirked. She swept her hand suddenly forward to cup his cock, rendering him instantly speechless. She had no patience this morn for his leisurely love play.

The dagger faltered in his grip. With her free hand, she easily knocked the weapon away. Then she seized the back of his neck, pulling him in for a kiss.

He groaned in pleasure.

She chuckled in lusty triumph.

She released his lips just long enough to gloat, "Now who's the hostage?"

Then she seized him by the arm and dragged him toward the stables.

To be honest, her abduction was met with very little resistance. They burst through the door, heedless of the startled horses. In a melee of kissing and groping and clawing at each other's armor, they managed to slam the door shut behind them.

Somehow they shivered out of their chain mail, sending up puffs of dust and bits of straw that glistened in the sunlight seeping through the cracks of the wooden door.

It had been far too long since they'd last coupled. Helena could feel her blood, already hot from battle, surge in her veins faster than a winter flood.

Colin was clearly swept up in the same raging current. He raked the linen from her bosom and feasted on her breasts.

She moaned and clenched her fists in his thick chestnut mane.

Curving an arm around her waist, he tumbled her into the pile of hay. In a mad rush of desire, he hiked up her underskirts and plunged forward. As he sheathed himself in her welcoming warmth, she sucked a sharp breath of awe between her teeth.

It wasn't the most graceful swiving they'd ever done. There was no sensuous seduction. No romantic finesse. No murmur of affection. No tender gesture. No heartfelt promise.

There was only a hasty, torrid coupling. The two of them thrashed and gasped and mated like wild beasts until they erupted in a roar of completion.

Then they collapsed in a weak heap, spent and satisfied. There would be plenty of time for honeyed words and loving gestures later. For now, their desperate tryst was perfect.

Until someone pounded on the stable door.

"Shite," Helena hissed, annoyed, but in no hurry to extricate herself from their sensual embrace.

"Are we going to answer that?" Colin whispered.

"Not if we can help—"

"Hel!" It was Deirdre.

Helena didn't respond.

After a moment, Deirdre said, "Helena, I know you're in there."

Helena scowled. "Well, if you know I'm in here," she yelled, "then you know you shouldn't be banging on—"

"Open up," Deirdre said. "I need you."

The command was subtle. But the understated concern in Deirdre's calm words struck Helena to the core, turning her ire to alarm.

She clambered up to locate her clothing. Colin followed her lead.

Something had happened. She didn't know what. But it was serious enough for Deirdre to risk the wrath of interrupting Helena in a tryst. It must be dire indeed.

DEIRDRE

Deirdre stood outside the stable door, sword in hand, biting her lip. She could no longer blame the mistletoe or her husband for what had happened. This was entirely her fault.

Deirdre was Laird of Rivenloch, after all. She had one duty—to look after the clan. And she'd utterly failed.

Of course, once she decided this was her battle to fight alone, Pagan insisted on lending aid. At present, her loyal husband and clan—and even the mummers and musicians—stood armed and assembled in the tiltyard behind her, breathing fog into the cold morning air, eager to help.

Deirdre was about to bang on the door again when Helena snatched it open. She was only half-dressed, but she had a dagger in her grip and a grim cast in her gaze.

"What is it, Deir?" she demanded hoarsely. "What's happened?"

Behind Helena, Colin was tying up his trews. Hay was strewn through his dark hair.

"The lasses," Deirdre breathed, "Hallie, Feiyan, Jenefer…"

The shirtless Colin pushed past Helena to bark, "Jenefer?"

Colin's aggression toward Deirdre was understandable, given the circumstances and how protective he was of his children.

But Helena wouldn't let her husband use such intimidation against Deirdre. She grabbed his arm to restrain him.

"What about the lasses?" Helena asked.

"They're...missing."

"Missing?" Colin aped. "What do you mean, missing?"

Miriel's high-handed servant Sung Li stepped in front of Colin. "Missing. It means they cannot be found."

Colin's eyes narrowed in anger. "I know that, you pesky..." He made a grab for Sung Li's throat.

Before anyone could intervene, diminutive Sung Li, with a quick flick of the wrist, somehow brought Colin to his knees in the snow with his arm bent behind him. The clan gave a collective gasp.

Helena, furious at seeing her husband laid low by Miriel's aged and irritating servant, targeted Miriel's husband. She stepped forward with her dagger, pressing the point against Rand's throat. "Call off your lackey, Miriel."

Rand froze.

"How dare you," Miriel bit out. "Besides, 'tis your husband's own fault. He should know better than to—"

Helena fumed. "If your pompous minion would stop interfer—"

"Sung Li was only defending—"

"Sung Li needs to be taught a lesson in—"

"Hel! Miri! Enough!" Deirdre shouted. "We need to work together...and quickly."

Still simmering with ire, Helena and Miriel nodded a reluctant truce. Helena lowered the blade from Rand's neck. Sung Li released Colin, and Pagan helped his fallen friend to his feet.

Deirdre glanced up at the sky. It had been cloudless at dawn. But a storm was fast approaching from the east. If the lasses got caught in it...

She didn't dare finish the terrifying thought. Fear only paralyzed a warrior. She had to do what she did best—take charge.

"We'll cover the most ground if we search in small numbers," she decided. "Archers, split up and take the north woods. Rauve, lead the men-at-arms and search the great glen to the south. Pagan, Colin, Rand, go west toward the loch. My sisters and I will head east. Lucy and Sung Li, gather the children and scour the keep for any sign of them. The rest of you, search all of the outbuildings—the mews, the smithy, the chapel."

As everyone left to do her bidding, Deirdre's sisters came to her side. Then she summoned all the Rivenloch children and hunkered down to speak to the oldest cousins.

"Gellir, Brand, Hew, Adam, I promise you we'll find your sisters. But I need your help. Are you certain they said nothing this morn about where they were going?"

The four lads solemnly shook their heads.

Deirdre nodded, swallowing back disappointment. "I need you lads to search every nook and cranny of Rivenloch. Can you do that?"

They nodded.

"I'll search the armory," Gellir offered, his eyes gleaming.

"Good."

"I'll look in the buttery," Brand said. "Maybe they got hungry."

"Good idea."

Hew chimed in, "What about the storeroom? The one where Da locked up Ma so she wouldn't have to wed that horrible—"

"Aye!" Helena interrupted before her son could finish the lurid story.

Adam screwed up his nose. "What about the secret passageway where Ma and Da were playing *Zhuōmí*—"

"Nay!" Miriel barked, startling everyone. She blushed and quickly explained, "Your da and I...already searched there."

Deirdre smirked. It seemed all three Warrior Maids of Rivenloch had been caught with their trews down—literally. And they needed to make things right before they'd ever let that happen again.

Helena quickly donned her armor and buckled on her sword. Miriel swirled her cloak over her exotic secreted weapons. Then the three of them struck out through the snow-frosted trees.

They traveled well into the woods, taking turns calling out their daughters' names, to no avail. Finally, Deirdre found the courage to tell them the rest.

"Listen," she confessed, "there's more."

"More?" Miriel and Helena replied in unison.

Deirdre nodded. "Laird Gellir is missing as well."

"What?" Helena exploded. "Da too? Bloody hell!"

"Why didn't you tell us?" asked Miriel.

"You know Da," Deirdre said defensively. "He's missing half the time, always wandering off."

On days when his wits were addled, which were more and more often of late, Laird Gellir roamed the halls of Rivenloch. Deirdre honestly didn't always know where he went. But without fail, he appeared in the great hall for supper every evening. Still, she felt guilty, not knowing precisely where he was.

"Most of the time he's safe enough," she added. "There are servants everywhere in the keep and guards posted around the castle wall."

"The guards should know where he's gone," Miriel deduced.

"And maybe they saw our daughters leave," Helena added.

Deirdre stopped in her tracks and shook her head. "With all

the festivities of Christmas, I gave the guards a reprieve. I allowed them to attend last night's feast and the mummer's spectacle. Then Pagan and I..." Then she bit out a foul curse. "I should never have let my guard down. This is all my fault."

Deirdre was prepared for her sisters' fury. She deserved every bit of it.

What she was *not* prepared for was their understanding.

"Don't be ridiculous," Miriel said. "You aren't the only one to blame. Rand and I...well..." She blushed. "I wasn't exactly... attentive to my children this morn."

"Nor was I," Helena added. "I'm certain the whole clan heard what transpired in the stable."

"Besides," Miriel said, "you can't watch over every clan member every hour of the day."

"I'm the Laird of Rivenloch, Miri," Deirdre reminded her. "That's my bloody duty."

"Ballocks!" Helena scoffed. "Even Da didn't do that. If he had, we'd never have had half the adventures we did."

"That's right," Miriel agreed. "Remember how we used to sneak off to bathe in the loch?"

"Oh aye," Helena said, smiling at the memory. Then she elbowed her little sister. "And your secret passage, Miri. I still can't believe you used it all those years, right under Da's nose."

Miriel shrugged. "Remember the overgrown crofter's cottage where we used to plan sieges?"

Helena arched a brow. "How could I forget? That's where I held Colin hostage." Then she gave Deirdre's shoulder a reassuring squeeze. "I'm sure the lasses are fine." Her smile wasn't quite as certain as her words.

"That's right," Miriel agreed. "Knowing our daughters, that's all they've done—gone off on some adventure." Her bravery too seemed forced.

Deirdre looked back and forth between her sisters. They

were obviously trying to make her feel less culpable. She loved them for it. She desperately hoped they were right.

But something else they'd said started a curious tingling at the back of her neck.

"The cottage." Her heart skipped. "Do you suppose they could be there?"

Miriel nodded. "Maybe."

Helen gave them a dubious frown. "Is it still standing?"

Deirdre shrugged and shook her head.

"Has your Hallie been there before?" Miriel asked Deirdre. "Could she have led them there?"

"I never showed it to her," Deirdre said. "But she's a curious lass. She may have found it on her own."

Miriel furrowed her brows. "'Tis been years since my last visit. Do you remember how to get—"

"*I* do," Helena said, charging past them. "Follow me."

Their hopes buoyed, the sisters set out at a brisk pace to find their daughters.

A few wrong turns tested Helena's temper.

The light onset of snowflakes made Miriel frown in concern at the sky.

Deirdre, unable to shake the feeling that this was all her fault, felt an ache start in her tightly clenched jaw.

Finally, they found the moldering hovel. It was much as they'd left it seven years ago. Nearly collapsed and covered with so many vines it was almost invisible. But even before Helena yelled out the lasses' names, Deirdre could tell they weren't inside.

Ivy had grown over the door. When Helena burst through it, tearing vines and shredding cobwebs, it made a grating screech of protest and sagged on its hinges.

For a moment, they gazed in silence at the damningly empty interior. It was much as Deirdre remembered it. Dirt-floored. Stone-hearthed. Sparsely furnished with a bed and a rickety stool that seemed ready to splinter apart. A few rusty pots and pans.

"Curse the Fates," Helena muttered.

Deirdre and Miriel sighed behind her. They'd been so sure they'd find the lasses here.

In the ensuing silence, Deirdre suddenly heard something she'd never heard before from Helena. A sniffle.

"Hel?"

Helena scowled at her own gathering tears. "Loki's ballocks," she cursed. "I'm so bloody mawkish when I'm breeding."

Miriel gasped. "You're breeding?"

"Aye. I meant to tell Colin right after we… But then…"

"But I'm breeding as well!" Miriel cried.

Helena squeaked, "What?"

"Impossible," Deirdre informed them. "You can't both be breeding." They looked at her as if she were mad. *"I'm* breeding."

"Nay!" Helena barked.

"Aye."

At that revelation, the still air was stirred to life by cheers of congratulations. They exchanged teary-eyed smiles and sisterly hugs.

Gradually, however, their mirth subsided, and they sobered.

"I intended to give Pagan the happy news last night," Deirdre said, "before we were…distracted."

"I haven't told Rand yet either," Miriel said. "But what kind of news will it be if we've lost our daughters?"

They silenced as the unthinkable possibility descended upon them like a heavy shroud.

Deirdre steeled her jaw. She couldn't let that happen. She couldn't ruin the best Christmas gift of all—three new Rivenloch babes—by paying for it with their precious daughters' lives. She *would* find the lasses.

Motioning her sisters out of the cottage, she wrenched the

door shut again and clapped snow dust from her gloves.

"Look. We've raised our daughters to be independent, aye?"

Her sisters nodded.

"Then we shouldn't be surprised when they exert that independence. We'll find them. We just have to think like they do."

"Like they do?" Miriel said.

"With hearts full of adventure and spirits full of courage," Deirdre said, "like we used to be."

Helena lifted a skeptical brow. *"Used* to be?"

Miriel snorted. "Deirdre, you may have engaged your husband in your bedchamber last night. But Hel and I are still trysting in secret tunnels and stacks of hay."

Deirdre smiled at that. She didn't need to tell her sisters, but there probably wasn't a wild spot in Rivenloch where she and Pagan hadn't knocked their sabatons together.

Helena sniffed and smeared the rogue tears from her cheeks. "So where to next?"

"Let's try the burn," Deirdre suggested. "Hallie knows to follow the current if she's lost."

A few tiny snowflakes began to filter down through the pine canopy as the maids hurried through the trees.

The silvery stream they sought wound through the wood, ultimately emptying into the double lake for which Rivenloch was named. If the young lasses were clever enough to follow it, they'd end up not far from the keep.

The sisters were only halfway to the burn when Miriel suddenly halted.

"Wait. Do you smell that?"

Deirdre and Helena sniffed the air. The scent was faint. "Fire."

"That has to be them," Helena breathed. She started to call out, "Jene—"

Miriel clapped a quick palm over Helena's mouth. Helena frowned in irritation and would have burst free. But Deirdre held her hand up for silence.

Of the three sisters, Helena was the least cautious. She preferred to dive headfirst into trouble and come out with her blade swinging.

Deirdre and Miriel, however, knew the benefit of stealth. Fire could mean anything. It might have been started by the lasses...or by outlaw captors.

Deirdre whispered, "Let's follow the scent."

Chastened but still scowling, Helena swatted Miriel's hand away from her mouth. Miriel glanced skyward and shook her head.

Deirdre carefully unsheathed and beckoned her sisters follow her. The three of them stole through the woods, as quiet as wolves on the hunt.

When Deirdre first detected the orange glow through the trees, she could see it was from a blaze much larger than a simple cooking fire. For an instant, she feared it might be a wildfire. But only a single broad column of white smoke, salted with bright sparks, rose up through the evergreens.

They approached in silence through the trees until Deirdre could hear the crackle and snap of pine pitch. In the clearing beyond, the golden flames of a great bonfire licked at the falling flakes of snow.

As she watched, three dark, devilish figures began cavorting before the fire like wee demons of hell. And reigning over their impish dance like the Viking god Hel himself was...

"Da?" Helena mouthed.

Miriel blinked in surprise.

Relief mingled with rage as Deirdre studied the macabre scene before her. The wee lasses were covered in blood, doubtless the blood of the goat that lay in grisly sacrifice before the fire.

While the sisters stared on in mute wonder, Laird Gellir hoisted a horn of beer in salute. "To Odin!" he shouted.

"To Odin!" the wee lasses echoed, tipping back their own horns to drain the contents.

Deirdre knew at once what this was about. Her father had brought the lasses into the woods to celebrate the Viking rites of Jul.

It was an innocent enough gesture. He obviously wanted to share his traditions with his granddaughters.

But she couldn't let him believe it was acceptable to abscond with the heirs of Rivenloch without a word to any of their mothers.

Before the laird could refill their horns and further intoxicate the wee lasses, Deirdre had to intervene.

As she sheathed her blade, her eye was caught briefly by its inscription, *Amor Vincit Omnia*. No matter how upset she was, it served to remind her that love conquered all.

"Come on," she murmured to her sisters.

The sisters pushed through the brush into the clearing, startling the celebrants.

Deirdre had never seen three guiltier-looking lasses. That guilt appeared to last about five heartbeats, at which point the spirited cousins grabbed hands to face their mothers in defiant solidarity. Deirdre couldn't decide if they were adorable or infuriating.

Before Deirdre could choose diplomatic words to chide their father, headstrong Helena shouldered her way past.

"What the devil are you doing, Da?"

Laird Gellir's blood-streaked face was menacing as he rose to his full height, fixing her with an icy blue gaze.

"Do you not know?" he growled. He narrowed his eyes. "I knew it. I knew you'd forgotten."

Miriel scolded Helena with a scowl. "'Tisn't true, Da."

The laird's blood-spattered white beard quivered as he

proudly raised his chin. "You've forgotten the old ways of your forefathers."

"Oh, Da," Deirdre's voice broke over the words, "we'd never forget."

She saw now that her father was hurt. In his mind, their Norman husbands had usurped his beloved Jul, replacing it with their foreign Christmas rites.

Laird Gellir shook his head. "How is it that my own granddaughters know nothing about Thor's battle with the frost giants of Jotunheim? About keeping Midgard from Fimbulwinter? About Odin leading the Asgårdsreien to keep the dead from the living?"

Deirdre stood in stunned silence. Was that true? She may have neglected some of the old rites. But every year she recounted the story to her children. She was certain her sisters did as well to their offspring. Were the lasses simply too young to remember the tales from year to year?

It turned out they were not. And it was the wee lasses themselves who brought comfort to all.

"Ach, I know, Grandda," Jenefer announced with pride, flipping her golden braid over her shoulder. "Ma tells me the story every Jul."

"Me as well," sweet, dark-haired Feiyan said. "We put gifts on the trees and burn a Jul log on the fire and have boar for supper."

"Aye, Grandda, we know," willowy, blonde Hallie gently assured him. "We just like the way *you* tell the story."

When all three lasses nodded in agreement, Deirdre's heart melted.

Beaming with pride, Laird Gellir straightened to his full height, looking like the mighty Viking warrior he'd once been.

Deirdre had never felt prouder of her Hallie. A lump lodged in her throat, making it impossible to speak.

Miriel pressed a hand to her bosom and gazed at her Feiyan with watery eyes.

Helena took one look at her Jenefer and burst out sobbing.

Deirdre took her sisters' hands. She shook her head. They were definitely breeding. Only pregnancy could make the fierce warrior maids so weepy.

Without another word, she pulled her sisters toward the bonfire. Crouching beside the slain goat, they painted their faces with blood. Laird Gellir poured beer into the wee lasses' horns, which they passed to their mothers.

"To Odin," Feiyan prompted in a whisper.

"To Odin!" the warrior maids called out together.

To Deirdre's amusement, the beer was so heavily watered, the lasses could have toasted every Viking god in Valhalla and still not have gotten drunk.

Draining the horns, all six maids squeezed onto a fallen log near the bonfire. Then Laird Gellir recounted the Jul story in all its splendor—with dramatic scowls, confiding whispers, triumphant laughter, and a wild waving of arms.

Of course, the tale culminated in his riveting rendition of the Asgårdsreien, the wild hunt.

He described the violence of the stormy night. The ferocity of Odin, mounted upon his eight-legged steed. The beauty and bravery of the Valkyries. He spoke of the fearsome horde of black horses, snapping hounds, and the terrifying specters of the underworld that loomed behind a frail curtain on this darkest day of the year. He praised the power of Odin, who drove the beasts across the sky, protecting the living from the dead.

By the end, even Deirdre was waiting breathlessly to see if the sun would once again triumph over the darkness.

As he finished the tale with an upraised fist and an affirmation of victory, Deirdre decided Hallie was right. No one told the story as well as Laird Gellir.

After a moment of quiet reflection, wee Jenefer jumped up abruptly with glee and cried, "Now the sunwheel!"

"The sunwheel!" the three lasses cheered. "The sunwheel!"

How her father had managed to build a sunwheel without her knowledge, Deirdre didn't know. He must have started it weeks ago. The thing was enormous, a great circle woven of wattle, with a heavy log cross that formed spokes in the middle. A hole was bored in the center of the cross, through which a long pole extended so it could be rolled.

The sunwheel was an earthly representation of the chariot Sol drove across the heavens. It was meant to mark the return of the sun after a long winter, the promise of life and birth and renewal. It was the culmination of the Jul celebration.

Studying the great wheel, Deirdre decided it was fortunate she and her sisters had come along when they did. Rolling the huge thing would have been dangerous and nearly impossible for one old man and three tiny lasses.

She quickly tasked the wee cousins with carrying the burning brands from the bonfire that would ultimately set the thing on fire. The three sisters would transport the wheel.

As it turned out, it was a challenge, even for the warrior maids. The wobbling wheel was hard to control and difficult to maneuver across the snow. But somehow they managed to steer the thing through the forest, finally emerging at the rise before Rivenloch.

Far below, Deirdre could see most of the clan had returned from their search. The search parties were gathered before the gates. Colin, Rand, and Pagan stood together before the crowd, addressing them.

"Wait." Miriel touched Deirdre's forearm. "Shouldn't we—"

"What?" Helena smirked. "Give them a warning?"

Before Deirdre could alert anyone, Laird Gellir plunged ahead. He touched his brand to the sunwheel, instantly igniting the dead wood. The wee lasses mimicked him. In a matter of moments, the whole thing was blazing. The flames leaped so high they licked the lower branches of the trees, threatening to devour them.

The warrior maids had no choice then but to begin rolling it down the hill.

In a thunderous charge, with loud cries and shrieks of triumph, they bolted down the slope.

Their husbands, seeing what appeared at first to be bloody savages rolling a fiery weapon toward the castle, froze in stunned wonder. The clan folk cried out in alarm and scattered out of the way. There was one awful moment when Deirdre wondered if Pagan would order the archers to fire upon them.

But soon enough everyone recognized the warrior maids, despite their macabre appearance. Cheers erupted from the clan.

The wheel slowed at the bottom of the hill, wobbling wildly on the pole. The sisters let it topple onto its side, where it hissed in the snow like a fallen dragon. A few defiant flames burned a while longer, sending white ash up to mingle with the thickly falling snowflakes.

But the sunwheel was already forgotten when the three lasses ran past it, tumbling over themselves to share their excitement with their fathers.

"Da!" Hallie called, her blue eyes alight. "Da! We had a big fire in the woods!"

"And Grandda told us the story of Thor and the Frost Giants!" Jenefer added, swinging an imaginary sword.

Feiyan gushed, "We drank beer to Odin!"

"And we danced," said Hallie, "to honor the Valkyries!"

"Grandda killed a goat!" Jenefer crowed.

Feiyan assured her frowning father, "Don't worry, Da. 'Tisn't our blood. 'Tis the goat's."

"And now we've brought the sunwheel," Hallie declared, "so summer can come back."

Breathless from the long run down the hill, yet still grinning at the husbands' baffled faces, Deirdre held up her hand. "Let's all go inside now, out of the weather."

As they made their way through the gates of Rivenloch, the lasses were still chattering to their fathers about the morn's adventures. Laird Gellir hadn't looked so proud and happy in weeks. As for Helena and Miriel, they wavered between smiles of smug pride and sobs of overwrought joy.

After everyone washed the blood from their faces, Deirdre ordered the servants to bring forth breakfast. The clan gathered by the fire in the great hall. A blissful peace fell over her as she gazed at their merry faces.

The spirit of Christmas and Jul was evident in everything around her.

The holly decking the tables.

The Jul log burning on the hearth.

The mistletoe hung over every door.

The sunwheel spent and smoldering in the snow.

The toasty Scots oatcakes.

The warm Norman wassail.

The mummers reenacting the birth of Jesus.

The laird telling the tale of Odin's hunt.

All of it was part of the same bright spirit of rebirth and renewal.

Deirdre lifted her hand and waited for silence. Once the hall was quiet and everyone had a drink at hand, she addressed the clan.

"I wish you all Joyeux Noël *and* Gud Jul," she said, "because the true meaning of the season is not one or the other, but a weaving together of both. Like the links in chain mail, our two traditions are stronger when they are joined."

She raised her cup and beamed at the gathering of her loved ones.

"To kith and kin. To love and light. To the end of darkness and the promise of new life."

The clan cheered and joined her in the toast.

Deirdre then called her sisters to her side, taking them by the hand. Her lips curved up in a secret smile as she gazed at her handsome husband, whom she was about to make very happy indeed.

"And speaking of new life..."

More books from the Warrior Daughters of Rivenloch series:

The Storming (novella)

Bride of Fire

Bride of Ice

Bride of Mist

the handfasting

A Knights of de Ware Prequel Novella

A French knight betrothed to a Highland heiress
falls in love with his spirited bride, then realizes
he's been tricked into wedding the wrong sister.

DEDICATION

*For all the people who weren't born perfect
and all those wise enough to
see their value anyway*

ACKNOWLEDGMENTS

Heartfelt thanks to:

Suzan Tisdale and Kathryn Le Veque
for nudging me to do a holiday novella

My BFF Lauren Royal
For convincing me to find a way to matchmake
my two legendary families

Birthe Hansen for OT brainstorming

Kit Harington and Emma Watson
for inspiration

CHAPTER 1

The Highlands
Yuletide 1199

Ysenda hated Yuletide.

All around her, the clan celebrated with feasting and cheering. Lively merrymaking filled the great hall. Laughter and music echoed from the rafters.

Yet she frowned into her half-drained wooden cup.

Her loathing had nothing to do with the supper. Who could complain about the sumptuous food gracing the table each night of Yule? Tonight there were succulent boar's head, smoked mutton, roast venison, rabbit pottage, cockles, hazelnuts, cheese, and endless cups of winter ale.

She didn't even mind the drunken revelry that inevitably followed. Raucous songs chased away the gloom. Lusty lads grabbed at giggling lasses. The music of pipes, harp, and tambors filled the air. Boisterous dancing encouraged the return of the sun after the solstice.

The boughs of holly decking the hall looked admittedly festive. So did the ivy draping the great hearth. Mistletoe hung in all the doorways for good luck. Luminous tallow candles set about the room made the rough wood beams of the keep look warm and welcoming.

For once, despite being crowded elbow-to-elbow into the keep, no one in the clan was bickering. Everyone was freshly-scrubbed, smiling, and dressed in their best finery.

Even Ysenda had made an effort. She'd bathed in lavender-scented water. She'd washed her long linen leine until it was as white as the snow outside. Atop that, she wore her best gown of soft gray wool. Flowing around her waist and across her breast was an arisaid of pale gray plaid, pinned at the shoulder with a silver brooch. Her normally unruly chestnut hair was harnessed by two narrow braids at the crown, tied at the back with a ribbon, and lightly scented with more lavender.

She felt bonnie...almost as bonnie as her sister.

"Caimbeul!" From across the hall, over the top of his bellowing friends, one of the many piss-drunk ruffians snagged a squirming lass by the arm and called out to Ysenda's older brother. "Caimbeul! Why don't ye come dance with Tilda here?"

Ysenda stiffened as Tilda pulled away with a horrified blush. Everyone laughed.

That was why she hated Yuletide.

Beside her, Caimbeul grinned at their jest. But Ysenda knew he was dying inside. He wanted so much to fit in, to be like them.

Most of the time, he could pretend he was. Most of the time, Ysenda forgot he was different. When the two of them were alone, he seemed as well-made and fit as any man.

It was only when they were forced to make a public appearance, like at Yuletide—seated beside their sister and father as if nothing were wrong—that his difference was made painfully clear.

Once the crowd gathered and the ale was flowing, the taunts and the laughter began. And to Ysenda's dishonor, their father, Laird Gille, did nothing to prevent the mockery.

Why would he? The laird had disowned his deformed son at first sight. Indeed, the only reason he'd let the boy live was because Caimbeul had been six months old when the laird came home from his travels to lay eyes upon him. Ysenda's fierce mother, descended from the infamous Warrior Maids of Rivenloch, had threatened the laird's life if he touched one hair on her precious son's head.

Beside her, Caimbeul sighed and lowered his half-eaten oatcake. Ysenda followed his gaze. A group of wee lads played beside the hearth. In imitation of their older brothers, they were making fun of Caimbeul's distinctive hobble.

Her grip tightened on her eating dagger as she muttered, "Those sheep-swivin' brats. What do they think they're doin'?"

He gave her a sad, forgiving chuckle. "They're only bairns, Ysenda. They don't know any better."

"Oh, I'd be glad to teach them," she said between her teeth. "Maybe I'll spit them and roast them slowly o'er the Yuletide fire."

That made him smile. "Ach, ye sound like our ma."

"'Tis disrespectful," she insisted. "Ye're the son o' the laird."

In fact, he was the *only* son of the laird. The firstborn. He should be the heir to the clan. But he might as well be invisible. His presence was expected at holiday feasts when the extended clan filled the hall. He was allowed to sit beside Ysenda when the laird flanked himself with his daughters. But Laird Gille paid him no heed. There might as well have been a mile-high wall between Caimbeul and his father.

Still, it was insensitive of Ysenda to remind him of that. She instantly regretted her words.

To make amends and lighten the mood again, she gave Caimbeul a conspiratorial wink. Then, when their father wasn't looking, she used her dagger to steal a slice of roast boar from the laird's trencher, dropping it onto Caimbeul's.

Caimbeul grinned and dug in.

Ysenda couldn't help but grin back. How anyone could overlook the gentle humor in Caimbeul's soft brown eyes—his kindness, his loyalty, his sweet nature—she didn't know. She supposed most people never saw past his crippled frame.

Calling him Caimbeul, which meant crooked mouth, had been polite. To be honest, it seemed there wasn't a bone in his body that was straight. His back was hunched. His spine was shaped like a slithering snake. His hips were twisted. And one shoulder was higher than the other. With each passing year, his deformity had gotten worse, as if the cruel claws of a dragon slowly closed around him, leaving his body more warped and useless.

Most people assumed his brain was likewise twisted. But Ysenda knew better. He might suffer from neglect. But he was bright, and he possessed a wry wit.

Sadly, their father had deemed it a waste to teach him anything. He said the lad would die young anyway, so an education was pointless.

To make matters worse, when Caimbeul was twelve years of age, their warring mother was killed, mortally wounded by a sword. While she lay dying, she made Ysenda swear to look after her older brother. It was no small task for a wee lass of nine. But Ysenda promised she would.

Once their mother was buried, however, things changed. The laird, ashamed of his son's infirmity, banished the lad from the keep. He was sent to live in a wee thatch-roofed cottage in the farthest corner of the bailey.

Looking back, Ysenda had to admit that had probably been for the best. For when the laird was in his cups and Caimbeul was underfoot, their father tended to use his fists, taking out his frustration and rage on the lad.

At the time, however, Ysenda had felt her brother's exile was unfair. And since she'd made that promise to her mother, she couldn't let him go alone. So, heartbroken at the thought of losing both her mother and the older brother she adored, Ysenda stubbornly packed up her things, left the keep, and moved in with Caimbeul.

Her father scarcely noticed her leaving. His attention was fixed on Cathalin, the one daughter who offered him hope. Cathalin was his middle child, the bonnie one, the one who would marry and inherit the lairdship.

Ysenda had done everything she could for Caimbeul. She'd taught him what she knew of reading, writing, and keeping accounts. She'd challenged him to learn about the running of the household and every man's part in it. She'd bribed visiting scholars to tutor him in history and philosophy.

Caimbeul may not have been blessed with a powerful body. But there was much power in knowledge.

And on those occasions when he needed physical defending, it was Ysenda who came to his rescue. She used the fighting skills her mother had taught her. Many a young lad earned a black eye or a bruised shin from daring to mock Ysenda's beloved brother. A few even learned their lesson at the point of her sword.

Caimbeul nudged her with his bony elbow as she slipped him another slice of stolen meat. "Hey." He nodded toward the door with a broad grin. "I think ye've got an admirer."

Ysenda glanced up. A tall, dark, handsome man was staring at her. He wasn't dressed like a Highlander. Instead of a leine and brat, he wore a long surcoat of deep blue covered by a brown tabard that was belted at the hips. By his brown hooded cloak, he appeared to have just come in from the cold. Snowflakes dusted his broad shoulders and his hood.

A hint of a smile touched the man's lips, alarming her. But that wasn't what made her most uneasy.

The truth was she'd never seen him before.

Ysenda was certain she knew every lad, lass, and bairn in the clan, as well as most of the neighboring clans. She would have remembered this one's face. He was striking, built like a warrior. His hair was the color of coal. His gaze was intense and steady enough to pierce iron.

What was a stranger doing inside the keep?

He lowered his gaze then, and she scanned the room.

He wasn't alone. Half a dozen unfamiliar men were scattered around the hall.

Who were they? And how the devil had they gotten in?

Sir Noël de Ware loved Yuletide.

It wasn't only because the holiday happened to mark his *own* birth as well as the Christ child's. He loved everything about the season. He loved the crèches in the church and the caroles in the hall. He loved feasting on roast goose and drinking spiced wine. Most of all, he loved snuggling up in the wintry weather with a warm woman by a crackling fire.

Which was why he was unhappy.

Instead of enjoying the holiday season in France, he was stuck here in the frozen Highlands, tracking down a reluctant bride.

King Philip had promised him a wife—the most beautiful lass in Scotland, if rumor was to be believed. Descended from the magnificent Warrior Maids of Rivenloch, she was the heir to a fine Scots holding.

But she'd been delaying him with letters and excuses for weeks now.

She was ill.

She was visiting kin.

The mountain was impassable.

The river was too high.

She was grieving over a lost kitten.

Meanwhile, he'd been stuck in the Lowlands, awaiting word that he could come for her.

Finally, he'd lost patience. He was weary of waiting for the lass to decide that he merited her company.

Part of the King's reason for awarding him a Highland bride was to assure the continuing alliance between Scotland and France. King Philip had recently made peace with Scotland's enemy, England. This had naturally caused a rumble of discontent among the Scots. The fact that this particular Highland bride was delaying their marriage strained not only Noël's patience. It strained the peace between their countries.

So, as archaic as it seemed, Noël decided he'd have to formally demand his bride.

Of course, he was no fool. The Scots might be allies of the French. But Highlanders were a different breed—wild and unpredictable. He couldn't afford to be caught with his braies down in the frozen north. He'd brought only a handful of men with him. He was ill equipped to wage war.

So he decided to use his brains instead of his brawn.

He chose to come at Yuletide. At Yuletide, the castle gates would be open in welcome. The keep would be teeming with people. Ale would be flowing. Spirits would be high. Nobody would be troubled by a few stray faces among the clan.

Once they were safely inside, Noël would announce to the laird that he hadn't been able to endure one more day without his betrothed. With any luck, the romantic gesture would soften his bride's heart. At the very least, with her entire clan as witness, it would make it difficult for her to refuse him.

So far, things had gone to plan. Even now, he and his men were dispersing peacefully through the crowded hall. They'd left their armor and swords outside the gates. There was no need to appear hostile. Still, as a precaution, they'd kept their daggers close at hand.

He scanned the hall and decided that the lass seated at the laird's right hand must be his betrothed.

She was as lovely as he'd heard. Her skin was fashionably

pale. Her cheeks were fashionably rosy. Her russet hair was swept up in an amazing labyrinth that must have taken hours to braid. Her chin had a proud tilt. Her stained lips were set in a knowing half-smile. The sweeping neckline of her gown revealed firm, round breasts. Her eyes smoked with subtle, sly desire as she sipped at her ale. She would definitely turn heads, even in France, which was filled with beauties.

Then Noël's gaze drifted to the lass seated on the laird's *left* side. And his heart tripped.

He must have been mistaken. Granted, the first lass was undeniably pretty. But the lass on the left was a maid to take a man's breath away. The rumors were true. He'd never seen a more beautiful female...anywhere.

Her skin glowed with health. Her long auburn hair, shining in the candlelight, fell in simple, gentle waves over her shoulders. She had large, captivating eyes, a pointed chin, and a sweet mouth. The soft wool of her muted gray gown seemed to swirl around her petite body like Highland mist.

As he observed her, the lass stole a slice of meat from her father's trencher. Then, with a crafty grin, she passed it to the man beside her.

The corner of Noël's lip twitched in amusement. It appeared his bride had a streak of mischief in her. That pleased him.

Indeed, as he watched the wayward lass continuing to steal more food right from under her father's nose, an interesting possibility occurred to him.

Noël had always expected to have a marriage of political convenience. Like all French nobles, he served as a chess piece for King Philip. Alliances were often established through strategic marriages. Love had little to do with it. He was just as likely to be wed to a withered beldame or a mere child as to a lovely maid his own age.

Learning that his bride was renowned for her beauty had been a welcome surprise. But the idea that he might actually grow to *like* this plucky new wife of his? That was quite intriguing.

He kept gazing at her until he caught her eye.

But instead of returning his friendly smile, her grin faded, and she regarded him with suspicion.

Not wishing to make a bad first impression, he quickly averted his eyes. When he next looked up, she'd left her spot at the table and was making her determined way toward him.

He straightened and tossed back the hood of his cloak, prepared to say whatever it took to ensure that he didn't leave the Highlands without a bride. Nothing could prepare him, however, for her bluntness. Or for her big, luminous, soul-searching gray eyes.

"Who are *ye?*" she muttered under her breath in her Gaelic tongue as the merrymaking continued around them. "And what are ye doin' here?"

Noël was taken aback by her fearless and forthright manner. The lass certainly wasted no words. Nor did she seem to be intimidated by the fact that he towered over her by nearly a foot.

"I asked ye a question," she said impatiently.

He fought back a smile. What a brazen lass she was. Noël knew how to speak her language, of course. But it was important that his wife know how to speak French. For over a hundred years, since the Norman conquest, most of the English and Lowland Scots had spoken French, and he planned to take her home to France. So he replied in his native tongue.

"I've come to speak with your father, my lady."

To his satisfaction, she understood him perfectly. But she still stubbornly answered him in Gaelic. "Have ye? Well, ye didn't answer my first question. Who are ye?"

He smiled. Beautiful, mischievous, *and* clever. He was beginning to like the prospect of being wed to such a spirited lass. Indeed, he was tempted to lean down and steal a kiss from her clever mouth.

But he was no fool. He'd been put off already several times. It would be no easy task to get the lass and her father to agree to the marriage. Noël would have to be careful about how he proceeded. So for now, he would defer to her and speak in Gaelic.

"I'd prefer to answer to the laird."

She raised fine, smug brows. "Indeed? And what makes ye so certain he wishes to speak with ye?"

"By my reckonin', he does not," he admitted.

She frowned up at him. Even that expression looked adorable, like the scowling face of a wee hawk.

He gave her a wink and confided, "But I'm goin' to speak with him anyway." Now that his men were dispersed throughout the crowd, he cleared his throat to address the gathering. "May I have your attention, please?"

The musicians ceased playing, and the hall quieted. All eyes went to him. Laird Gille frowned from his seat, looking very much like the wee hawk, before he slammed his cup on the table and rose to his feet.

"Who are ye, and what is the meanin' o' this?"

Noël eyed his men, whose hands rested upon the hafts of their sheathed daggers. Then he gave the laird a respectful bow.

"My laird, I apologize for interruptin' your revels," he said. "I am Sir Noël de Ware. I've come to claim the bride I was promised by King William o' Scotland and King Philip o' France." He smiled and set a subtly possessive hand upon the shoulder of the lovely lass beside him. "I couldn't stay away a moment longer. I hoped my arrival would be a welcome Yuletide surprise for Lady Cathalin."

Ysenda stiffened. Cathalin? He thought she was Cathalin? How could anyone have mistaken her for her beautiful sister?

From the great table, Cathalin—the real Cathalin—gasped.

Ysenda had heard gossip about Sir Noël de Ware, her older sister's betrothed, for some time now. He was a noble French warrior. He meant to take her sister to France to live with him at his castle. Upon Laird Gille's death, Cathalin would return to Scotland with Lord de Ware to inhabit the keep and rule the clan.

For weeks, neither her father nor Cathalin had been happy about the arrangement. True, there was an alliance between Scotland and France. But Laird Gille didn't trust Lowlanders, let alone Normans. He wanted a Highlander to inherit his land and title. And so he'd ignored the king's command. He'd plotted to hastily marry Cathalin to a Highland laird before her Norman bridegroom arrived.

But the Highlander hadn't yet come.

And the Norman had.

And now he'd mistaken Ysenda for his bride.

Upon hearing Cathalin's gasp, Sir Noël hastened to reassure her. "There's no cause for alarm, my lady. I will take good care o' your sister, I swear." He glanced down at Ysenda with fondness. "I will honor Lady Cathalin and guard her with my life."

There was an uncertain silence in the hall.

Ysenda pulled away from the knight. This wasn't right. Her sister and her father might not want a wedding between Cathalin and Sir Noël. But it was what two kings had decreed. Ysenda would not be a party to such deception, a deception which amounted to treason.

"I'm afraid ye've made a mistake," she told the Norman. "I'm not—"

"Daughter!" her father called out.

For the first time in his life, Laird Gille had wrapped a companionable arm around Caimbeul's shoulders. Caimbeul had a look of confused hope on his face, as if his father had suddenly realized he had a son whom he loved very much.

Only Ysenda noticed the eating dagger that dangled casually from the laird's fingers, an inch from Caimbeul's throat. And there was no mistaking the threat glittering in her father's eyes.

"Cathalin, darlin'," he said, addressing Ysenda. No one in the hall corrected him. Not even Cathalin herself. She only bit her lip and stared intently into her ale. "'Tis no mistake. 'Tis the king's decree. And how fortunate ye are to have your betrothed arrive at Yuletide. The two o' ye shall have a weddin' feast fit for a king."

Ysenda blinked in disbelief. Did her father really believe he could pass her off as Cathalin? Couldn't the Norman see that her sister was the bonnie one? She waited for someone to speak up, to say it was all a jest.

But no one did. No one wanted to contradict the laird. Caimbeul was aware now that his father held a knife to his throat. They both knew if he uttered a word, the laird wouldn't hesitate to make it his last.

Finally, her sister stood and raised her cup, saying pointedly, "Congratulations, Cathalin, dear sister. No one is more deservin' o' this great honor than ye. And no one could be happier for ye than I am."

Ysenda's eyes flattened. No doubt. Things couldn't have worked out better for her sister. It appeared Cathalin would get the Highlander husband she and their father wanted. And Ysenda would be sacrificed to the Norman.

Worse, nobody in the clan was brave enough to come to her defense. She was being thrown to the wolves. And there was nothing she could do about it.

But what was her father thinking? Sir Noël had obviously agreed to marry Cathalin for the title and land that came with her. What would happen when he discovered he'd inherit neither? And what would happen when the two kings found out their alliance had been sabotaged?

It seemed Laird Gille was courting war.

Here and there, the clan folk began to cheer in tentative congratulations. The laird nodded to the musicians to resume playing. Everyone returned to eating and dancing and making merry, welcoming the Normans to their revels. And her father beckoned Sir Noël forward with an affable wave of his hand.

The Norman offered Ysenda his arm. She didn't dare refuse him, for fear of endangering Caimbeul. So she rested her forearm lightly atop his.

She tried not to panic. Surely her father wasn't serious. He wouldn't *really* defy the king. Surely he'd marry the real Cathalin to this Norman. His proud boasts of finding her sister a proper Highland laird were only that—boasts.

The laird couldn't hide the truth from Sir Noël forever. He must know that the instant Ysenda knew Caimbeul was safe, she'd confess to the Norman that she was not his true betrothed. After all, it was far better to face her father's anger than to invite the wrath of two kings.

Besides, she reasoned as she stole a sidelong glance at the knight escorting her forward, her sister should be grateful. Lots of political alliances were made with doddering old men. At least Sir Noël was fit and handsome. He had broad shoulders and thick, curling hair. His jaw was strong, and his dark eyes sparkled with life. He even spoke perfect Gaelic.

Laird Gille narrowed his eyes at the Norman. "So ye're the one who's come for my most precious prize."

Sir Noël gazed down at Ysenda. The tender sincerity in his eyes made her heart flutter. "I'm honored to have her entrusted to me."

Laird Gille guffawed at that. "I was referrin' to my castle." He picked up his cup of ale with his free hand, the one that wasn't holding a dagger to Caimbeul's neck. "But aye, I suppose my daughter is a prize worth havin' as well." He took a drink, and a foamy trickle dripped down his beard.

Sir Noël smiled at her. "She's even more beautiful than I imagined."

Ysenda's breath caught. He couldn't be talking about her. Had he even *looked* at his real betrothed? Cathalin was flawless. Next to her perfect rose of a sister, Ysenda looked like a common thistle.

By Cathalin's sour expression, she did not appreciate the slight. That anyone would praise Ysenda's looks while Cathalin was in the room was unthinkable. Ysenda could almost see the steam coming out of her sister's perfect ears.

But to be honest, it was pleasant having an attractive man gazing down at her with such appreciation. No one had ever looked at Ysenda like that before. She'd grown accustomed to hiding in the shadow of her breathtaking sister.

Of course, that bewitched look on the Norman's face would vanish once he learned his bride came with no inheritance. But she wasn't going to give him the bad tidings until Caimbeul was out of her father's clutches.

Meanwhile, her brother scowled in frustration. She could see he wanted to help her. But he didn't dare. One slip of the knife, and he'd be good to no one. Her father had been drinking heavily. He might do something foolish, something rash, something he couldn't undo...

"Why wait?" the laird bellowed. "Let's have the handfastin' now!"

Like that.

CHAPTER 2

Sir Noël couldn't have been more satisfied with the laird's idea. Preparing for an elaborate ceremony weeks in advance seemed like a waste of time to him.

The betrothal had been made. The laird had agreed to the marriage. There was already a sumptuous feast laid out at the table. Why not get the deed done?

Besides, he'd seen enough of his bride to suspect there was a splendid body under all that wool. The sooner the wedding, the sooner the bedding.

Then he glanced down at his bride.

A look of sheer panic filled her silvery eyes.

"So soon?" she squeaked.

He placed his hand atop hers in concern. Obviously, haste did not appeal to her. But why?

Surely, she'd been prepared to be a wife. It should come as no surprise. She'd known about the betrothal for some time.

Did she not find him suitable?

True, he was no golden-haired Adonis. He had a few battle scars. And he'd been told he could sometimes look fierce and menacing.

But he was young and strong, capable of defending a lady's honor. And most women found him attractive enough.

"What's wrong?" he asked her gently.

The laird answered for her. "Ach, she's only an anxious bride. All the more reason to make it quick, aye?"

His bride was growing more agitated. But she couldn't seem to find the words to adequately explain why. "Wait. I'm not... Ye can't... This isn't... Da, please... Don't ye see 'twill only make matters worse if ye—"

"Sir Noël, I should introduce ye to your kin," the laird interrupted. He turned to his second daughter, who sat fidgeting beside him. "This is Cathalin's sister, Ysenda."

"My lady, 'tis an honor." Noël made a slight bow.

The laird swung an arm out toward a red-bearded bear of a man. "That's my sister's son, Cormac." He pointed to a smaller version of Cormac. "And that's Dubne, his brother." He waved a hand toward three curly-headed maids who were whispering together. "And those wee gossips are her daughters—Bethac, Ete, and Gruoch."

"Ladies." Noël inclined his head. "Gentlemen. I'm pleased to make your acquaintance."

He lost track of all the kin. Most of them were short and sturdy. Most of them had reddish-brown hair. And most of them were half-drunk. Finally he turned his attention to the young man around whose neck the laird's arm was locked and waited for an introduction. "And ye?"

"This? This is Caimbeul."

Noël could see there was something amiss with the lad. His body was woefully misshapen. But that wasn't all. Distress furrowed the young man's brows. Maybe it was because the laird was waving his dagger about, dangerously close to the man's throat.

"Caimbeul," Noël repeated.

"Sir," the man tightly replied.

Before the laird could continue, his bride interrupted. "Da, please listen to me." Her words spilled out like the falsely calm surface over a turbulent river. "I think 'twould be best if we delayed at least till the morrow so ye can—"

"Nonsense, daughter," the laird chided. "Can ye not see how eager your bridegroom is to have ye by his side?"

"But—"

"And he's come all the way from France."

"Aye, but—"

"I'll hear no more of it. 'Tis best ye're wed right here and now." Then he turned till he was almost nose-to-nose with Caimbeul. "Wouldn't ye agree?"

Noël's bride lowered her head then. But it wasn't in submission. Her eyes were darting about madly, as if she were trying to come up with a clever ploy.

"My lady?" Noël said softly in French. "Is this not your wish?"

She lifted her eyes. They possessed all the colors of a winter sky, shifting from ominous pewter to stormy gray to serene silver. How pleasing it would be to look into those eyes every day for the rest of his life, watching their changing hues and moods.

Then she looked back at her father, who still had a possessive grip on Caimbeul.

"Da, please. Don't—"

"Ye'll do as I say, lass," the laird scolded. "Ye know your place. We all make sacrifices. Look at poor Ysenda here. Even if the unsightly wench somehow manages to snag a husband…" He paused, his eyes twinkling, and Noël was certain the laird must be jesting. The lass was almost as beautiful as her sister— even when she frowned, as she did now. "'Twill probably be no better than a Highland sheepherder. But ye… Ye'll be the wife of a Norman lord. Ye'll be Lady Cathalin de Ware."

Noël's bride clenched her hand atop his now, digging in to the muscle of his forearm. "But Da, the king will—"

"Hush! I'll hear no more!" her father interrupted as he tightened his grasp on the man, hugging him closer. "Ye should be more like Caimbeul. He knows when to hold his tongue. Don't ye, lad?"

Caimbeul lowered his eyes in anger and shame. The hand atop Noël's arm clenched even tighter.

Noël wasn't sure what was going on. Did Caimbeul object to the marriage? The man had been seated beside his bride. Was it possible he had feelings for her? And did she return those feelings? Perhaps she preferred the sweet-faced Scottish lad, despite his crooked body.

Surprised by the pang of jealousy that shot through him, Noël suddenly longed to whisk his bride away from this place. He didn't like the idea of anyone else desiring his wife.

He didn't like Laird Gille either. Didn't like the fact he seemed to be irresponsibly drunk. Didn't like the way he kept cutting his daughter off. Or how he was manhandling Caimbeul. In fact, until the laird died and surrendered his keep, Noël would just as soon remain as far away from the Highland holding as possible.

But to his own amazement, more than anything, he wanted to please his bride.

He spoke for her ears alone. "My lady, is somethin' amiss? Do ye find marriage to me repulsive? Are ye afraid o' me? I won't beat ye, I promise." Then he thought of something else. "Are ye afraid o' the marriage bed? Is that it?"

He saw that calculation in her eyes again, as if she were winnowing wheat from chaff. She turned to him with new determination.

"Aye," she decided. "That's it. I'm afraid o' the marriage bed." There was an eager light in her eyes now as she clutched his sleeve in both hands. "So if ye vow not to bed me tonight, I'll go through with the handfastin'."

She was up to something. He could see that. He doubted the intrepid lass was afraid of *anything*. But though her notion didn't please him—already his body stirred with desire for her—if it was what she wanted, he supposed he could wait another day.

"As ye wish," he said.

Ysenda sighed in relief. She'd bought herself a day. No handfasting was official until it was consummated. Hopefully, in the morn, when her father was sober, he'd realize what a grave mistake he'd made and correct it. Their sham of a marriage would be nullified, and Cathalin, the *real* Cathalin, would take her place as Noël's bride.

Part of her was not happy about that. Already she could tell that Sir Noël was too good for her sister. Cathalin was selfish and spoiled, accustomed to getting her way. Noël was considerate, noble, and polite. He'd likely try to accommodate her, and she'd end up running him ragged.

Cathalin would never appreciate his gentlemanliness. She was used to forceful Highlanders who took what they wanted. She would probably mistake Noël's kindness for weakness and belittle him at every turn.

It was a pity really. But Ysenda could say nothing about it. She was the youngest daughter, without power and without a voice.

Her father still had a dagger at Caimbeul's throat. He obviously didn't expect Ysenda to go through with the ceremony willingly.

But now that she had the Norman's promise—and she trusted the word of a noble knight—she knew she was safe, at least for tonight. So she'd oblige her father and recite the damned handfasting vows.

The ceremony would be brief, doubtless briefer than the lavish weddings of France. Highlanders had little use for religion and no patience for church approval when it came to unions. Matrimony was achieved simply by mutual consent.

Sir Noël's men made a formidable appearance as they gathered round him. They were large and powerfully built. Their manner was grave and guarded. Ysenda thought they looked ready to unsheathe and do battle if anyone so much as cocked an eye at them.

She wasn't sure why, but that gave her strange comfort.

Sir Noël had brought the marriage agreement with him. One of his men unfurled it across the table between the roast venison and the smoked mutton, along with a quill and ink. Sir Noël penned his mark on the document, as did Laird Gille.

Ysenda swallowed hard. The heavy black scrawls on the parchment made the marriage seem all too real...and permanent.

Before the ink was even dry, Laird Gille stood at the table to preside over the rite, and the hall again hushed.

"Join your right hands," he directed.

Sir Noël faced her and clasped her right hand, which felt dwarfed within his. She could feel the calluses that marked it as the sword hand of a seasoned warrior. His palm was warm and dry. She feared her own was sweaty. Yet there was something reassuring in his grip.

"Here," her sister offered, tugging a long scarlet ribbon out of her hair and passing it forward. "To make it fast."

Her father wrapped the ribbon around their joined hands, binding them loosely together.

Then she lifted her face to look at her bridegroom. She was startled. In the low light, she'd assumed his shadowed eyes were brown. But standing this close, she could see they were actually blue—a blue as deep as the ocean, as dark as the falling night. For a moment, she only stared at him, lost in the heaven of his gaze.

And then she saw he was waiting uncertainly as the silence dragged on.

"Say your piece, lad," Laird Gille urged.

A tiny furrow formed between Noël's brows. Ysenda realized he didn't know the vows for a handfasting. They probably had no such thing in France. It was up to her then.

Her voice shaking, she began. "I, Lady Ysen—" Heat flooded her cheeks as she recognized her blunder. She coughed to cover the mistake, whispering to Noël, "Forgive me. I'm a wee bit anxious." Then she cleared her throat and began again. "I, Lady Cathalin ingen Gille, Maid o' Rivenloch, take ye, Sir...Noël de Ware...to my wedded husband, till death parts ye and me. And thereto I pledge ye my troth."

She gulped. That hadn't been so difficult. And yet those simple words held such great weight.

His voice sounded much surer than hers. "I, Sir Noël de Ware, take ye, Lady Cathalin ingen Gille, Maid o' Rivenloch, as my bride—"

"To my wedded wife," she corrected in a murmur.

"To my wedded wife...till death...comes..."

She fought back a giggle. "Till death parts ye and me."

"Till death parts ye and me..."

"And thereto I pledge ye my troth," she prompted.

"Aye," he said, finishing with a triumphant smile. "And thereto I pledge ye my troth."

"'Tis done then," her father said in satisfaction, clapping the matter from his hands.

Ysenda hardly heard him. Her attention was riveted on the man before her—the man who had somehow, improbably, just become her husband. A warm twinkle glimmered in his eyes. His smile was captivating. And the thumb he stroked softly over the top of their joined hands sent a curious tingle through her veins.

The laird raised a cup of ale in salute, and the clan followed with cheers.

But Noël wasn't finished. He held his hand out to the man on his left, who placed a gold ring in his palm. Unwinding the handfasting ribbon to free her hand, Noël then gently slipped the ring onto Ysenda's third finger.

She stared down at it. It was heavy, carved with the figure of a wolf's head.

"'Tis the great Wolf o' de Ware," he told her.

She bit her lip, troubled by its scowling face. The ring was loose on her finger. She hoped that it wouldn't slip off, that she wouldn't lose it, for it rightfully belonged to Cathalin.

He bent his head down to murmur, "I vow, my lady, from this time forward, ye shall have the protection o' the Wolf."

For one foolish moment, she wished that could be true. She wouldn't mind having an army of fierce wolfish knights at her beck and call.

She gave him a faltering smile, which he returned with a wide grin that made her heart skip. But this was Cathalin's husband, not hers. And part of her burned with envy at that truth.

He was still clasping the fingers of her right hand when he lifted his left hand to cup her cheek. He tipped her head up, commanding her gaze. His dark eyes sparked at her like a smoldering coal. She had trouble drawing breath. His thumb brushed at the corner of her mouth, coaxing her lips apart. In a sensual daze, she let her jaw relax as her eyes lowered to his tempting mouth.

He was going to kiss her.

Cathalin's bridegroom was going to kiss her.

She should have stopped him. But she had to play out this fiction, for her brother's sake.

At least that was what she told herself as he closed the distance.

But it wasn't completely true.

She wanted to see what it felt like to kiss a man. And she wanted to pretend, even if only for a moment, that she was just as worthy and desirable as her sister.

When he touched his lips to hers, the cheering clan seemed

to fade away. There were only the two of them, connected by their joined hands and their searching mouths. Her eyes fell closed. His light breath upon her cheek sent a current of pleasure rippling through her.

And then he leaned closer, increasing the sweet pressure.

She expected, by his formidable appearance, that his kiss would be rough and aggressive. But the warrior somehow reined in his strength. His lips were soft, tender, and deft. His fingertips gently caressed the sensitive flesh beneath her ear, making her shiver.

As he kissed her, he entwined the fingers of his right hand with hers and drew her closer, until their tangled hands formed a lover's knot between their hearts. Ysenda felt like warm candle wax, melting into him. Her heart beat forcefully against her ribs. A quiet, joyful moan sounded in her throat as he inclined his head to deepen the kiss.

Noël never wanted the kiss to end.

It was mad—the strong, inexplicable attraction he felt to his new bride. His heart was pounding. His mouth was ravenous. He didn't dare ponder what was happening below his belt.

He supposed he should withdraw soon. He wasn't even sure public kissing was proper among the Highlanders. Yet he couldn't pry himself away.

Lady Cathalin was irresistible. Soft and sweet, young and lovely, passionate and willing.

She was the best Yuletide gift he'd ever received.

What he'd done to deserve such a treasure he didn't know.

But she was his now.

And he didn't plan to ever let her go.

CHAPTER 3

I t took the taunts and jostling of his men and the clan to break them apart at last. But when Noël, hot and breathless, peered down at his bride, she appeared as stunned as he felt.

Her cheeks were flushed. Her silvery eyes were glazed with desire. She lifted trembling fingers to her rosy lips. If he hadn't been holding her by the hand, she might have staggered backward in dizzy surprise.

The thought gave him immense pleasure. One corner of his lip curved up as he gazed down at her. He fought the powerful urge to whisk her off her feet, carry her up the stairs, and claim his husbandly rights at once.

But he'd vowed he would not—not tonight. And if there was anything that defined the Knights of de Ware more than their healthy appetites for women, it was their honor.

So he leashed the beast in his braies and stepped back with a respectful nod of his head.

"Eat! Drink!" the laird encouraged. "Ye'll need strength tonight, lad, to wield your braw claymore." He made a nasty gesture that caused a roar of raucous laughter and made his new bride blush.

Noël, with a sudden surge of protectiveness, clenched his

jaw. No one—especially not her own father—should speak so crudely in the presence of a lady.

But he didn't wish to upset her more, so he wouldn't challenge the laird for his lack of courtesy. Still, he was inclined to pack up his wife and his men and leave the keep at once.

He settled for guiding her to her place at the table and seating himself between her and her father, where he could shield her from the drunken laird's vulgarity. The last thing a skittish bride needed was more fuel for her fear.

And more delay.

Noël might agree to put off the consummation of his marriage by a day. But more than that was bordering on unreasonable. He wanted to get home. Besides, if his wife *did* harbor feelings for that young man, Caimbeul, it was probably best to make a quick, clean break of it.

Still, he knew he couldn't leave until their wedding was official. And so he intended to employ his considerable powers of seduction to ensure that, come tomorrow night, he'd bed a very willing bride.

Ysenda was still reeling from that earth-shaking kiss when Caimbeul leaned toward her, clearly upset.

"Oh, sister, why?" he whispered in despair. "Why did ye do it? Why did ye agree to marry him?"

She rested a comforting hand on her brother's forearm. "Caimbeul, I couldn't let ye be hurt."

He looked miserable. "I'd rather die than have ye wed to a stranger."

"'Twill be fine. Ye'll see," she promised in a murmur, hoping she was right. "The Norman has vowed not to touch me tonight. The handfastin' won't stand. On the morrow, Da will see the error of his ways. He'll realize he can't defy the king. 'Twill be undone faster than ye can blink."

Caimbeul didn't look convinced, especially when he glanced past her at Sir Noël. But he nodded. "Promise ye won't let him touch ye."

She gave him a scheming grin. "I'll sleep with a dagger in my hand."

But Caimbeul didn't return her smile.

In the next moment, her attention was drawn away by Noël's men. As if by magic, they'd produced a cask of wine. Noël said it was the finest from Bordeaux, which he wished to share with his new clan.

Ysenda was impressed, both by the gesture and by the wine. She'd never had wine before. In the Highlands, they drank cider, ale, and, on special occasions, mead.

Noël filled a cup for the two of them to share. She took a sip of the ruby-colored liquid. It was clear, smooth, and sweet. It was also quite strong.

She handed the cup back to Noël. He clasped his hands over hers to drink. His callused palms were warm on her knuckles. She felt that warmth travel along her arms, up her throat, into her face.

Perhaps the wine was stronger than she thought.

He gazed at her as he swallowed. His midnight blue eyes sparkled with delight.

After he lowered the cup, a droplet of red wine lingered on his lips. Ysenda fought a wild urge to steal it with a kiss. Thankfully, he lapped it up before she could do something so reckless.

His hands were still wrapped around hers on the cup. And she was in no hurry to cast them off.

"Do ye like it?" he murmured, lowering his smoky gaze to her lips.

She gulped. "Aye."

His lip quirked up into a wry smile. "Would ye like more?"

Oh, aye, she thought, gazing at his delicious mouth. She'd

like much more. More of his smiles... More of his kisses... More...

"Cathalin?" he prompted.

She blinked, then nodded, startled by the strange name and by how quickly astray her thoughts had gone.

But she didn't dare let them wander. This was her sister Cathalin's husband, not hers, no matter what vows they'd exchanged. She'd do well to remember that.

Silently toasting her serious intentions, she downed the second cup all at once.

Noël chuckled in amazement. "Ye *do* like it." Then he curved a brow in warning. "But beware, lass, 'tis a wee bit stronger than what ye're used to."

She licked her lips. It *did* seem as if her skin was growing rather hot.

He refilled her cup a third time, giving her a coy wink that made her heart race.

Her sister was damned lucky. She hoped Cathalin realized how lucky she was.

Ysenda glanced over at her. Somehow, despite the haughty lift of Cathalin's brow and the knowing smirk on her lips, she was still beautiful. Ysenda wondered if she ever looked ugly.

Sighing, she lowered her eyes to her wine. Her father was right about one thing. One of his daughters was probably going to wed a grizzled old sheepherder. And it wouldn't be Cathalin.

"Are ye not pleased, *cherie?*" Noël asked.

Cherie. He'd called her *cherie.* And the concern in his furrowed brows was sincere.

Damn! It wasn't fair that demanding Cathalin was going to win such a prize. Men like him should be loved and adored, not scorned. She felt sorry for the sweet and noble knight.

"I'm fine," she assured him, instinctively touching his chest in pity. When she realized what she'd done, she tried to pull her hand back. But he caught it and clasped it against his chest, over his heart.

"I am yours, *cherie,* heart and soul, from this day forward."

Maybe it was just the wine, but his words made tears gather in her eyes. How she wished that could be true. And how she wished she could hold on to that promise forever.

He gave her hand a gentle squeeze. "I want nothin' more than to keep ye happy."

Her heart melted. Bloody hell. Her sister was going to make mince out of the poor man.

It startled Noël to realize that what he'd said was true. He wanted to please his new wife. He wanted to watch her lovely gray eyes light up with joy and see her pretty pink mouth widen in a smile.

He wasn't the sort of man to believe in love at first glance. But there was something about his bride that bewitched him.

Meanwhile, she was draining her third cup of wine with astonishing haste, like a warrior bracing for battle. He feared the wee lass would drink herself into oblivion if she wasn't careful.

He gently took the empty vessel from her and set it on the table. Maybe a bit of fresh air would clear her head.

"Would ye like to go out?" he whispered.

"Out?"

"Outside."

"'Tis night." Her brow creased. "'Tis wintertime."

"Ye don't strike me as the kind o' lass to be put off by a wee bit o' darkness or snow. And I've got a cloak to keep us warm."

Her eyes sparked as if he'd asked her on a forbidden adventure.

Without waiting for her reply, he took her hand and nodded toward the door. "Let's go."

Most of the clan were too distracted to note their departure. Caimbeul, however, had his scowl fixed on them. Noël gave him a nod that acknowledged the man's disapproval. But that didn't stop him from taking his bride's hand and stealing out the door into the night with her anyway.

The air was crisp and cold. The snow had stopped falling. White drifts draped the ground like a linen sheet. Noël swirled his woolen cloak over his bride's shoulders as they stepped into the courtyard.

She hesitated, glancing down at her feet. He realized she was wearing soft slippers meant only for the great hall.

Without hesitation, he swept her off her feet and into his arms. She gasped, clinging to him as if she feared he'd drop her. But she was no heavier a burden than his chain mail. He sauntered easily across the courtyard, past the outbuildings nestled against the bailey wall. His boots squeaked in the newly fallen snow.

"I suppose 'tis hard to think o' leavin' the place o' your birth," he said. "But I think ye'll grow to like France. And we can return here now and then if it pleases ye."

"That's very kind."

He smiled. "So tell me, what should I know about this land we're to inherit?"

Noël knew the Highlanders followed curious customs. One was that the oldest daughter could inherit the land and become laird in her own right. His brothers had shuddered at the notion. They'd warned him that ere long, his wife would be wearing trews and he'd be forced to don a kilt.

But the idea didn't trouble him. He'd always admired capable women. In fact, he was looking forward to sharing the responsibilities of the holding, particularly since he knew so little about clan life.

"The land?" She wrinkled her brow in thought. "Well... centuries ago, 'twas settled by Vikings."

"Vikings? Invaders?"

"Nae. They were peaceful enough. They came mostly to build homes. Indeed, many o' my ancestors came from Viking stock."

"I see."

"There's little left o' their settlement now, just a few stones here and there."

"What about the land? Does it provide well for ye?"

"Aye. There are fish in the loch and game in the forest—enough to keep the clan fed all winter. We keep sheep, cattle, and chickens. And we sow oats and barley. When summer comes, there are wild berries everywhere." She thawed just a little when she mentioned summer, relaxing against him.

"I'd like to see it in summer."

"'Tis a bonnie time. The braes are cloaked in green grass and wildflowers." Then a crease touched her brow. "Though they're also full o' ankle-bitin' midges."

He chuckled. "What's your favorite place?"

"My favorite?" She mused for a moment. "The Viking well, I suppose."

"The well?"

"'Tis an old stone ruin. But some say 'tis enchanted."

Noël felt enchanted himself. His bride fit into his arms as if she were made just for him. Her voice was soft and compelling. Her body felt warm and yielding against his. "Enchanted? And why is that?"

"Accordin' to ancient legend, two lovers hid in the well from those who would prevent their marriage. A storm arose, and the lovers drowned. They were cursed to live apart in the afterlife. But 'tis said that at Yuletide, if two lovers tie together locks o' their hair, weight them, and toss them into the well, the spirits o' the ones who drowned will bless them with magic, bindin' their souls together for eternity."

"Is that so?" Noël didn't believe in magic. Everything he'd

won, he'd earned—not by magic, but by the sweat of his brow. Still, he didn't want to dampen her spirits. "And is the legend true?"

She shrugged. "I wouldn't know."

"Maybe we should go and try it."

She stiffened in his arms. "Now?" She cleared her throat. "Nae, 'tis late. And 'tis too far away. There may be wolves about."

Noël knew a feeble excuse when he heard it. He might have fallen in love with his bride in an instant. But that didn't mean she shared his sentiments. He'd just have to be patient and win her affections in time.

"Perhaps on the morrow?" he asked.

"Perhaps."

Ysenda knew she should be cold. The air was frosty. The clouds were thick. There was a dusting of snow on all the tree branches. But she felt pleasantly cozy, tucked into the knight's arms, enveloped in his cloak, snug against his firm chest.

She could feel the flush in her cheeks. Whether it was from the Bordeaux or the fact that a handsome man was carrying her across the courtyard, she wasn't sure.

But when she suddenly succumbed to the irrational desire to steal a kiss, she blamed the wine.

It happened in an instant. In one moment, they were speaking reasonably, discussing the history and resources of the land. In the next, she pulled herself up by the edges of his cloak and pressed her lips to his.

Despite surprising him, he responded with levelheaded calm. Then, as if she'd done nothing untoward, he kissed her back.

After that, Ysenda—knowing full well she had no right to do it, no claim on him whatsoever—took his head between her hands and deepened the kiss.

The liquid warmth of their tangled tongues seemed to melt the icy night. Their fervent breaths mingled, making white mist against the black.

Suddenly, her hands were acting of their own will. Her fingers spanned his wide shoulders. They caressed the cords of his neck. They wove through the thick locks of his hair.

He pulled her closer. The pads of his fingers pressed into her back. His mouth ground against hers, tasting of wine and lust. And she liked the flavor.

"Ah, *mon dieu, cherie,*" he muttered between kisses.

As they continued feasting on each other, he tilted her body, letting her slip down to stand atop his boots. He took her head tenderly in his hands. He tipped up her chin, brushing his thumbs along the corners of her mouth. Then he drew her lower lip between his own, sucking gently.

Through a haze of desire, she felt his fingers drift down her throat and across her bosom. While he clasped the back of her head in one hand, the other strayed along the neck of her gown. When he delved beneath the linen, she was too delirious with desire to refuse him. And when his hand closed over her bare breast, she sucked in an awe-filled breath at the divine sensation.

She should have pushed him away. She should have clouted him. If she'd been in control of her senses, she would have shoved him into a snow bank to cool his loins.

But she wasn't.

All she could do was float on a heavenly vessel of lust, neither knowing nor caring where she was bound.

"Ah, *mon amour,*" he murmured against her mouth. "Let's go inside."

She nodded. Anything that whisked her away from this mad and perilous place would be a wise choice. Once they were inside, surely reason would prevail.

He gave her breast one last fond caress. Then he picked her up and carried her swiftly toward the keep.

Luckily, she could blame her ruddy lips and cheeks on the cold weather, though no one paid the couple much heed as they came in. Everyone was too busy passing around the Bordeaux.

Ysenda's breast still tingled where Noël had touched her. But her gown was safely in place. She'd checked it three times to be sure.

Sir Noël excused himself for a moment to confer with her father. The laird pointed up the stairs toward Cathalin's room, and Noël nodded.

Ysenda swallowed hard. This was not going to be easy.

Her brother glowered at her, as if he could read her mind.

She glowered back.

He shook his head.

She stuck out her tongue.

Unfortunately, Noël turned at that moment and caught her in the childish gesture. She quickly withdrew her tongue, but not before his face split into a grin.

She'd hoped their escape to the bedchamber would go unnoticed. But it was not to be. Four Frenchmen gathered round with great pomp to carry Noël on their shoulders. And before she could protest, two more had hoisted her up. With the clan cheering in noisy celebration, the couple were carried up the stairs and deposited before Cathalin's chamber.

Noël opened the door. Ysenda, unwilling to risk further humiliation, hurried in. She counted herself lucky his men didn't push their way past her to make themselves welcome in the bedchamber. Noël waved goodnight to the celebrants and secured the door.

The room was dim. While she stood beside the door, he hung up his cloak and crossed to the hearth, using the poker on the wall to jab the banked coals to life. Then he added a few chunks of peat to keep the fire going.

It had been a while since Ysenda had been in this chamber. Living in her cottage, she'd forgotten how luxurious the castle was. The carved wood bed was fitted with a thick pallet of feathers and draped in a deep blue brocade canopy. A heavy chest containing Cathalin's gowns crouched at its foot. A large wooden trestle table stood against one wall. Its top was littered with vials and jars of the oils, powders, and potions Cathalin used to maintain her beauty.

The window was shuttered at the moment. But she knew it afforded a magnificent view of the distant brae and the forest where the old Viking well stood, because once, this chamber had belonged to Ysenda as well.

While she was lost in her thoughts, Noël came up behind her. When his hands settled lightly on her shoulders, she jumped.

He chuckled. "I didn't mean to frighten ye, lass."

"I'm not frightened," she scoffed. It wasn't quite the truth. But showing fear was never wise. At least that was what her warrior mother had taught her.

He slid the edges of his thumbs along the tops of her shoulders. "I'm beginnin' to suspect ye're not frightened of anythin'."

He was wrong about that. At the moment, she was a bit frightened of herself.

"Ye made me a promise," she breathlessly reminded him. "I'm trustin' ye to be a man o' your word."

"I'm a de Ware," he said, as if that should explain everything.

Then he turned her in his arms to face him, holding her in his indigo gaze. "But ye know ye can only bend a man so far. I'm your husband now. On the morrow, I won't take nae for an answer."

She nodded. His demands were perfectly reasonable. But by morn, everything would be sorted out. And tomorrow night, in this very chamber, he would claim his husbandly rights...with her sister.

The idea turned her stomach.

Her eyes lowered to his mouth. She couldn't abide the

thought of Cathalin kissing Noël. Her brat of a sister didn't deserve to wrap her arms around his neck, to taste his sweet lips.

While she continued to stare, his mouth curved up in a slow, sly smile. "Go on then."

"What?"

"Kiss me."

"What?"

"I can see ye want to."

Flustered, she gave her head a wee shake.

"Go on," he urged, crossing his arms over his chest. "I won't even kiss ye back."

Kissing him again would be a mistake. She knew that. Yet she lowered her gaze to his mouth, considering the idea.

"Come on, lass. I can't wait forever," he teased.

On the other hand, this might be the last kiss she ever got...at least until she married whatever coarse and smelly sheepherder her father lined up for her.

It was that depressing thought that convinced her to take the chance while she had it.

"I suppose I can give ye one kiss goodnight," she decided.

"O' course."

"But only one."

His eyes twinkled with laughter. "Whate'er ye can spare."

Resting her hands on his crossed forearms, she rose onto her toes. She lifted her chin and closed her eyes. He lowered his head to meet her halfway. When she felt his faint breath upon her face, she moved toward him until their lips touched.

If this was to be her last kiss, she wanted to remember it. So she focused on the supple warmth of his lips and the coarse brush of stubble on his chin. She inhaled his masculine fragrance—all leather and iron and spice. Daring to let her tongue venture out, she savored the tempting taste of his mouth. She sighed against him with bittersweet longing.

And then he began to respond.

His mouth moved over hers, gently at first, and then with more urgency, as if he sought to drink the last bit of her before she was gone.

She too was filled with a strange desperation—a craving for more of him, for all of him. A soft moan of longing built in her throat. Frustration creased her brow.

His arms came unfolded. He pulled her into his embrace.

It was utterly thrilling.

It was also dangerous.

"Ye're...kissin' me...back," she cautioned between kisses.

"Am I?"

"Aye."

"Should I stop?"

She paused. "Nae."

CHAPTER 4

Scarcely realizing what she did, Ysenda began gliding her hands beneath his surcoat. His collar bone was hard and smooth under her fingers. His pulse beat forcefully at his throat. The muscles of his chest flexed beneath her touch. She slid her palms outward. The garment loosened, slipping from his massive shoulders.

Encouraged by her boldness, he rewarded her in kind. He tugged the neckline of her gown lower and lower until it perched precariously on the tips of her breasts.

When their tongues began to entwine, she lost all hope of propriety and control. An erotic vibration began in her ears, blocking out the voice of reason. She pulled at his clothing, eager for his flesh.

He growled inside her mouth like a hungry, wild beast. And she let him feed upon her. She leaned against him, yearning to be closer. At last he pushed her sleeves down, baring her breasts so he could press his warm skin to hers.

It was heaven—this feeling—and she never wanted it to end. Where their naked flesh made contact, it seemed to melt together. Their tongues mated, creating the most intoxicating ambrosia.

She let her hands roam over him with abandon. They swept across his sleek muscles and delved into his lush hair. She tried to memorize every inch of him with her fingertips.

It wasn't enough. She wanted more.

Breaking away from his mouth, she left a trail of kisses...from the corner of his lip...along his jaw...down the side of his neck where his pulse pounded.

He groaned and then sucked a hard breath between his teeth. He drew her closer, until she could feel the rigid length beneath his tabard.

She should have been appalled. Such a blatant display was improper, crude, disgusting. Yet disgust wasn't at all what she felt as he pressed against her.

Instead, a heady thrill coursed through her, as if the Bordeaux filled her veins, warming her blood and making her drunk.

She'd done that. *She'd* made him harden like that.

But wrapped up in her exhilarating triumph was also her surrender. Her bones were melting. Her heart was softening. Her resolve was weakening.

She didn't mean to retreat toward the bed. Somehow it just happened. Suddenly the back of her knees made contact with the wooden frame.

Noël, in his eagerness, continued to advance, covering her face with kisses, not realizing she had nowhere to go.

They toppled together onto the feather pallet.

In the small sliver of her mind that wasn't drunk on wine and desire, Ysenda knew she should resist him.

But a bigger part of her mind knew there was no hope of return. They'd leaped into the raging sea and were being carried away. And every sense she possessed told her to seize the moment.

So she did.

When he was a lad, one of Noël's brothers had tricked him into sitting astride an unbroken horse. The steed had bolted off across the countryside, taking him on a wild ride. And all he could do was hang on for his life.

Which was how he felt now.

He'd resigned himself to spending a tame and quiet evening with his new bride, convincing her with reasonable examples that he'd make a decent husband.

But when she began kissing him, his good intentions went right out of his head.

It wasn't as if he'd never been kissed. He was a de Ware, for heaven's sake. But he'd never been kissed with such passion, such enthusiasm, such genuine enjoyment.

It was his clumsiness that made them fall onto the bed. And once he was horizontal, it was hard to resist doing what came naturally any time he was horizontal with a woman in a bed.

Still, he tried to resist her.

But when the lovely lass began putting her hands on him—clutching at his tabard, tearing at his surcoat—she was difficult to ignore. When she rained feverish kisses all over his face, he was compelled to answer them. And when she rolled him onto his back, all his self-control vanished.

Afraid of the marriage bed?

Hardly.

His new bride was clearly no trembling novice. He wondered what game she played, trying to make him believe she was.

Perhaps she feared he wouldn't wed her if he found out she wasn't a virgin.

She needn't have worried on that account. Noël had always preferred voracity to virtue.

He chuckled low in his throat as she moved her hungry mouth along his collar bone. Now that he knew the truth, he couldn't help teasing her a bit.

"I thought ye said just one kiss."

"Did I?" she said breathlessly.

He grinned. No longer concerned about keeping a rein on his lust, he tangled his hands in her glorious hair and opened her mouth with his. He let his tongue dance on her lips, then plunge within, relishing her wine-sweet flavor.

It had been months since he'd lain with a lover. Once he'd learned of his betrothal to Cathalin, he'd sworn off coupling with other women.

But he was paying for his abstinence now. He was as hard as stone. Indeed, he felt as if he might explode at any moment.

Which would be a mistake. Nothing would disappoint a bride more than discovering her new husband spilled his seed quicker than a twelve-year-old lad.

So taking a sobering breath, he rolled her over, sitting back on his knees to straddle her so he could have more control. He slipped his hands beneath the neckline of her gown and slid it down past her shoulders, leaving kisses along the way. Then he pulled her garments lower, to her waist, trapping her arms beside her.

"Ye're so beautiful," he murmured. "They said ye were the bonniest lass in all Scotland. They were right."

She gasped as he slowly ran the pads of his thumbs down her soft breasts until they rested above her taut nipples.

Noël smiled as she arched up to force his touch, brushing the peaks of her breasts against his thumbs. Then he lowered his head to replace his thumb with his tongue, flicking lightly at each nipple before drawing the lovely nubbin into his mouth.

She groaned and clenched her fists.

Desire surged between his legs. But he had to temper his lust, at least until hers matched his.

He glided his hands slowly up her silken legs, raising her skirts. She lifted her head and jerked her arms as if she might try to stop him. But her hands were caught in her sleeves. And judging by the smoldering gray smoke of her gaze, he could see she didn't truly want him to cease.

Sure enough, when his fingers crested the tops of her knees and continued upward, she dropped her head back onto the pallet with a sigh of rapture.

When he reached the crease of her thighs, he pushed back her gathered skirts. There he stole a glimpse of heaven. Dark, curling hair made a small, perfect triangle against her fair skin. His loins ached with longing as he perused her lovely body.

Swallowing back his ravenous desire, he gently urged her legs apart. Slipping his fingers into her nest of curls, he opened her as tenderly as a flower.

Ysenda sucked a sharp breath between her teeth. Why was she letting him do this to her? She didn't know. But she couldn't form the words to stop him. Nor did she want to.

She wanted this.

Nae, she didn't want it. She *needed* it.

Yet it wasn't hers to have. He didn't belong to her.

Still, she wanted him so badly.

And when she felt his mouth upon her...down there...all rational thought abandoned her. Stricken by erotic lightning, she could form no words. His lips caressed her with delicious intimacy, flooding her with heat. His tongue bathed her with care, making her gasp in blissful wonder.

She squeezed her eyes closed, too ashamed of her own pleasure and weakness to face him. But her shame came with a curious joy. A powerful force began to build within her. Her veins filled with brilliant fire. Her blood surged with glorious energy. Her flesh warmed and swelled and longed.

Just when she thought she would burst with craving, the world seemed to stop for a timeless instant. Then, with a silent scream, she lost control.

She was rocked by waves of ecstasy as the most divine sensation encompassed her. It seemed she sailed along on a deep ocean of pleasure.

But it lasted for only a moment.

And then he plunged into her.

She cried out, feeling the sudden searing heat of his trespass like a knife.

Noël bit out a curse and froze. What the devil?

He'd been so sure his new bride was not a virgin.

Ah, god, he'd made a terrible mistake. An unforgivable one.

"Oh *non, non*," he lamented. "I'm so sorry, *cherie.*"

Her knuckles were white. Her eyes were tightly shut. And her lips were compressed into a tense line.

He ached with remorse. He'd give anything to undo what he'd done.

But he couldn't.

All he could do was to withdraw and leave her alone, as he should have done all along…as he'd promised her he would.

Yet if he withdrew, it would only make things more difficult. The next time, she would be even more reluctant, and with good cause.

That was no way to start a marriage.

Nae, if he wanted to repair the damage he'd done, he had to help her through the pain and bring her back to pleasure. So he remained within her.

"I'll make it better," he promised, smoothing the hair back from her troubled brow. "I didn't mean to hurt ye, lass. Truly I didn't."

He tugged her sleeves off, freeing her arms. Her hands relaxed. But she still wouldn't look at him. And it broke his heart. He had to fan the flames of her desire quickly before his own subsided.

"Ye aren't afraid, are ye?" he asked. "Because if ye are..."

That got her attention. She opened her eyes and furrowed her brow. "Nae."

She *was* afraid. He could see it in the way she sucked her lower lip under her teeth. But she wasn't going to admit it. And he rather admired her for that.

"I can make the pain go away," he said, "if ye'll allow me."

She looked doubtful. Then she gave him a nod.

Holding himself up on his elbows, he lowered his head to kiss her. But this time, he kissed her softly, tenderly. And when she answered too eagerly, he drew back. It was essential this time that she be completely ready.

It didn't take long. Soon she was reaching for him. She clasped the back of his neck to hold him close. She gasped against his throat and arched up until her bosom grazed his chest.

Then, to his relief, she began grinding her hips slowly against him. He closed his eyes as a ripple of desire coursed through his loins. Even a virgin instinctively knew the dance of love.

The sweet friction was almost too much to bear. He clenched his teeth against his release as she sought her own.

When she finally stiffened, opening her mouth in joyous awe, he groaned her name and drove deep within her. Together, they shuddered out their bliss.

For a weightless moment, Ysenda felt like a hawk, soaring high in the sky. There was no more pain, only freedom. Then she dove through clouds of pure pleasure, plummeting down so swiftly that her wings shivered on the air.

It would have been a moment of perfect bliss...if only he hadn't cried out her sister's name.

The word struck her like a slap in the face, snapping her back to reality.

Bloody hell! What had she done?

Noël, utterly spent, sank down upon her, careful to support his weight on his forearms. He heaved a contented sigh against her neck.

"Ah, lass, I'm so pleased to be your husband."

Ysenda gulped, wrapping her arms around him in an awkward hug.

She didn't know what to say.

She couldn't even pretend this was his fault. She'd encouraged him. She'd been the one who had to have that goodnight kiss. If he hadn't kept his promise, it was only because she'd led him to believe she was no longer holding him to it.

He'd done nothing wrong. He'd only made love to the woman he thought was his wife.

But Ysenda had committed a sin. She'd knowingly and intentionally consummated a counterfeit marriage.

"Are ye all right, *cherie*?" he murmured, lifting his head to look at her.

Nae, she was not all right. She'd behaved like a wanton. And she'd stolen her sister's bridegroom.

But she didn't dare confess to him. So she gave him a bleak smile and nodded.

He eased away to lie beside her, still holding her close.

"The next time," he promised, "'twill be better."

The next time? There could be no next time.

She bit her lip. She supposed she was ruined now. But she wouldn't make Noël pay the price for that. On the morrow, when her father came to his senses and handed over Noël's *real* bride, Ysenda would do the right thing, the merciful thing. She'd deny she'd ever bedded him.

The handfasting would be broken. Noël and Cathalin would be free to wed. He'd whisk his new wife away to his castle in

France. And Ysenda would probably never see him again.

She glanced over at the handsome knight with the dazzling smile and the kind heart. If he hadn't drifted off to sleep, he would have seen the childish tears gathering in her eyes.

It was silly, she knew. But she wanted him for herself. She didn't care that he wasn't a Highlander. She didn't care that he was Cathalin's. She didn't even care that she had nothing to offer him—no castle, no land, no title.

She'd given him her maidenhood already. And if she believed for an instant that he'd take it, she'd offer him her heart as well...for she was sure she'd fallen in love with him.

As mad as it sounded, it was true. Though she'd known him only a few hours, she knew he was everything she'd ever wanted in a husband. He was loyal, brave, sincere, fair. He commanded the respect of men and earned the admiration of women.

But her heart wasn't what Sir Noël had come for. He'd come for a political alliance. Besides, a man like him could have any maiden he chose. Why would he choose Ysenda when he'd been given the most beautiful woman in all of Scotland?

She turned away and sulked herself to sleep.

CHAPTER 5

Ysenda woke before the sun. In her sleep, she'd somehow wrapped her arms and one leg around her bedmate. She paled, realizing she had to untangle herself both from Sir Noël and from the mess her father had created before it was too late. She also had to make sure nothing bad had happened to Caimbeul.

She carefully extricated herself and glanced at the man sleeping beside her. She couldn't resist a fond grin. One side of his face was distorted where it was smashed into the downy mattress. His hair stuck out every which way, like a tree struck by lightning. His mouth hung open, and great snores issued forth. The noble knight didn't look quite so noble now. And yet his unguarded sleep made her adore him all the more.

How pleasant it would be to wake up each day to such an endearing sight...to hear the reassuring sound of his breathing...to peruse the sculpted contours of his...

She almost choked when she beheld the bold silhouette poking up the linen sheet. How could that be? How could he be aroused when he was fast asleep?

Her cheeks flaming, she crept out of the bed before things could get worse. She cast one last despondent glance at the man she was leaving behind. Then she left the chamber to seek out her brother.

"Where is he?" she demanded. "What have ye done with him?"

The laird grimaced as her sharp words pierced his aching head. "He's fine." He shooed her away and continued to poke among the kitchen stores for something to soothe the pain.

She found the vial of willow bark extract and shoved it into his hand. "Father, listen to me. What happened last night was a mistake. Ye can't go against the king. 'Tis..." She glanced around the cellar, even though it was too small to conceal spies. Then she whispered, "'Tis high treason."

"Ach!" he scoffed. "The king won't come marchin' all the way up here to enforce one wee marriage." But Ysenda detected a hint of uncertainty in his eyes. "Besides," he said, uncorking the vial and sniffing at the contents, "'tis too late now."

"But that's just it. 'Tisn't too late." She licked her lips, hating to lie. "We didn't...that is...there was a weddin'...but there was no beddin'."

He screwed up his face in disbelief. "What?"

"The handfastin' can be broken now. He'll be free to marry Cathalin."

He stared at her as if she were stupid. "He's not marryin' Cathalin."

Ysenda's heart plummeted. "But he has to. The king decreed it. Ye signed the papers yourself."

"I'm not givin' my land to a Norman, no matter what the king decrees."

"But my laird...Da...don't ye see? Ye've been given a second chance."

He narrowed his eyes. "Ye wily wench. Ye refused him on purpose."

"Aye, I did. I did it for the good o' the clan. I could see ye weren't in your right mind last night. And I knew if I didn't—"

The back of his fist cracked suddenly against her cheek, rocking her head and making her stagger sideways. She caught herself on the shelf, knocking over a row of bottles that clattered on the stones.

She blinked in shock and worked her jaw, making sure he hadn't knocked out any teeth. Her instincts told her to repay him with a solid punch of her own. It wouldn't have been the first time she'd given as good as she'd gotten from a man.

But for once she had to resist the urge.

After all, he was the laird.

He was her father.

And he had Caimbeul locked away somewhere.

"How dare ye speak to me like that," he snarled. "I know what's best for the clan. And 'tisn't havin' a laird that's not even Scots."

She ignored her stinging cheek. Somehow she had to convince him he was making a mistake. "But Da, he must be a decent man. The king himself chose him. He'll be good to Cathalin and provide for the clan as well as—"

"Nae, 'tis settled." He took a tiny sip from the vial, wrinkling his nose. "Cathalin's bridegroom, her *Highland* bridegroom, is due to arrive any day now. I'll simply say we couldn't wait any longer for their Norman knight, that by the time he arrived, her weddin' had already taken place."

"You'd lie to the king?"

"'Tisn't a lie. 'Tis a stretch o' the truth."

"And what will ye tell Sir Noël when this Highlander arrives?"

"He'll be long gone. Your husband seems very keen to get home." He toasted her with the vial, took a generous swig, shuddering at the bitter taste, then stuck the cork back in. "Ye know, ye should count yourself lucky, lass. In France, ye'll be a proper lady."

"But Sir Noël will find out I'm not Cathalin."

"Not unless ye tell him."

Her thoughts raced. "And what if I tell him now?"

"Oh, I don't think ye'll do that."

"And why not?"

"Because I'm holdin' that hunchback pet o' yours, and ye don't want to see anythin' bad happen to him."

Ysenda clenched her hands at her sides. She wanted to think he was bluffing, that he wouldn't do anything to harm his own flesh and blood. But she knew better. The laird had been wanting to get rid of his embarrassing son from the moment he'd first seen him.

Laird Gille chuckled. "Ye know, ye're just like your ma. Strong-willed and weak-hearted. Don't think I don't know about your sneakin' in tutors to teach that halfwit."

"He's not a..." She managed to stop herself, but only because she knew it was hopeless.

"Ye'll do fine in France. And if ye get too headstrong for Sir Noël's taste, he has an army o' braw lads at his command to keep ye in line."

If he was trying to scare her, it wasn't working. She trusted Sir Noël completely. What she couldn't anticipate was his reaction when he discovered he'd been gulled by her father...and by her, for that matter. Would he believe the truth—that she'd been in fear for her brother's life? And if not, what would he do to exact revenge? Would he toss her aside and demand his true bride? Would he make war on the clan and lay siege to the keep?

A voice came from beyond the door. "Good morrow?"

Ysenda sucked in a quick breath. It was Sir Noël.

Her father arched a brow. "Your husband's callin' ye." He smirked. "Probably comin' for somethin' ye forgot to give him last night."

"Cathalin?" Noël called.

Ysenda winced.

Her father snickered.

"In here," she called back, swinging open the door.

Noël was even more magnificent than she remembered. He'd finger-combed his hair. His face was freshly scrubbed. He was dressed again in his dark blue surcoat, which set off his sparkling eyes.

Unfortunately, he looked nothing like a man who'd been forced to spend his wedding night in unrequited passion. And the memory of what they'd done washed over her like a warm wave, heating her cheeks.

"Ah. Good morn...son," her father said. Somehow he managed to make the word sound like both an insincere welcome and an insult. He'd never called Caimbeul "son." Not once.

"My laird," Noël replied with a nod. Ysenda got the distinct impression Noël didn't care to call Laird Gille "Father" either.

Already there was animosity between them. If Lord Noël found out that the laird had tricked him, it would get ugly. She couldn't afford to let that happen, not before Caimbeul was safe.

"Have ye broken your fast, Sir Noël?" she asked, taking his hand, eager to separate the two men. "Are ye hungry?"

"Aye." Noël was hungry, to be sure. He wanted to feast on his wife's lovely body again.

His wife. He loved the sound of that. And to think he'd been dreading meeting his Highland bride.

When he'd awakened to find her gone, he feared it might have all been a dream. But the rumpled sheets smelled like her—fresh, warm, and womanly—and that scent had stirred him to life.

Now, walking beside his lovely new wife, he had to resist the urge to sweep her up the stairs, toss her onto the bed, and make love to her...all day long.

"There should be bannocks in the bakehouse," she said, ushering him out the door of the great hall.

The courtyard was still covered in white. But the sun had peeped out this morn. Icicles dripped from the thatched roofs of the outbuildings. The snowy expanse twinkled like crystals.

His bride was still in her slippers. So he scooped her up to carry her toward the bakehouse.

She squeaked, startled.

He grinned down at her. Then he noticed something that made his smile vanish. One side of her face was red, as if someone had clouted her.

He stopped walking and tipped up her chin to examine the mark. He clenched his teeth. "Your cheek—did someone strike ye?"

She frowned, tugging her chin away. "Nae," she told him. "I probably just slept on it."

He suspected she wasn't telling him the truth. "Ye know that I'm your protector now." Indeed, he was surprised by just how fiercely protective he felt. "If anyone touches ye, he'll have to answer to me."

Her eyes went all soft and dewy when he said that. But he was serious. Any man who laid a hand on a defenseless woman deserved to be beaten to a bloody pulp.

"'Tis very chivalrous," she said. "But ye know *I* come from a long line o' warrior maids."

"So I've heard."

Still, he had a hard time believing his wee wisp of a wife could fend off a grown man. If someone *had* struck her—and he suspected it might be her father—perhaps it was a good thing he was taking her away from this place.

He carried her to the bakehouse. As she'd promised, there were oat bannocks, fresh out of the pan. They were warm, buttery, and filling. He ate three of them. But he saved his last bite for her. He fed her from his hand, letting his fingertip linger on her lip.

He'd appeased one hunger, but the other still nagged at him. He stared at her beautiful mouth. Then, not caring whether it was proper in Scotland, he pulled her close, lifted her chin, and placed a soft kiss on her lips.

She responded at once, letting her eyes drift closed. Her lips were pliant beneath his as she dissolved against him. He pulled her closer, reveling in her warmth. Her arms traveled up around his neck. And then he felt a strong surge of lust in his braies, one he had trouble concealing.

She gasped lightly, and he knew she felt it as well. Without another word, he finished the kiss, nodded to the baker, picked up his bride, and headed back to the keep.

Thankfully, no one stood in his way—not her unpleasant father, not Noël's knights, not the Caimbeul lad. He climbed the stairs and pushed open the door to her chamber.

Then he stopped. Her sister was there, rummaging through Cathalin's clothes.

"Oh!' she exclaimed in surprise, looking back and forth between the two. "I...I just needed to...borrow a gown...from Cathalin. Is that all right...Cathalin?"

Ysenda had never felt more awkward. There was no question now. They were all conspiring together to fool the Norman knight. When he found out...

She glanced at him and gulped. Considering the breadth of his chest, his powerful muscles, and the formidable men who followed him about...she didn't want to be there when he found out.

But there was nothing she could do about it now. As far as Cathalin, it seemed that as long as her sister was granted access to her extravagant gowns, she wasn't in the least perturbed that Ysenda might be swiving the man who should have been *her* husband.

"Cathalin?" her sister prompted again.

"O' course," Ysenda said. "Help yourself."

She gave them a knowing smirk. "I can come back later if—"

"Nae," she said. "We're only—"

"Aye," Noël said simultaneously. "Come back later."

Cathalin left with a wink, coyly waving the stockings she'd picked out.

This was a disaster. Ysenda had still hoped she could persuade her sister, if not her father, to see reason. Surely Cathalin wouldn't wish to be the target of two kings' wrath. But now it would be impossible to convince her sister that she'd never consummated the handfasting.

Noël didn't seem to note her distress. He had only one thing on his mind. And the longer Ysenda gazed into his smoldering azure eyes, the more she had to agree that nothing else seemed important.

What started as feathery, inviting kisses grew urgent and demanding. Against her better judgment, she began caressing his flesh and then grasping at his clothes. By the time they tumbled headlong onto the bed, they were already half undressed.

She told herself it didn't matter if they made love again. After all, they'd consummated the handfasting. What difference did it make whether they coupled once, twice, or a dozen times? A lie was still a lie.

But the truth was she was too overwhelmed by desire to think straight. She wanted him. She wanted this. And when Noël peeled off his surcoat and tossed it aside, the sight of him left her breathless.

There was no time for the play in which they'd indulged last night. They both knew what they needed. There was no reason to delay.

He pushed up her skirts and smoothly sheathed himself inside her. She welcomed him with shivering desire.

This time it felt like they were running together up the slope of a great brae. They panted with exertion as they neared the top. When they reached the peak, they paused to admire the beautiful glen below. Then they tumbled down the other side as fast as a waterfall, rushing over the rocks and diving into a deep, refreshing pool.

Afterward, as they caught their breath, Ysenda thought she'd never felt as contented as she did, lying in Noël's arms. A brilliant glow seemed to surround them, protecting them from regret and guilt and sorrow. She closed her eyes and enjoyed the peace of utter satisfaction.

But all too soon, it faded away. Then she was left with remorse and worry.

What would he think when he found out she was a pretender? Would he think she was no better than a wanton harlot who had used him for her own gratification? Or just a heartless betrayer?

She bit her lip as an even worse thought occurred to her.

What if he'd gotten her with child?

He leaned on one elbow, gazing down at her with adoration and gratitude, two things she knew she didn't deserve. But she forced a smile to her lips.

"Let's get out o' here," he said with a lopsided grin.

"Now?" For an awful instant, she thought he meant to leave immediately for France.

"Aye." He brushed her hair back from her brow. "Why don't we pack a wee feast, and ye can show me this wishin' well o' yours?"

She let out the breath she'd been holding. Brilliant idea. She needed to get away from the temptation of the bedchamber. There was still a chance that Cathalin would decide to do the right thing and agree to wed her intended husband. Ysenda didn't want to jeopardize that possibility any more than she already had.

Still, it was with great regret that she donned her sister's warmest clothing and boots. She bid a silent farewell to the downy bed and to the ecstasy she would never have again...yet never forget.

Noël knew his men were restless, eager to be home. And now that the handfasting had been sealed, there was no reason to remain in Scotland. If they left on the morrow, there might even be some of the holiday left to enjoy.

He smiled at the thought of sharing his new bride with his family. He couldn't wait to show Cathalin the beautiful Christmas crèches. He wanted her to see the jongleurs performing caroles in the hall. And on his birthday, he wanted to drink warm mulled wine with her beside the fire.

Still, he didn't wish to appear rude to her clan. One day, all of this would be his, and he hadn't even given it a decent inspection. So as much as he'd prefer to lie in bed with his delectable wife all day, he decided he should do the proper thing and make a tour of the land.

Now, as they slogged through the snowy field toward the forest, Noël had to admit he was surprised by just how extensive the holding was. It appeared the king had been quite generous. They'd been hiking for some time.

"How much farther is it?" he asked.

"Not far. Just through those trees, in the clearin'."

Her cheeks were rosy with the cold. Her breath made fog on the air. And her gray eyes shone with excitement. It almost seemed a pity to tear her away from the land she loved so much.

"There," she breathed when they finally reached a small clearing in the wood where stray beams of sunlight seemed to cast glittering gems in the snow.

The well wasn't much of a well anymore. It was a ruin. A winding stream ran into what was left of the stone walls and trickled down the other side. Ferns grew up around the moss-covered rock. Snow-laden pines crowded near, their tops bent inward as if to shield the well from intruders. If Noël didn't know better, he'd say it *was* a magical place.

As they drew near, he saw a curious stone disk sitting askew atop the well. It looked like a dislodged lid.

"There's an inscription on top," she told him. "See the Viking runes?"

"What does it say?"

"'Tis a blessin'. For a quiet journey, joyful days, and strong deeds for Odin."

"Odin?"

"The Viking god." She ran her fingers across the carved runes. "And here it says, 'May your love stay true to your noble heart'."

He nodded. "That sounds like a good blessin'." He drew his dagger. "Do ye think we should try it? Shall we cut locks of our hair and—"

"Oh, nae!" she blurted out. "I don't think so."

Her response set him on his heels. Yesterday he expected her to have some qualms about staying true to a man she'd never met. But they were properly married now.

And they'd made love.

Twice.

"Nae?"

"'Tis just...I guess..." she said, stumbling over the words, "I guess I don't much...believe in wishes."

"Hmm." She wasn't being completely forthcoming with him. But he supposed it didn't matter. Wish or no wish, he intended to stay true to his noble heart. And he intended to keep his new bride so satisfied that she wouldn't even *think* of straying.

He sheathed his dagger, and then peered over the stone lid

and into the abyss of the well. It seemed like a perilous thing to leave open. A small child could fall in and drown. *Their* small child.

"'Tis deep," he said with a frown. "If I were laird now, I'd seal it up."

"Oh, ye mustn't do that."

"And why not?"

"Because the spirits will be trapped inside. Besides, at this time o' year, all the lasses toss their wishes in it."

"I thought ye didn't believe in wishes."

"Well, *I* don't, nae," she said, coloring a little. "But the others..."

"I see," he said with a grin. He crossed his arms over his chest. "Ye know, ye're quite bonnie when ye blush like that."

She gave him a teasing push. "I'm not blushin'. 'Tis only the cold."

"Well, I'll have to warm ye then, won't I?" He didn't wait for an answer. He opened his cloak and swept it around her, enfolding them both. "Better?"

Ysenda nodded. She had to admit it *was* better. But not because she was cold. She had the thick blood of a Highlander, after all. And her sister's fur-lined wool cloak and sturdy leather boots were good protection against the snowdrifts.

It was better because she felt...protected...in Noël's arms.

She could protect herself, of course. Her mother had passed on enough of her fighting skills to ensure that her daughter wouldn't be left vulnerable.

But there had never been anyone to champion Ysenda. She'd fought against the prejudice of her father. She'd battled the arrogance of her sister. She'd defended her brother when he was too weak to defend himself. But she'd always fought alone. No one had ever stepped in and taken her side.

Now, for the first time, snuggled in the arms of this Norman warrior, she felt absolutely safe.

"How long have ye been a knight?" she asked.

"I'm a de Ware. I was *born* with a sword in my hand."

She chuckled and gave him a poke in the ribs. "That must have been painful for your mother."

"Oh, aye, the poor woman had eight of us wee knights."

"Eight? 'Tisn't a family. 'Tis an army."

"France's best," he said proudly. He wrapped his arms tighter around her. "I can't wait to show ye off to my brothers."

He began to rattle off their names, too many to remember, giving a humorous description of each. And with each name, Ysenda grew more and more despondent. They sounded so wonderful. But she was never going to meet them. And she had to face that fact.

Indeed, the reason she wouldn't wish at the Viking well was that she didn't want to indulge in the false hope that she could somehow keep him for herself.

As she watched the stream in silence, her eyes mirrored the well, filling with water. A secret tear trickled down her cheek as she longed with all her heart for that which she couldn't have. Then, ashamed of her selfishness, she quickly wiped it away.

His voice was full of affection as he continued speaking about his family. Meanwhile, the water gurgled over the rocks. The ice at the edges of the rill made soft cracks as it yielded to the sun. Snowmelt dripped from the trees.

Ysenda closed her eyes, wishing she could stay here forever, enfolded in his arms.

She wished a lot of things.

But what she'd said was true. She didn't believe in wishes.

CHAPTER 6

Noël spent most of the morn with his new bride, hiking across braes and moors, through the pine forest and past a great loch. They stopped along the way to share the small feast of oatcakes and soft cheese they'd packed, washing it down with cider.

Afterward, she pointed out the best fishing place and the spot where the lasses liked to bathe in summer. She showed him the rotting remnants of a Viking longhouse where she used to play and the holly grove where her mother had once frightened away two wolves. He saw how much she loved the land. It made him love it as well.

But there was also a touch of sorrow in her gray eyes. He wondered... Was it the idea of leaving her home that saddened her? Or something more?

He thought again about the young man who'd sat next to her at the table. They'd seemed very close. Did her heart belong to him? Jealousy pricked at Noël again.

He supposed it didn't matter. They'd journey to France in a day or two, leaving everyone she knew far behind.

Still, that didn't change the way she *felt.* And Noël wanted his bride to be in love with *him.*

The idea was laughable. He'd come to Scotland for one purpose—to make a political alliance. Falling in love had never been part of his plans.

But that didn't change the fact that he wanted to win her heart now. He wanted to make her smile. He wanted to bring the joy back into her eyes.

"So, lassie, when was the last time ye made a snowwoman?" he asked.

She quirked her brow at him. "I've made a snow*man.*"

"Oh, aye, everyone's made a snowman. But have ye made a snow*woman?*"

She gave him a skeptical grin. "I don't see how there could be much difference."

"What? O' course there's a difference. Come on, I'll show ye."

Together they piled and packed the snow until they had a vertical mound that was about her size. He rounded the top into a ball for a head. She formed two stubs to serve as chubby arms. Then she sought out two small pine cones to make eyes. He made a small snowy nose, and he stuck a curved twig under it, turning it into a frown.

"Why is she so unhappy?" she asked.

"Because she looks like a snow*man.*"

"I told ye there was no difference."

He scowled and stroked his chin, studying the sculpture. "Perhaps if ye found some beautiful flowin' hair for her."

She perused the glen and found golden drifts of fallen pine needles near the trunks of the trees. While she was busy gathering them, he set to work. He patted together two small globes of snow and plucked a holly berry to perch in the middle of each one. These he affixed strategically to the front of the body. Then he waited for her return.

First she gasped. Then she giggled. It was a delightful sound.

"Shame on ye, Sir Noël," she scolded, unable to keep the laughter from her voice.

"Shame?" he asked, all innocence. "Why?"

Her silvery eyes danced as she came up beside him. "Ye aren't goin' to leave her like that."

"Like what?"

She gave him a chiding elbow. "Undressed."

"She'll be fine," he assured her. "She won't get cold. She's a snowwoman."

"'Tisn't the cold I'm talkin' about, and ye know it."

He reached out and turned the frowning twig into a smile. "But look how happy she is now."

She shook her head. "Ye're a naughty lad."

He winked at her. "Ah. Wait till ye see my snow*man.*"

For a moment, she only stared at him. Finally her eyes went wide, and her mouth formed a shocked "O." She started pelting him with the pine needles.

He laughed and shook off the deluge. Then he caught her about the waist and hauled her to him.

Kissing her felt as natural and instinctive as breathing. Her lips opened to his as readily as a lock to a key. Her laughter spilled into his mouth, and he lapped up her joy. Their tongues touched, and the current bolted through him, making him instantly hard and eager.

If it were summer, he would have spread his tabard on the soft grass and made sweet love to her, right there and then.

But the world was wet and frozen.

So, between kisses, he gasped out, "Let's go back...to the keep...before I turn *ye*...into a snowwoman."

Shaking off his lust, he took her hand and began the short hike home, happy he'd made her smile. But by the time they emerged from the wood, in view of the keep, he was already thinking about her warm bedchamber.

"I'll race ye," he said.

"What?" She giggled.

"Come on. Whoever is first to the gate gets to undress the last."

She was still puzzling out whether it would be better to win or lose when he bolted off across the snow.

"Wait!" she cried. "Ye cheated!"

"Hurry up!"

"But ye never said go!"

"Go!" he yelled.

He gained several good yards. But then he made the mistake of turning around to gloat. While he was running backward, his heel caught on a tree root, and he fell smack on his arse.

She burst into laughter, charging past him as he scrambled to get up.

"Come back here, wife!" he bellowed after her.

"I don't think so!" she crowed.

"But a wife's supposed to obey her husband!"

She only laughed.

Chuckling, he dusted the snow off of his surcoat and let her get a short distance ahead. He was enjoying the view, after all, watching her bustling backside and catching a glimpse of her lovely calves as she picked up her skirts to scurry through the snow.

He couldn't get over the fact that she was his. That breathtaking, vibrant, fresh-faced Highland lass belonged to him. How he'd gotten so lucky, he didn't know. But he didn't intend to let her get away from him. Now or ever.

In the end, he let her win, but only by an instant. He nipped at her heels the whole way, making her squeal in panic one moment and giggle at his antics the next. By the time they collapsed against the gate, they were breathless from running and giddy with laughter.

He grinned into her shining gray eyes and bent to give her a bold kiss, deciding he didn't care whether it was proper or not. What should it matter if a few curious clansmen saw how much he loved his bride?

Her lips were cool. Her tongue was warm. Her breath

mingled with his as they kissed, then caught their breath, then kissed again.

"You win," he whispered, cradling her face with his palm. Then he stepped back with his arms outstretched. "Go ahead. Undress me."

She gasped in delighted shock, shoving at his chest. "Ye're a wicked, wicked man."

She'd add a few more "wickeds" if she could read the lusty thoughts coursing through his head right now. Of course, he wasn't about to act on any of them. By now there were several sets of eyes on them.

Instead, he escorted her politely through the gate, walking hand-in-hand with her.

The courtyard was bristling with Yuletide preparations. Cooks roasted haunches of mutton on a great spit. Maidservants tied together clumps of evergreen with red ribbon. Kitchen lads carted baskets of bread into the keep. And in one corner of the yard where the snow had been shoveled away, his men were sparring, providing lively entertainment for the laird and for the wee lads gathered round.

When Noël lifted his gaze, he saw someone else was watching. At the highest window of the tower, intently studying the knights, was Caimbeul.

"They're very good," his bride exclaimed as she saw his men crossing blades.

He smiled. "Aye." The Knights of de Ware were the best swordsmen in France.

He peered up again at the window. Caimbeul had spotted him. The young man was staring back at him with a venomous glare.

Noël frowned. Was that jealousy? He had to find out. He might not be able to mend the lad's broken heart. But he could at least try to make peace with him and make the truth—that Cathalin was his wife now—easier to bear.

"Would ye like to watch them for a bit?" he asked her.

"Aye, if ye don't mind."

"Not at all." Kissing her knuckles and releasing her hand, he glanced up again at the scowling Caimbeul. "I'll be back. I've somethin' to attend to."

Ysenda admired good swordsmen. It was a trait she'd doubtless inherited from her mother. And the Knights of de Ware were far superior to any fighters she'd seen in Scotland.

But that wasn't the real reason she wanted to watch them.

She mostly wanted to avoid going to Cathalin's bedchamber.

Ysenda's will was weaker than ever now. Not only did she desire this Norman knight with the handsome face, unruly black hair, and dazzling blue eyes. But now she also adored him.

He made her laugh. He made her feel beautiful. He made her feel loved.

She glanced down at the Wolf of de Ware ring on her finger. Giving him up was going to be painful. And the more intimate they became, the harder it would be.

Cathalin was watching the knights battle as well. Maybe if Ysenda could get her sister alone, talk to her, she could make her see reason.

After Noël left, she approached.

"Cathalin," she whispered, tugging on her sleeve.

Cathalin whipped her head around. "Don't call me that," she hissed. "They might hear ye."

"We need to talk."

"There's nothin' to talk about."

"'Twill take but a moment. We likely won't see each other again for years. Can we not at least say farewell?"

Cathalin rolled her eyes. "Ach, very well. I've grown weary o' watchin' these French bairns playin' with their wee blades anyway."

Wee blades? Their broadswords might not be as big as a Scots claymore, but Ysenda was sure an agile Norman with a light blade had a definite advantage over a Highlander with a heavy sword.

They retreated to a spot along the back wall of the keep.

Cathalin crossed her arms over her bosom. "What did ye wish to say?"

"I need ye to think about what ye're doin'."

"I know exactly what I'm doin'. I'm marryin' a Highlander. And he and I will inherit the castle and rule the clan when Da is gone."

"But don't ye see? The kings won't allow it. They've betrothed ye to a Norman because they want a Norman to hold the land."

"It doesn't matter if they'll allow it. 'Twill be done. I'll be wed ere they can have their say." She smirked. "Besides, ye've already made good on the handfastin'."

"We can say I haven't," Ysenda said, clutching her sister's sleeve in desperation. "We can say 'twas never consummated. Then ye'll be free to..." She almost choked on the words. "To wed Sir Noël."

"I don't *want* to wed Sir Noël."

"Ye must. 'Tis the will o' the king."

"I don't care," Cathalin said with a pretty pout. "Besides, Da said the royals wouldn't dare come to the Highlands to—"

Ysenda grabbed her sister by the shoulders. "They *will* come. They'll send men like those," she said, pointing toward the Knights of de Ware. "And they'll kill everyone in the clan if ye don't do as the king wills."

Cathalin pried Ysenda's hand from her shoulder. "Then ye're goin' to have to keep pretendin' *ye're* Cathalin. 'Tis the only way to keep the peace."

Ysenda sighed in exasperation. "He'll find out. Even if I say nothin', it won't be a secret for long. As soon as Da dies, the secret will be out."

Cathalin straightened with pride. "By then my Highland husband will have raised an army to defend the keep." She scoffed. "His men will slaughter every last one o' these wee bairns with their wee blades."

Ysenda could only stare at her sister, mortified. How could Cathalin be so delusional, so reckless? She would bring destruction down upon their clan. And for what? So she could wed the man of her choice? A man she'd never even met?

She wanted to wring her sister's perfect neck.

But maybe she could try a different approach. Ysenda had no intention of going to France in Cathalin's stead, leaving Caimbeul and their clan behind to be killed by the king's army.

"Ye know, Sir Noël would be a very good match for ye." The words were hard to push past her throat. "He comes from a wealthy family. Ye'd live in a beautiful castle. Ye'd have everythin' ye desire. Servants at your beck and call. All the new gowns ye want. Jewels, furs, falcons. Sir Noël would grant your every wish, I know. And your bairns... They'd be the most beautiful children in all o' France."

"That may be." Cathalin sniffed. "But I refuse to marry such a blind and stupid man."

She blinked. "What do ye mean?"

Cathalin lifted her haughty chin. "How could the fool have thought *ye* were the most beautiful lass in all o' Scotland?"

While Ysenda stood with her mouth agape, Cathalin picked up her skirts and stalked off in a vexed huff.

Ysenda could only stare off after Cathalin. She couldn't argue with her. That *was* what Sir Noël had thought. And once Cathalin's pride was insulted, there was no way to assuage her feelings.

Hell. Now she didn't know what to do.

Noël rapped lightly on the door. "Caimbeul?"

There was no answer. But he heard a startled scrape on the other side.

He slowly opened the door, preparing to defend himself if necessary.

Caimbeul was sitting on the floor below the window, scowling up at him.

"I need to speak with ye," Noël said.

Caimbeul's frown turned mistrustful.

Noël closed the door behind him. Caimbeul made no move to rise, but perhaps the young man's twisted frame made it difficult for him to stand. He obliged the lad by hunkering down before him.

"I think 'tis best we speak plainly," he told him, "so I'd like the truth from ye. Do ye have...feelin's for my bride?"

Caimbeul's face twisted. "Feelin's? What do ye mean?"

"Romantic feelin's."

Caimbeul's eyes narrowed with rage. Before Noël could dodge aside, the young man shot out a furious fist. Fortunately, it missed Noël's nose, but only because a heavy iron chain around his wrist brought it up short. Still, Noël instinctively recoiled, falling backward onto his hindquarters.

"How dare ye!" Caimbeul yelled. "She's my sister, ye horse's arse!"

Noël didn't know what shocked him more—the fact that Caimbeul packed an impressive punch for a crippled man, that he was chained like an animal, or that he was his bride's brother. He held up a hand in peace.

"Wait. Ye're her brother? The laird's son?"

"Aye," he ground out.

Noël sat forward, resting his forearms on his knees. He

remembered the laird's attitude toward Caimbeul at the table. He'd never introduced him as his son. And he'd treated him with a distinct lack of respect.

"Is your father the one who put ye in chains?"

Caimbeul didn't answer. His frown of shame was answer enough.

Why would the laird do such a thing? Was he afraid his son would interfere with the wedding? Maybe Caimbeul thought he was protecting his sister.

"Tell me, man to man," Noël said. "Do ye disapprove o' me? Do ye think I'm not good enough for your sister?"

Caimbeul's eyes burned with silent anger. "Which sister?"

It was a strange question. "The one I'm married to, o' course."

Caimbeul stared at him in silence for a long while, as if deciding whether to say anything further. Finally he did. "Ye're not married to the right one."

"What do ye mean?"

Instead of answering, Caimbeul focused on the ground and said tightly, "Ye've slept with her, haven't ye?"

Noël let the lad's words sink in. What did he mean, "the right one"? Was it possible he'd married the wrong sister?

"She's Cathalin. Aye?" he asked, fearful of the answer.

"She's not."

Noël felt the breath freeze in his chest. How could that be? How could he have wed—and coupled with—the wrong sister?

Then he glanced again at the young man. Perhaps Caimbeul was mad. Perhaps he was confused. Perhaps that was why his father had chained him up.

"Are ye certain?" he asked.

"O' course I'm certain. I know my own sisters. Ye've wed...and bedded," he added with a sneer, "Ysenda, not Cathalin."

Noël couldn't comprehend it all. He rose slowly to his feet. "But why would..."

"My father wanted a Highlander, not a Norman, to inherit his land."

"But 'tisn't up to your father. Two kings have decreed this marriage."

"Aye, and ye've seen it through. As far as ye know, ye're wedded to Cathalin."

"But that's ridiculous. If she's not the real Cathalin, then when the laird dies—"

"Ye'll inherit nothin'. The land will go to the *real* Cathalin and her Highlander husband."

Noël was astounded. "That can't be true. Every member o' the clan would have to be privy to the deception in order for—"

"No one said a word when you mistook Ysenda for Cathalin. They were too afraid to gainsay the laird. My father was overjoyed. Ye played perfectly into his hands."

All the air went out of Noël's lungs. How could this have happened? Had his honest mistake become an act of rebellion? He shook his head, which was spinning as he recalled the events of the past day.

"Your father was afraid ye'd speak out," he realized. "That's why he had a knife at your throat."

Caimbeul nodded.

"And why he's put ye in chains now."

"Aye."

"Then he mustn't know I came to speak with ye." Noël straightened and placed a hand of reassurance on Caimbeul's forearm. "I don't know how, but I promise ye...brother...I'll make everythin' right."

With that, he left the chamber. But his mind was far from settled. And as he descended the stairs, he began thinking—not like a suitor, but like a warrior.

By offering him the wrong bride, Laird Gille had intentionally broken an oath to two kings. By rights, Noël should drag him before the royal court.

But the clan would turn on him if he made a prisoner of their laird. That was the last thing he wanted to do, considering that some day these people would be his responsibility. He'd always ruled his knights, not by force, but by earning their respect. And that was how he wished to rule the clan.

Besides, he'd only brought a small contingent of his men. True, they were Knights of de Ware. But they were no match for a hundred angry clansmen.

There had to be another way. And he was determined to find it.

Still, that wasn't the most troubling aspect of the deception for Noël. The worst part was knowing his bride had lied to him. She'd held his hand, kissed him, spoken the handfasting vows.

His brow creased as he remembered she'd asked him not to consummate the marriage. Perhaps she'd had one moment of regret then.

But they *had* consummated the marriage. She'd let him... Nae, he corrected, he'd imposed himself upon her. It had been an accident, but it *had* been his fault. Maybe she hadn't wanted for it to happen.

Still, she'd never told him the truth—that she was not his real betrothed—even though there had been ample opportunity for her confession.

She'd laughed with him.

She'd slept with him.

She'd made him fall in love with her.

Was it all a lie? Did she have no feelings for him?

He frowned, swallowing down the lump lodged in his throat.

It didn't matter, he told himself. They were not intended to be husband and wife anyway. He would find some way to annul the marriage. No one had seen them in the bedchamber. He could claim he'd never consummated the handfasting. That way she could continue her life, unburdened by their sin.

But his heart felt like it was breaking in two. He couldn't get her laughing gray eyes out of his mind. Nor could he think about the other sister, the one he was supposed to marry, without a shudder of distaste.

He would do his duty, for king and country, no matter how painful it was. But he would never be happy about it.

CHAPTER 7

senda watched with the rest of the clan as the Yuletide bonfire was lit in the courtyard. Sir Noël stood beside her. The flames illuminated his face. But his expression was still inscrutable, as it had been since he'd returned from the keep. She didn't know what was wrong. Somehow he seemed...distant.

It was probably just as well. After failing to convince Cathalin to do the right thing and marry Noël, Ysenda figured her only hope was to make Noël fall in love with Cathalin. Once he saw her sister in her best light, surely he couldn't help but be charmed by her. All men loved Cathalin. And of course, Cathalin would fall madly in love with him, for what woman would not? Maybe then Ysenda could repair the damage that had been done.

Of course, the whole idea made her sick at heart. She couldn't bear the thought of losing Noël, especially to her spoiled sister. But for the sake of her brother, whom she'd vowed to protect, and for her clan, to whom she owed allegiance, she'd make the sacrifice.

"Ysenda!" she called softly to her sister, nudging her when she didn't respond to the unfamiliar name.

Cathalin scowled.

Undaunted, Ysenda touched Noël's forearm and smiled back at her sister. "I was goin' to tell Sir Noël about the time we tried to save the pups in the pond."

Cathalin stared silently back. Finally she shrugged and said, "Go on then."

Ysenda gave her sister a pointed look. "But ye tell it so much better."

Cathalin sighed. "What's to tell? We saw the pups in the pond, and we jumped in to pull them out."

Ysenda's face fell. "Aye." She turned to Noël to explain. "But 'twas silly, because the mother hound was only tryin' to teach them to swim." She grinned. "We didn't know they could swim, so we dove in to save them. And when Ca-, my sister found out, she was furious, because she got her new gown soakin' wet."

Cathalin managed a small smile then. "After 'twas ruined, I gave *ye* that gown."

"So ye did," Ysenda said with a chuckle.

She glanced at Noël. His expression was one of polite interest, no more.

Ysenda tried again. "Your hair looks lovely tonight, dear sister."

That worked. Cathalin touched her locks. "Do ye like it? It took Tilda half the morn to braid."

"'Tis beautiful. Don't ye agree, Sir Noël?"

He nodded.

Cathalin, clearly annoyed by his lack of praise, pursed her lips.

Ysenda wrung her hands. What more could she do? What would impress Noël?

"Ye know, Sir Noël, my sister is quite skilled with a needle."

Noël lifted a brow. "Sewin' cloth or jabbin' people?"

With a huff of irritation, Cathalin picked up her skirts and whirled away to stand beside someone else.

Ysenda turned to Noël in accusation. "Why did ye do that?"

"She's like a spoiled hound. Someone needs to bring her to heel."

Ysenda thought about his words as the flames flickered high into the night sky.

"Someone like ye," she decided. "Someone who could take her in hand, teach her patiently, bring out the best in her." She gulped. "Do ye think ye could be happy with...someone like my sister?"

His mouth tightened as he stared into the fire. "Not nearly as happy as I am with ye."

Ysenda's eyes filled. She tried to blame the smoke. But her heart was breaking.

"I... I've grown tired. I'm goin' to go up to bed."

She didn't wait for his reply. She needed to get away before she burst into tears. Maybe Noël would speak again with Cathalin. Maybe not. But she would at least give them the opportunity.

After she left, Noël tried valiantly to fall in love with Cathalin. He stared at her from afar in the bonfire's glow, admiring her perfect profile, her creamy skin, her pouting lips. He watched her laugh when someone whispered in her ear. He saw her toss pine cones onto the fire with delicate grace.

But she wasn't her sister. She didn't have Ysenda's honest face, her sweetness, her endearing awkwardness and innocent charm. Cathalin was haughty, coddled, and hopelessly vain. Life with her would be unpleasant.

Noël watched his chance at happiness float away, like one of the bright sparks from the bonfire, rising and becoming swallowed by the black sky. All he could think about was the irresistible lass who waited in her bedchamber even now, less than a hundred steps away.

She'd pledged him her troth. She'd spoken the words to bind them as man and wife. At least, that was what she wanted the world to believe. And if she wished to keep up that appearance, why should he deny it?

If tonight was to be their last night together...if tomorrow he would confront the laird and demand his true bride...then perhaps he should seize what joy he could before he resigned himself to a lifetime of misery.

He gave the woman he was supposed to wed one last glance. She was beautiful. There was no doubt. But she was no match for the lass he'd married.

Against his better judgment, he took those hundred steps to the bedchamber.

When he softly entered the room, his wife was crouched by the fire, stirring the coals. She shot to her feet in surprise. The flames crackled to life behind her, illuminating the sheer linen of her leine, leaving nothing to his imagination.

"I thought ye were stayin' below a while." Her voice was cautious.

His eyes never left her as he closed the door behind him. "And I thought ye were goin' to bed."

"I was. I am."

This woman had lied to him. She'd deceived him, earning his trust now so she could exploit it later. Worst of all, she'd made him fall in love with her. By all rights, he should feel hurt and betrayed.

But seeing her in the hearth's soft glow—her face alit, her eyes shining, her lips so tempting—made him feel only longing.

Had her affection for him been a ruse? Did she feel nothing for him?

He had to find out.

"Then let's go to bed *together*," he said.

She gulped. "Don't ye want to watch the Yule fire?"

"Nae. I've seen enough." He took a step toward her.

She fidgeted with her gown. "They make a circle round the outside..."

He took another step.

She licked her lips. "And they walk..."

He took a third step.

"In the direction o' the sun, so..."

His fourth step brought him close enough to detect the smoky desire in her eyes. And when he lowered his gaze, he could see the sweet curve between her breasts where the linen gapped away.

"Tell me somethin'," he whispered, almost afraid of the answer.

"Aye?" Her voice cracked.

"Do ye love me at all?"

As she stared up at him, her eyes filled with tears, and her chin began to tremble.

He felt his heart crack. She might not want to say the words. But the answer was there in her silence.

He clenched his jaw against bitter disappointment.

But just as he would have turned and left her alone—perhaps to drown his sorrows in a barrel of Bordeaux—she collided against his chest with a great sob.

"Oh, aye, god help me, but I do, Noël. I love ye so much."

She rained kisses and tears on him in equal measure. The warmth of her admission was a soothing balm to his heart. He held her close, too lost in relief and joy to think beyond the moment.

Their kissing quickly fanned the flames of love from affection to desire, then from desire to desperation. Noël didn't want to think about tomorrow. Or his king. Or his *real* bride. All he wanted was one beautiful night with this irresistible woman who, aye, loved him.

Ysenda knew she was playing a perilous game. Yet she brazenly continued, like the lads who leaped through the Yule bonfire. She couldn't stop herself.

The situation was impossible. She hadn't been able to make Cathalin fall in love with Noël, any more than she could make *herself* fall *out* of love with him.

And now that she'd admitted she cared for him, she couldn't confess that she'd deceived him. It would break his heart.

Yet even as the deadly knot of lies and deception wrapped around her, all she could think about was making love to him. She didn't want to think about her sister. Or Noël's return to France. Or what would become of Caimbeul. All she wanted was to live for this moment.

Somehow their clothes fell away. Somehow they wound up on the bed. In a delicious tangle of limbs, they let the rest of the world disappear.

His lips kissed away her guilt. His fingers caressed away her cares. And with his bare flesh pressed to hers, there was no room for remorse.

She floated in heavenly oblivion. For now, all that mattered were the two of them and their compelling quest for pleasure.

This time, it was more than mere coupling. She wanted to show him how much she cared for him. She wanted him to feel her love in the deepest recesses of his soul. And she wanted to feel cherished in return.

When he pressed gently into her, she sighed in relief. Looking up at him with a languid gaze, she saw the same sweet satisfaction in his midnight eyes.

When he began to move within her, she met him, thrust for thrust. Just as they had hiked hand-in-hand across the snowy fields, they traversed the landscape of desire together.

His gaze burned into hers. His breath sent shivers along her skin. His tongue bathed her with intoxicating nectar. His fingertips teased and coaxed her to greater heights.

Wanting to keep him with her forever, she wrapped her legs around him. She dug her heels into his buttocks, making him groan with bliss.

He laced his fingers through hers, anchoring her to the mattress. She caught her breath as her lust sharpened to a fine point. Then it exploded into a hundred beautiful fragments. She arched up and clenched her fists in his.

He answered her, surging into her with a ragged cry of release.

Then she stiffened.

He'd called her by name.

Her *real* name.

She sucked in a panicked breath, but he wouldn't release her. His fingers were still entwined with hers. And when he slowly opened his lust-glazed eyes, she saw the truth.

He knew who she was.

He knew everything.

For a long moment, they only stared at each other.

"How did ye find out?" she whispered.

He didn't answer her. Instead, his gaze hardened. "How could ye lie to me?"

"I had to," she confessed. "I had no choice."

He was still holding her down. She wasn't afraid of him, not really. He was a man of honor, a knight who'd never harm a lady. But she could see by the glower in his brow and the strength in his arms that he could be a fearsome foe.

"When did ye plan to tell me?" he demanded.

"I've wanted to tell ye all along. I tried to stop the handfastin'. I never meant to consummate it. I hoped to convince my sister to wed ye." She added quietly, "I still do."

"Why didn't ye just tell me that first night?"

She swallowed hard, lowering her eyes. The truth was humiliating. But she owed it to him. "The laird said if I told ye, he'd hurt Caimbeul. He's been wantin' to kill my brother ever since he was born. He can't abide havin' a son who's...who isn't perfect. When my mother died, she made me vow to look after Caimbeul. I've always taken care o' him."

His fingers loosened around hers. The grim line of his mouth relaxed. "Ye could have told me. Your father wouldn't have known."

She gave him a rueful smile. "And what would ye have done then? Insisted on marryin' my sister? And when my father refused, would ye have taken on the whole clan with your six knights?"

He compressed his lips.

"I never wanted to deceive ye," she told him. "'Tis pure madness to go against the king. I've tried to tell my father so. But he won't listen. He wants a Highlander to hold his lands."

"When the kings find out—"

"They'll send an army to quell the clan. I know. My father refuses to believe that. And my sister thinks her Highland husband will bring men to defend the keep."

"So he'd rather start a war than see a Norman inherit his lands."

She nodded.

He unlaced his fingers and rolled off of her then, lying on his back to stare at the ceiling. She pulled the linen sheet up over her breasts.

It pained her to say the words, but she did. "I wish my sister loved ye."

He didn't hesitate. "I could never love her. Not the way I love ye."

Her heart flipped over. And then it sank. "What are we to do?"

"*Mon dieu*, I don't know."

A good night's sleep solved nothing.

Noël wished he'd never learned the truth. He could have lived happily in France with his counterfeit bride for years before her father died. By then, it would be too late to undo what had been done. Not that he even wanted to. He'd begun to dream less about inheriting the Highlander's land and more about stealing off with the man's daughter.

But, short of kidnapping her, he still didn't know how to solve the problem of his marriage.

One problem he *did* know how to solve. A young lass like Ysenda shouldn't be burdened with watching over her brother for the rest of his life. This morn, Noël intended to prove to her that Caimbeul was not some helpless creature who needed to be hand-fed and fussed over. If Noël could do nothing else, he could at least give Ysenda the gift of freedom.

He crept out of the bedchamber without waking her. Most of the clan were in the great hall, breaking their fast with buttered oatcakes. He approached Laird Gille.

"My laird, I haven't seen your man, Caimbeul, about lately."

The laird grunted. "Why should ye be interested in him?"

Noël shrugged. "I was wonderin' if ye think he'd be up for a wee bit o' sport this morn."

The laird's eyes lit up. "Sport?"

"Aye. My men have issued me a challenge. They say I can't make a fighter out of a cripple. I say I can."

"Indeed?" The laird stroked his beard in speculation. "And have ye put coin on it?"

He waved away the idea. "Nae, 'tis only a matter o' pride."

The laird's eyes were glittering now. "Pride? Ach! There's coin to be made on a wager like that."

"Perhaps."

Laird Gille chortled. "Not to mention it could be an amusin' sight—Caimbeul with a sword."

Noël bit back his distaste. "So do ye think he'll agree?"

"Oh, aye, I can get him to agree."

"After breakfast then? In the courtyard?"

"Aye." The laird gleefully rubbed his hands together and left to fetch Caimbeul.

Noël didn't tell Ysenda what he was up to. She'd only try to interfere, to protect her brother. She'd find out soon enough anyway.

The knights were exercising in the courtyard, and the sun was dancing along the tops of the distant pines when Caimbeul, no longer in chains, came limping and lurching briskly across the yard, leaning on a gnarled staff.

Noël studied him. But instead of noting the flaws in his gait, he looked for the man's strengths.

Of course, Noël's men hadn't really issued that challenge. They knew Noël well enough to realize he could turn any man into a fighter. Instead, they welcomed Caimbeul onto the field with open arms and ready blades.

Laird Gille had servants bring him a chair so he could sit on the sidelines. He probably imagined he was about to see a horrific and entertaining spectacle. A small crowd of men gathered around. Noël could see them exchanging coins, betting on the outcome.

By the time Caimbeul reached Noël, his face was an angry shade of red, and his eyes were full of rage.

"Is this how ye repay me for tellin' the truth?" he bit out. "By makin' sport o' me?"

"Not at all, brother," Noël said in quiet reassurance. "I'm goin' to teach ye to fight properly...so ye won't have to be afraid o' your father anymore."

Caimbeul blinked in surprise. For an instant, hope flared in his eyes. Then they darkened with cynicism. "I'm a cripple. I can't fight."

"Ye threw a fair clout at me last night. If it hadn't been for the shackle, ye would have flattened me."

Caimbeul almost looked pleased at that.

"Come on," Noël urged, clapping him carefully on the shoulder. "Let's show your father what ye've got."

The lad fell a few times. His father laughed. But each time, Noël and his knights bolstered the young man's courage and heart, assuring him he was making good progress.

And he was. He might not have the stature to wield a broadsword with great precision, power, or speed. But he had surprise on his side.

Anyone looking at Caimbeul would imagine he couldn't defend himself. But even with his twisted frame, he could thrust forward with a dagger, cuff a man squarely on the nose, and kick an attacker's legs out from under him.

Indeed, Laird Gille started to frown as Caimbeul managed to not only stay on his feet, but to knock a few of the knights off theirs.

It was then that Ysenda arrived.

But to Noël's chagrin, the wide grin of triumphant pride and cheery salutation he gave her was withered by her scowl of pure fury.

CHAPTER 8

Ysenda's heart had fluttered in panic when she'd awakened to find Noël gone. Had he decided it was too painful to say goodbye? Had he simply left without a word?

Even though that would probably be best—even better if he'd absconded with Cathalin—she hoped with all her heart he had not.

She scrambled to the window and peered out through the shutters. Noël's men were still here, sparring in the courtyard below.

With a sigh of relief, she turned back toward the bed. Her gaze caught on the foolish prize she'd collected last night while Noël lay sleeping—the black curl she'd snipped from his head and tied into the red handfasting ribbon.

She tucked her lip under her teeth. She'd forgotten about that. It had been a childish gesture. But she'd wanted a memento of him.

Someone scratched at the door. With a little gasp, Ysenda snatched up the incriminating lock and stuffed it down the bodice of her leine. She opened the door to Cathalin and her maid, come to choose Cathalin's attire for the day.

After they'd gone, Ysenda threw on her own gown and went downstairs. She meant to make one more attempt to convince her father to make things right. She grabbed a buttered oatcake in the great hall, and made her way outside to speak to the laird, who was watching the Norman knights practice.

Now she'd reached the edge of the field where her father was seated. She halted in her tracks.

What she saw made her jaw drop. She let the oatcake fall to the ground.

In the midst of the fighting stood Caimbeul. He was dragging a sword behind him as he hobbled toward two of Noël's men.

He suddenly swung the weapon around. The first knight dodged it. The second shoved Caimbeul aside with his shield, pushing him off balance.

Caimbeul tumbled backward onto his arse. Beside her, her father snorted in laughter.

Her blood boiled.

Clenching her jaw, she strode forward. She shoved her clansmen out of her way, stealing a sword from one of them before he even realized it, and kept charging.

Caimbeul had recovered now and was back on his feet, hacking away at his attackers. But it would only be a matter of time before he fell again.

She elbowed aside one of Noël's knights. He instinctively drew his blade. Then, seeing she was a woman, he sheathed the sword and backed away with his palms raised.

"To me!" she yelled at the knights attacking her brother.

Like most strangers to the Highlands, the French knights were unaccustomed to facing a woman with a weapon. Startled, they turned to her. One of them lowered his shield. The other was forced to raise his when she came at him with a blow forceful enough to lop off his head—had it landed.

Jarred by the impact of his shield on her steel, Ysenda staggered back a step. But she recovered quickly enough to intervene between the knight and her brother and took another swing.

From across the field, she heard Sir Noël shout, "Nae!"

Too late. She gave his man a punishing clip on the shoulder. He stumbled backward, clutching his bruised arm, while his companion quickly retrieved his shield.

But then she was caught around the waist from behind. Before she could squirm away, her sword was wrenched from her grip. An instant later, her captor swept her off her feet with a swift kick to the back of her heels. Instead of letting her fall, he caught her on his arm and lowered her with exaggerated care onto the wet grass.

She immediately rose on her elbows, scowling up in sputtering rage. But her anger vanished when she saw who had disarmed her.

"Caimbeul?" She blinked in astonishment.

He grinned down at her. "Good morn, sister."

"What did you...? How did you...?"

It seemed impossible.

He gave her a wink. "'Twould appear ye're not the only one whose veins run with the blood o' warriors."

She was still speechless with wonder when Noël hunkered down beside her. His brow was heavy.

"*Mon ange,* are ye hurt?"

She glanced back and forth between the two men. Noël's eyes were filled with concern, Caimbeul's with gleeful pride. "What the devil is goin' on?" she snapped.

"She's fine," Caimbeul assured Noël.

Noël looked doubtful. "'Twas quite a spill she took."

Caimbeul shrugged. "I've seen her take worse."

Noël shook his head. "How can ye bear to watch your own sister fight?"

"She's tougher than she looks."

Noël's brows raised. "Is that so?"

"Oh, aye. And 'tisn't the first time she's fallen on her arse."

Ysenda frowned. "That'll be quite enough, ye two. I'm right here, ye know. I can hear ye."

She struggled to her feet, batting away their helpful hands.

Noël murmured, "Are ye sure ye're all right?"

"I'm fine," she bit out, though her pride was bruised. "Now one o' ye had better tell me what's goin' on."

"Sir Noël's teachin' me to fight," Caimbeul said.

"Oh, he is, is he?"

Her eyes burned as she turned slowly to face Noël. Then she seized him by the front of his tabard and dragged him out of Caimbeul's hearing. "Teachin' him to fight?" she hissed. "Against battle-tested knights? A...a cripple?" She hated to use that word, but there was no other term for it. "Why? Did ye think 'twould be entertainin' for my father?"

Noël's eyes grew dark. He lowered his cool gaze to rest on her fists, still clenched in his tabard. His unspoken message was clear. He wouldn't allow her to belittle him in front of his men and her clan. And he wasn't going to reply until she unhanded him.

So she did.

But she still needed an answer.

"How could ye be so cruel?" she whispered. "Can ye not see how the laird mocks him?"

"He's not mockin' him now."

She glanced at her father. Noël was right. The laird wasn't gloating. He was glowering.

"Your brother is more capable than ye think. He's more capable than even he believes."

"Ye don't understand. He's...he's crippled."

"He's a wee bit twisted up," Noël admitted. "But he can still fight. He knocked *ye* on your arse." One side of his mouth lifted in a smile.

"Maybe he can trip up his sister. But he can't fight against seasoned warriors." A wave of dread washed over her as she considered the consequences. "If ye make him believe he can, ye'll get him killed."

"And if ye make him believe he cannot, ye'll keep him weak."

Her shoulders drooped. "I can't let harm come to him. I made a vow."

His eyes softened. "Ye were children when ye made that vow. He's a grown man now. He can take care o' himself."

Ysenda bit her lip. Part of her wanted to believe that. But Noël didn't know Caimbeul like she did. He didn't see how Caimbeul had been mocked and belittled all his life, how he longed to be normal. He couldn't understand her brother's pain.

"Watch him for a wee bit," Noël suggested. "And if ye don't agree that he can fend for himself, ye can go back to wipin' his arse."

She gave him a shove for that remark, but it only made him grin. Then she peered past his shoulder at Caimbeul, who was already back to sparring with one of Noël's knights. She couldn't remember a time when her brother had looked so bright-eyed, eager, and alive.

It was a difficult decision. But she finally nodded her assent. Noël returned to the field.

Her knuckles were white as she clenched her fists in her skirts, resisting the urge to rush forward in Caimbeul's defense while he dodged slashes from men with arms as thick as oaks. She gasped several times when a blade narrowly missed his head. And her heart dropped to the pit of her stomach when one of the knights sent him sprawling in the grass.

But then, in the midst of the fighting, Noël called out a few instructions. Caimbeul suddenly executed an unexpected spin to duck backward under one man's sword arm, pushing him forward into the second attacker.

As the two knights fell in a tangle of chain mail, Caimbeul crowed in victory. Noël rushed forward to clap him on the back.

"Well done. Ye see? Your best weapon is the element o' surprise."

Intrigued now, Ysenda watched as Noël continued to train her brother with a unique style and technique. Of course, once Caimbeul began to improve and his antics were no longer amusing, the laird lost interest and retired to the keep. But Ysenda remained to watch in fascination, glimpsing a side of her brother she'd never seen before.

Gradually, over the course of an hour, Noël transformed Caimbeul into an impressive and lethal fighter. Even more significant, the Knights of de Ware became Caimbeul's companions in arms. They challenged him, jested with him, boasted and cursed together. Her brother finally had friends who treated him as an equal.

Yet to what end?

Her heart sank. The knights might be his brothers now. But soon they would desert Caimbeul to return to France. Then he'd be left once again with clansmen who mocked him.

It wasn't fair. It was bad enough that she had to surrender a perfect husband to her selfish sister. It was beyond cruel to make Caimbeul sacrifice his happiness as well.

She had never felt more like fortune's foe.

In the shadows of the armory, Noël unbuckled his sword belt and tossed it aside. He was filled with regret. As if choosing between his duty to his king and the dictates of his heart wasn't difficult enough, now he had to grieve over losing a young brother whom he'd quickly come to admire.

Noël had never had a more enthusiastic and attentive student than Caimbeul. The young man not only learned fast, but he was clever and inventive. If only Noël had more time with him, he was confident he could mold him into a respectable warrior.

Noël slipped his tabard off over his head, then bent forward to shiver off his chain mail, letting it pool on the ground.

Behind him, he heard someone enter the armory. The uneven gait—the stab of a staff and the foot dragging across the floor—was instantly identifiable.

"I came to thank ye, Sir Noël," Caimbeul said quietly, "for givin' me somethin' no man's ever given me before." He stopped in the middle of the chamber. "Hope."

Noël's shoulders lowered. Hope? He feared he may have given Caimbeul only *false* hope. What would become of the lad once the knights left? Would he go back to cowering before his father?

"Ye've made me see that I'm more than just a cripple," he continued. Emotion thickened his voice. "I'll never forget that. And I'll never forget ye."

Noël nodded and turned to Caimbeul. But he couldn't look him in the eyes. "I'll never forget ye either."

However, another pair of eyes floated into his thoughts. Eyes that glowed like soft gray fog. Eyes that shimmered like the sleek silver sea. They were eyes he'd never be able to banish from his mind. With a sigh, he sank down on the wooden bench and hung his head.

Caimbeul limped over and sat beside him.

"Ye love her, don't ye?" he guessed. "Ysenda?"

Too weary to lie, Noël nodded.

"And ye don't want to leave her."

Noël swallowed back despair and answered gruffly. "'Tisn't my choice. I'm honor-bound to do the king's will."

Caimbeul shook his head. "'Tis my own damned fault. If I hadn't told ye ye'd wed the wrong sister…"

Noël smile ruefully. "'Tisn't like sparrin', Caimbeul. Ye can't feint and fool and deceive your way through life."

"Can't ye?" he grumbled.

Noël shook his head.

"But if ye truly love my sister, isn't that all that matters?"

Noël clucked his tongue. "Ye've got skills with a blade now. But ye still have much to learn about duty and honor."

Caimbeul heaved a sigh. Then he drew his dagger and began idly carving the top of his wooden staff.

"Besides," Noël said, "would ye not prefer I take the real Cathalin and leave Ysenda here? I know ye're very close to your sister. And she loves ye very much."

Caimbeul continued carving in silence, but Noël saw his lips compress with an unasked question.

"Ye were hopin' to come with us," Noël guessed, "weren't ye?"

Caimbeul shrugged. "Maybe." He dusted the wood chips from the top of his staff. "I could make myself useful now."

His words broke Noël's heart. There was nothing worse for a man than not feeling useful. He wished he *could* take Caimbeul with him.

But if he did the right thing and married the real Cathalin, he had to leave Caimbeul behind. He couldn't be so heartless as to steal Ysenda's brother from her.

With a growl of frustration, he shot to his feet, raking his hands back through his hair.

The abrupt movement spooked Caimbeul, who lurched from the bench in surprise and almost fell. As he grabbed Noël to regain his balance, his dagger grazed Noël's neck.

"Ach!" Caimbeul cried. "Forgive me. Ye startled me. Are ye all right?"

"Aye," he said, clapping his hand to his bloodied neck to make sure his head was still attached. Then he gave the lad a wink of reassurance. "'Tis only a scratch. But ye'd better put away your weapon before your warrior blood gets the best o' ye."

"Sorry." Caimbeul sheathed his dagger and bent to retrieve his dropped staff. "Are ye sure ye're all right?"

Noël sighed. Nae, he was *not* all right. He was brokenhearted and discouraged. He could see no way out of this predicament.

There would be no happy ending...for anyone.

After Caimbeul limped off and Noël was alone again in the armory, his thoughts began to drift.

The Viking well suddenly materialized in his mind. Why, he didn't know. He didn't actually believe in enchantments. Only a fool would imagine an ancient ruin held some magical power.

Yet Ysenda's words haunted him. What had she said? That the well could bless two lovers, binding them together for eternity.

Which was ridiculous. But he supposed every place had its local legends—the Highlands probably more than most. For the superstitious, all it took to keep such a legend alive was enough inexplicable coincidences.

Noël, however, was neither superstitious nor gullible. Shaking his head over his absurd imagination, he left the armory.

As he entered the great hall, he glimpsed Ysenda near the far wall. She looked as beautiful as...as a Viking goddess.

He frowned. A Viking goddess? What had made that pop into his mind? He knew nothing about Viking goddesses.

He straightened and made his way through the crowd toward Ysenda.

Her smile was melancholy. Her eyes looked like heavy clouds about to loose their store of rain as she murmured, "I can't thank ye enough for what ye did for Caimbeul."

"He's a good fighter. If he puts his mind to it, he'll one day be a great Viking warrior."

"A what?"

Noël furrowed his brows. What had made him say that? "Highland, a great Highland warrior."

Ysenda's eyes were moist. He could see his praise of her brother meant a lot to her. But the longer he looked at her, the more miserable he felt. Standing beside her was torture when he knew he couldn't keep her.

He had find an excuse to get away, if only for a moment.

There was a keg of ale at the opposite side of the hall.

"I'm goin' to fetch myself a drink from the well. Would ye like me to get one for ye?"

She gave him a quizzical look. "From the well?"

"What?"

"Ye said ye were fetchin' a drink from the well."

"Nae, I didn't."

"Aye, ye did."

Had he said that? What was wrong with him? "I'm fetchin' a drink from the keg there, on the far...wall. Aye, that's what I said, from the wall."

That wasn't what he'd said, and he knew it. But he couldn't explain why his mind was fixated on that damned Viking well. And he didn't want to try.

Without waiting to see if she wanted a drink, he left to fill two cups.

By the time he brought her ale back, he'd forgotten all about the well. He nodded toward her father. The laird was speaking to three of the de Ware knights and Caimbeul.

"It looks like your father has new respect for his son."

"Aye," she replied, taking a sip, "at least while he's surrounded by your men."

The reminder of Noël's imminent departure brought a scowl to his face.

Just then, Cathalin breezed down the stairs and into the great hall. Not a hair was out of place. Not a wrinkle creased her gown. Even his own men, accustomed to the great beauties of France, turned their heads as she entered the room.

But looking at her only made Noël's heart sink. A weight descended on his shoulders. And he knew he had to do something about it.

"We need to talk," he told Ysenda.

"I know."

"We need to decide what to do. I planned to leave today, and—"

"Today?"

"Waitin' any longer won't make it easier."

"I know."

She was trying to be brave. He could see that. But her eyes were wet. And it was making his throat ache.

A tendril of her hair fell forward against her cheek, and he brushed it back, tucking it behind her ear. But his gaze locked on it in speculation.

A lock of her hair and a lock of his, tied together with a ribbon.

He frowned. He was *not* going to do it. It was a silly ritual. A waste of time.

And yet, he thought as she clamped her jaw to keep her chin from trembling, what harm would it do? He'd tried everything else. Why not try this? As long as no one caught him at the well, no one would be the wiser.

But how would he get a lock of her hair?

"And who will ye be leavin' with?" she choked out. "My sister? Or me?"

She was on the verge of tears. He knew she didn't want to cry in front of her clan. So he took her hand and guided her toward the stairs.

When they reached the shadows of the stairwell, he swept her into his arms. He kissed her deeply, passionately. It was a bittersweet embrace of loss and longing, of fond farewell and ill-fated desire.

It was also an opportunity for Noël to sneak out his dagger and steal a wisp of her hair. Feeling foolish, he nonetheless managed to collect it without her knowledge. He closed it in his palm and then broke off the embrace to hold her at arm's length.

"I need to be alone for a wee bit...to think."

She nodded.

He looked into her eyes again, imparting his love for her with a glance. And then he left.

CHAPTER 9

After he'd gone, Ysenda's eyes filled and spilled over. Sobs lodged in her throat, too painful to swallow away.

She never wept—at least not where anyone could see her. Weeping was a sign of weakness. Or so her mother had always believed. So she sat on the step, indulging her sorrow in secret.

Was there no way to undo what had been done? Was there no choice that would satisfy everyone? Was there nothing she could do to change their destiny?

As she continued sniffling into her hands, she felt an itching between her breasts. With tear-damp fingers, she reached into her bodice.

The lock of his hair. She'd forgotten it was there.

She withdrew it by the red ribbon and stared at it. Suddenly a strange tingling started at the back of her neck. A wee hope blew through her soul like a stray wind.

Locks from each lover's hair, tied together with a ribbon.

Was it possible? Could she call upon the magic of the Viking well?

She didn't even know if she believed in the magic. Some of

the clan swore by it. But she didn't put much faith in old legends and ancient enchantments.

On the other hand, something had compelled her to snip the lock of his hair last night. Why else would she have done that? She must have known, deep in her heart of hearts, that she would end up visiting the well.

She ran her thumb over the silky strands of black hair. She was being childish. It was only a Yuletide story, after all. Nobody even knew if the story was true. Going there was probably a reckless waste of time.

Still…what was the harm? She had to try.

Wiping away her tears, she went upstairs and donned her cloak. She didn't want Noël to see her going. He would guess what she was up to. And he would think she was a fool. So she left the keep quietly and took a roundabout path to the well.

Halfway there, she stopped to rest. Drawing her dagger, she cut off a small piece of her own hair and tied it together with his. Her auburn and his black made an interesting contrast. She couldn't help but think about what their children's hair might look like.

She gulped. What if a child was already growing in her belly? The thought was at once thrilling and horrifying.

Closing the precious strands in her hand, she continued on her journey, hoping no one would catch sight of her.

In fact, she was so busy making sure she wasn't followed that when she arrived, she didn't notice at first that she wasn't the only visitor to the well. A mere ten paces from the stream, she finally saw she wasn't alone.

She gasped in surprise.

Noël glanced up with a frown. "Ysenda?"

"What are *ye* doin' here?"

He hid something behind his back and cleared his throat. "I could ask ye the same thing."

She realized she was holding the bound locks of hair where

he could easily see them. But she couldn't exactly tuck them back into her bodice. "I needed...fresh air."

He wasn't fooled for an instant. And his gaze went immediately to what she was holding in her hand. "What have ye got there?"

A dozen lies crossed her mind. She opened her mouth to speak one of them. But none of them were believable. So she closed her mouth again. She might as well confess. She shook her head. "Locks o' hair."

"Whose hair?"

She raised her chin in challenge. "Yours and mine."

She expected him to make fun of her. He'd doubtless have a good chuckle at her expense. And just as she anticipated, he began to laugh.

But then he held aloft what he had behind his back. "Like these?"

She frowned. He was holding strands of black and auburn hair tied together with a green ribbon. Her hand went instinctively to her head as she wondered when he'd stolen a lock of her hair. "How did ye...?"

"While we were kissin'." One side of his mouth curved up in a grin. "And ye?"

She gave him a sheepish smile. "While ye were sleepin'."

He shook his head. "Come on." His eyes twinkled as he summoned her with his free hand. "We may as well get it over with."

She joined him where he stood over the well. "Do ye think 'twill work?"

"I have no idea, but 'tis worth—"

There was a sudden movement through the trees. They both froze. Someone was coming their way. Damn! The last thing Ysenda wanted was an audience for their foolishness.

But after a moment, she blinked in surprise. She recognized the lurching motion of the intruder.

Noël recognized it as well. "What the devil? Caimbeul?"

Caimbeul was struggling through the snow. His staff slipped on the slick surface. He was out of breath. But he had a wide smile on his face.

"Caimbeul!" she said, handing the locks of hair off to Noël before rushing forward to meet her brother. "Are ye all right? How did ye walk so far? And in the snow?" As far as she remembered, he'd only been to the well once before, and he'd had to ride part of the way on a vendor's cart.

He shrugged off her questions to ask his own. "What are the two o' ye doin' here? Are ye wishin' on the well? Is that what ye're doin'?"

"Nae," she said.

"Aye," Noël said.

Ysenda frowned. She wasn't exactly proud of what they were doing.

But Caimbeul only laughed and hobbled forward, then dug something out of his satchel. For an instant, Ysenda couldn't speak.

"Is that what I think 'tis?" Noël asked.

Caimbeul grinned. "Locks o' your hair? Aye."

Ysenda blinked at the white-ribboned bundle. "I'm beginnin' to think I'm lucky I haven't been plucked bald. How did ye…?"

"Remember when I knocked ye on your arse in the courtyard?" Caimbeul asked, clearly acting the braggart. "I might have stolen a few strands while ye lay helpless."

Noël narrowed his eyes and nodded. "And ye took mine when ye had that 'accident' in the armory, didn't ye?"

"Ye said trickery was my strength." Caimbeul beamed with pride. "So what do we do now?"

It had seemed silly enough when Ysenda was thinking of making the wish by herself. Now, with three of them reciting the wish, it seemed absolutely ridiculous.

On the other hand, what did they have to lose? The fact that they all wanted the same thing touched her. And it made her more than willing to indulge the two most important men in her life.

"I suppose we weight them with rocks and drop them into the well together," she said.

Noël nodded. "That should give our wish three times the power."

Once they'd secured small rocks to each bundle, they stood together over the well.

"What are we supposed to say?" Noël asked.

"I'm not certain," Ysenda admitted. "I suppose we wish for a way to bind our two spirits together for eternity?"

"I'll do it," Caimbeul offered when they stood above the well. "I think ye should hold hands." They did. "In the name o' the unfortunate lovers who once drowned in this well, I make this Yuletide wish that the two souls to whom these locks o' hair belong to be blessed in their marriage and joined together forever and aye."

They all nodded, pleased with his choice of words. And then they dropped their tokens, one by one, into the water, where they disappeared into the inky depths.

The heavens didn't open up to let angels descend.

The air didn't stir with the breeze of faerie wings or fill with the sound of ancient pipes.

No Viking ghosts appeared.

Indeed, the moment was remarkably unremarkable.

"What do we do now?" Caimbeul asked.

Noël answered. "I suppose we wait."

As the moments crept by, Ysenda became more and more despondent. Nothing was happening. The spell wasn't working. She should have known better than to believe in magic.

After an uncomfortably long silence, she finally spoke. "Maybe we should be gettin' back."

"Do ye think it worked?" Caimbeul asked.

"Nae." The word scraped across her throat, like a sword blade on a sharpening stone.

Caimbeul's brows came together. "So what do we do now?"

Noël's chest was tight. He'd hoped he wouldn't have to answer that. He'd hoped, impossibly, that somehow the well would give him an answer. But there had been nothing.

"What we must," he decided.

Caimbeul straightened, as much as his crooked frame allowed. "Whatever happens, I'm goin' to France with ye," he blurted out. "That is," he amended, "if ye'll have me."

From the corner of his eye, Noël could see Ysenda had clenched her jaw.

He shook his head. "I can't take ye from Ysenda, Caimbeul. Ye may be her younger brother, but now that ye're grown, *she* needs *your* protection."

Caimbeul scowled, simultaneously disappointed and flattered. In the end, all he did was mutter, "I'm not her younger brother. I'm the oldest."

There was a long, melancholy silence.

Finally, Caimbeul's words sank in. Noël blinked, wondering if he'd heard wrong. "What? What did ye say?"

"I'm older than Ysenda. Three years older."

He frowned. "Ye are? And what about Cathalin?"

"I'm two years older than Cathalin."

He rattled his head. Surely that wasn't right. "Ye're the oldest?"

"Aye."

Noël closed his eyes. Was he missing something? "Ye're the *oldest?*" he repeated.

"Aye," the siblings said together.

"The oldest, as in the rightful heir to the laird?"

"Oh. Well, nae," Ysenda explained. "The laird has never...he's never claimed Caimbeul as his heir."

"Hold on." Noël's heart started to race. He didn't want to get prematurely excited. But something was awry here. "Are ye sayin' ye're the next in line?"

"In principle, aye, but—"

"Nae, nae, nae, nae," Noël interrupted. "Not in principle. In actual fact." Now his heart was pounding. This could be his answer. "Exactly why has he not claimed ye? Are ye not his son by blood?"

"I am."

"Are ye a bastard?"

"Nae."

"Why then?"

Caimbeul flushed and lowered his gaze.

Ysenda answered for him. "He's never claimed Caimbeul as his son because he's a cripple and unfit to rule."

"But he's not unfit," Noël insisted, beginning to pace eagerly now as he considered this new piece of information. "Ye saw him on the field. Not only is he bright and clever, but he can even hold his own with a sword."

Ysenda and Caimbeul stared at each other. Clearly, the thought of contesting the inheritance had never crossed their minds.

He supposed he could see why. The Highlands were so remote that a clan laird was essentially the ruler of his own domain. The Scottish king might lay down the law of the land. But the laird felt he had the power to bend that law as he saw fit.

In truth, however, laws were a matter of record. No man could alter what was written down by a king to suit his own wants or needs...not even a laird.

"It doesn't matter whether the laird wishes to claim him or not," Noël explained. "Caimbeul is his son. As long as he's fit to rule—and anyone can see he is—by law, Caimbeul is the true heir."

"So ye're sayin' the holdin' doesn't rightfully belong to

Cathalin," Caimbeul mused aloud, "no matter who she weds? It belongs to me?"

"Exactly." Noël crossed his arms over his chest in satisfaction. "Which means—"

"Which means we can all have what we want," Ysenda gushed. "We can stay married and go to France. Cathalin can wed her Highlander..."

"And I can come to train with your men," Caimbeul inserted, for fear he might be excluded.

Noël gave him a slow grin. "Aye."

Caimbeul rubbed his jaw, thinking this over. Then his brow creased. "It doesn't seem possible. Do ye truly think 'twill come to pass? My father is very strong-willed. And the Highlands is a long reach for the arm o' the law."

"Which is why the king sends men like the Knights o' de Ware to enforce the law," Noël said.

"Ye'd do that?"

"Aye, o' course. Ye're one of us now."

"But what about the clan?" he asked. "I don't want war with the clan."

"They're my clan as well," Noël assured him. "When the time comes, we'll find a way to keep the peace. Ye're a clever man. Ye'll think of somethin'."

Ysenda's beautiful silver eyes shone with hope. But there was wisdom and caution in her voice. "'Twill all have to be kept a secret. If the laird suspects that Caimbeul has a claim to the holdin'..."

She didn't finish the thought. But they all knew the risk. Laird Gille wouldn't hesitate to eliminate his heir if Caimbeul proved to be...inconvenient.

"Aye," Noël said. "'Twill be a secret between the three of us."

They nodded in solemn agreement.

And then, with a soft cry of victory, Ysenda threw herself into Noël's arms.

He chuckled with pleasure and held her close.

But as their lingering embrace went on and on, Caimbeul finally rolled his eyes and turned to leave.

"Where are ye goin'?" Ysenda asked him.

"Back to the keep," he said over his shoulder. "There's somethin' I've been meanin' to do for a long while. But don't fret. By the time ye get finished...celebratin'...ye can catch up with me."

Noël bid him farewell. Then he grinned and kissed the top of his lovely wife's head. "It looks like we'll have our whole lives to celebrate."

"Not just our lives," she murmured. "Eternity."

"It worked, didn't it?" he asked her softly. "The Viking well. It granted us our Yuletide wish."

She nodded. Then she gazed up at him. Her smile was as sweet as mulled wine. Her eyes glowed with the warmth of Christmas candles. "For ever and aye."

epilogue

Leaving her Highland home to travel south with the Knights of de Ware, Ysenda had never felt so well protected. Of course, that hadn't kept her from packing her own chain mail and weapons. Old habits were hard to break. It would be a long while before she'd grow to accept that she had an army of knights at her command and that her brother could take care of himself.

Caimbeul had certainly proved that upon their return to the castle.

Ysenda had had a lot of time to think on the way home from the well. Now that she was no longer beholden to her father, years of anger over Caimbeul's mistreatment began to fester within her. All the laird's past abuses—his mocking, violence, and cruelty—congealed into a single, hard knot of rage and injustice that stuck in her craw. With each step she took toward the castle, fury flowed hotter in her veins.

When they finally arrived at the keep to face her father, he was alone in the great hall and deep in his cups. His drunken sneer as the three of them approached only added fuel to the almost irresistible desire Ysenda had to pay him back for all the pain he'd caused.

But she'd held her tongue as Sir Noël explained that they wished to take Caimbeul with them to France.

Her father's eyes lit up. "Ach, aye!" he crowed. "I've heard the French courts like to use dwarves and such for entertainment."

Ysenda longed to curse her father for his brutal words.

But then she heard the echo of her mother's voice. Above all, the warrior maid had taught Ysenda to maintain control of her emotions. Losing one's temper was never wise. Besides, she and Caimbeul would leave soon and likely never see the laird again. There was no point in stirring up trouble. So she tensed her jaw against the urge to fire off a biting retort.

The laird eyed Caimbeul speculatively over the top of his cup. "Or maybe ye're plannin' to sell him along the way? The lad has a decent voice. No doubt a singin' cripple could bring ye a good price."

Ysenda clenched her teeth until they hurt. But she kept mentally repeating her mother's advice. One must take a deep breath, harness all the anger, and choose one's battles wisely.

The laird took a drink and then smacked his lips. "He's probably got another five or six years o' life at most. Still, ye'll get your coin's worth."

That made Ysenda's blood boil. But no matter how much she yearned to claw that smug smirk off of the laird's face, no matter how gratifying it would be to tear the beard from his chin, no matter how her fist ached to...

Crack!

Ysenda lifted a brow as her father's head snapped back under Caimbeul's solid punch. The laird staggered backward, dropping his cup and clutching his nose.

As Ysenda stared in wonder, Caimbeul shook his bruised knuckles. Then he grinned in satisfaction. "That's for a lifetime o' sufferin'...Da."

Those had been Caimbeul's last words to the laird, who'd

shuffled off to have someone tend to his bloodied nose. Ysenda had never been prouder of her brother. And she thought their mother would agree that he'd chosen his battle wisely.

Now they were headed to France—to freedom and to family. As impossible as it seemed, Ysenda thought Caimbeul looked taller as he traveled beside his new companions-in-arms. Perhaps he no longer felt crushed by the weight of his infirmity.

As for her husband, though his men laughingly insisted Noël was the ugliest of the de Ware brothers, Ysenda could not have been happier to be wed to such a handsome, kind, noble, brilliant, and honorable man. Noël had promised that when her father died, he and his men would return with Caimbeul to help him claim the Highland holding without shedding a drop of blood.

Their path from the keep took them past the Viking well. Ysenda requested a private moment before they continued on their journey to visit one last time. Gathering her cloak about her, she clambered across the snowdrifts until she reached the silvery stream and the crumbling stones of the ruin.

There, she ran her fingers over the ancient runes carved into the lid of the well. She whispered thanks to the lost lovers for granting her wish. Then she sent up a silent prayer of her own—that somehow, some way, no matter how long it took, the doomed couple might eventually have their own curse lifted.

By the time she returned to the company, the knights were speaking with a dozen strangers—travelers headed in the opposite direction. The band of ragged Highlanders said they were on their way to the keep of Laird Gille.

The wee lad at the fore licked his chapped lips and raised his beardless chin, boasting in his high, sweet voice that he was going to marry the bonniest lass in all of Scotland.

Ysenda's brows lifted. But she wisely held her laughter. She wished she could see her sister's face when Cathalin beheld the bridegroom she'd wanted so badly—all four feet of him.

Instead, she smiled up at Noël, whose lips were twitching with amusement. He gave her a wink, and she sighed with pleasure.

This was going to be, without a doubt, the best Yuletide ever.

More books from the Knights of de Ware series:

My Champion

My Warrior

My Hero

tbe stowaway

A California Legends Prequel Novella

A notorious Scottish rake, scuttled aboard a ship bound for America, has to rely on a spirited young botanist to restore his good name.

DEDICATION

For the America I know and love,
where science is welcomed with open arms
and new beginnings are possible

ACKNOWLEDGMENTS

A special thank you to my shipmate Lauren Royal,
who suggested a cruise just when I needed it most;

Holland America Cruise Line, which, by pure serendipity,
featured 19th century ship models and orchids on board;

My sister Jewel authors, Cheryl Bolen, Erica Ridley,
Brenda Hiatt, and Darcy Burke, for inviting me
into their Regency world for a brief visit;

Amy, Kirby, and Jill, expert time jugglers;

The real Travis Jameson,
for letting me borrow his uber-cool name;

and Tatiana Maslany and Nikolaj Coster-Waldau
for their inspiration.

CHAPTER 1

"Oamn, George! Are ye sure ye want to do this?"

"'Tis a rather large sum, old boy."

"Aye, and ye're already down a wee fortune."

Charlotte knew it wasn't proper to eavesdrop. The young gentlemen had retired to the library after dinner. They expected privacy. It was none of a lady's affair what the brandy-and-cigar set did while the females were left to their own devices in the drawing room.

Unfortunately for Charlotte, those feminine devices included chattering endlessly on and on. About the latest fashions in London. The romantic eligibility of various Edinburgh bachelors. And who'd been invited to which Christmas ball. All of which she found incredibly shallow and deadly dull.

Besides, as her father oft remarked, Charlotte had been born with inexorable curiosity. It was that curiosity that gave her a scientific mind. And sometimes got her into more than a wee bit of trouble.

She'd excused herself from the ladies, ostensibly to powder her nose, mostly to give her ears a rest. But as she breezed past the library, she couldn't help but be intrigued by the conversation drifting through the open crack of the door.

Hearing her brother George's name, she naturally felt compelled to stop and apprise herself of the situation.

Their parents had gone to Oxford to visit her oldest brother, William, at university. The second oldest, John, was an officer in the Navy, fighting in the Baltic Sea. In their absence, George had been left in charge of the household.

Despite her brother being only a year older than she, Charlotte was well aware that George and Responsibility weren't the best of companions. Thus, she felt it was her duty to make sure Tragedy didn't ensue.

Even if that involved a bit of subterfuge and listening at doors.

Tucking a stray lock of her short brown curls under her bandeau, she peered through the crack of the door, searching the group of lounging dandies until she spotted George at cards.

Cigar smoke hovered like a halo over the six young gentlemen at the rosewood card table. But they hardly looked angelic. Their jackets were slung over the backs of their chairs. Their white sleeves were rolled up and their cravats undone. Brandy sparkled in their cut crystal rummers. They slouched over a game of *vingt-et-un.*

Charlotte narrowed her eyes in disapproval. Every night this week, George had met with his friends to play cards—drinking, smoking, and gambling long into the wee hours. It seemed her brother was intent on squeezing all the debauchery he could into the weeks their parents were away.

She wouldn't have minded if the games were a casual entertainment. But George seemed to be obsessed with wagering of late. Eager to play. Feverish to win.

If he wasn't careful...

George took a swig of brandy and slammed down the empty glass, motioning for a servant to refill his rummer.

"Are ye in or out, lads?" he challenged, his words slurred by drink. "Put up your damned markers."

"Not so fast, old boy," the *banquier* warned, placing a hand on George's forearm. "Are ye sure ye're good for the wager?"

Righteous indignation crackled off George like lightning as he cast off the *banquier*'s hand. He snarled, "O' course I'm good for it! I'm a bloody de Ware, aren't I?"

His vehement outburst silenced the room. Charlotte bit her lip. She felt sorry for her brother, even though he could be a complete cad when he'd been drinking. George was embarrassing himself in front of his peers.

In the next moment, he seemed to realize that. One corner of his lip curled up in a mischievous grin, and his eyes twinkled as he glanced around the library—at the distinguished portraits on the wall, the shelves full of leather-bound books, the gilt mahogany furnishings. "Ach! I'm growin' weary o' this shabby hovel anyway."

His jest broke the uncomfortable silence and made everyone laugh. Everyone but Charlotte. She found no humor in the notion of George gambling away their home.

A young man warming his hands by the fire called out, "Well, if ye happen to lose it all, Georgie, I know a lady who'll keep ye in fine style for five years at least."

A conspiratorial "ooh" circled the room.

"As a concubine?" George asked, stroking his chin as if considering the option.

"Nay," the man replied. "As an indentured servant."

More laughter filled the room, disgusting Charlotte. Debt was not a laughing matter. She knew of more than one family that had been ruined by gambling debt, forced to sell off their possessions, one by one.

The *banquier* tapped his finger on the table. "Let's see what we've all got then, gents."

Charlotte held her breath as the players began to reveal their hands.

Then, just as George was reaching to flip over his card, Humphries the butler barked out behind her. "Miss!"

She gasped and whirled around.

They both knew what she'd been doing.

His eyes were flat with disapproval.

Her face was pink with guilt.

But the servant was wise enough not to scold her.

And she was wise enough not to try to explain.

He cleared his throat. "The ladies are inquiring about your absence, Miss."

"I was just on my way back."

He gave a nod of his head. "Very good, Miss." He reached past her and silently closed the door.

Charlotte smoothed her rose satin gown, which she realized probably matched her face at the moment. Trying to salvage her dignity, she walked toward the drawing room.

Somehow, she managed to fritter away another hour, pretending to enjoy the inane conversation. As usual, she failed to engage any of the women in her own topic of interest—botany.

Once the purview of females, botany had fallen out of favor with proper ladies. Prudish Johann Siegesbeck had deemed the sexual classification of flowers "loathsome harlotry," too offensive to a woman's delicate sensibilities. What might have been common ground in years past was now considered outré by decent society.

And so, as always, Charlotte ended up having little to say and was left feeling awkward. Out of step. And socially exhausted.

It had been George's idea to have his university friends over this eve, dignifying the gathering by including several of their sisters. Thus it had fallen to Charlotte to serve as hostess, no matter how much she resented the task.

She'd much rather have spent the evening studying the Caledonian Horticultural Society report. The latest installment had arrived this afternoon and was sitting on her father's desk, unread.

The report was sent to her father after every meeting. Not because Charles de Ware was interested in horticulture. In all honesty, he couldn't tell a dandelion from a daisy.

But Charlotte's application for membership in the newfound Caledonian Horticultural Society had been turned down. Not because she was a hobbyist. The Society was accepting those with or without formal education. It had been turned down because she was a woman.

Her father would hear none of that. Refusing to bow to what he deemed archaic rules, he promptly gave a hefty donation to the Society, obliging them to send him the notes from their meetings, which he then handed over to Charlotte.

Charlotte looked forward to perusing the report. Though it dealt mostly with crops and propagation, horticulture was a world she understood. Reading the latest discoveries made her feel like part of the scientific community.

Sadly, by the time the gentlemen came round to collect the ladies, the night was half gone. Charlotte's smile was worn thin with overuse. Her eyes drooped like the petals of an overwatered rose.

She bid the guests goodnight and dismissed Mrs. Scott, telling her she could clean up in the morning—an order the fastidious housekeeper predictably refused. When Charlotte finally mounted the stairs to her bedroom, she found her brother had already retired. She'd have to wait until tomorrow to learn how he'd fared at cards.

Charlotte woke long before George, of course. After his night of carousing, she imagined her brother would sleep till afternoon.

She threw on her white muslin morning dress, splashed water on her face, and raked back her unruly mop of dark curls. Then, snapping up the notebook she kept by her bed, she hurried to the first of the three south-facing windows, which were lined with flowerpots.

She smiled in satisfaction. The sky was cloudless. Her plants would get a good drenching of sunlight today.

She was aware her collection of two dozen specimens of *Orchidaceae* was impressive. The fact that she'd managed to keep the tropical flowers alive and blooming, some for as long as fifteen years, was even more remarkable, given the inhospitable clime of Scotland.

To a wee lass, the colorful flowers had been treasures her Grandfather de Ware brought back for her from the exotic places he sailed. With every ocean voyage he took, he collected a plant for her. Soon she'd acquired an assortment of beautiful blooms in every color of the rainbow.

When her father obtained the translated volumes of Linnaeus' *A System of Vegetables* for his library, she began to learn the taxonomy of the flowers she possessed.

And two years ago, when he'd gifted her a copy of Olof Swartz's *Genera Orchidacearum* for her birthday, she'd been able to finely tune that identification and classification of the various genera and species.

Only then did she realize what a true treasure they were.

Stopping at the first flower, the *Oncidium punchellum* with its lavender *labellum* and maroon guide markings, she turned the pot to count the blooms and check for new growth.

Some orchids went dormant in autumn. But those of the *Oncidium* genus flourished in winter. Sure enough, a new nub of a rhizome protruded perhaps two millimeters off the base of the stem.

She carefully dug her finger into the soil at the edge of the pot, checking the level of moisture.

Outdoors, the flowers would never have thrived. The weather was too cold and rainy. Tropical orchids preferred lots of sunlight, just enough humidity to keep the roots damp, and at least a modicum of warmth. She found keeping them on the windowsill was ideal for protecting them against chill and dehydration.

It took her nearly an hour to record her daily observations. But it always thrilled her when she could measure the slow progress of a plant, catalog the birth and death of a blossom, and, best of all, witness the surprising revelation of an orchid's first bloom.

She'd already filled several books with meticulous notes and sketches. They were observations nobody but she had ever read. Observations nobody would *ever* read, she supposed.

Yet she'd always sensed that her notes were somehow important. That they would one day be of use. She considered it her scientific duty to record each day's statistics. Even when it meant missing breakfast and having to raid the kitchen for a mid-morning roll with marmalade.

Because most of the plants were dormant at this time of year, she fulfilled her obligations in short order. She managed to take her morning tea and toast well before noon. Then she went to her father's study to fetch the Caledonian Horticultural Society's report, bringing it to the drawing room to read.

Some hours later, lost in an article on the cultivation of French pears, she nearly jumped off the settee when Humphries suddenly appeared with a silver tray.

"The post, Miss," he announced. "Shall I...?"

Before Humphries had to face the uncomfortable decision of whether to hand the day's post to *her* instead of the Man of the House, George came hurtling down the stairs.

"I'll take that, Humphries," he said.

George looked dreadful. His valet had managed to dress him in a clean shirt and breeches and comb his hair. But his skin had a pale cast, almost like the color of her *Vanilla planifolia* orchid, and his hands were shaking as he reached out for the letter on the tray. His eyes were rimmed with red, and there were dark circles around them, as if he'd lain awake all night.

She waited until Humphries was gone to address him in concern. "Are ye feelin' well, George?"

"Aye. Fine."

Shuffling through the envelopes, he selected one and stared at the thing, as if he were afraid to open it.

"What is it?" She lowered the report to her lap. "Not the Navy?" she asked, her heart in her throat. She frequently worried about her brother John, away at war.

"Nay," he muttered, "'tis just business."

She lifted a brow. Business? George? That was news to her. George didn't seem to be interested in business of any kind.

George, still staring at the envelope, wiped away the sweat above his lip with the back of his fingers.

Disturbed by his sickly appearance, Charlotte rose from the settee. "Perhaps ye should have somethin' to eat, George. 'Twill make ye feel—"

"I don't need anythin' to eat," he snapped. Then, remembering his manners, he lowered his eyes. "Thank ye for the offer," he murmured. "I'll be fine. I'm just tired."

No doubt, she thought, considering he'd been up until all hours of the night, five nights in a row. Too much brandy had likely taken its toll as well. Then she recalled the conversation she'd overheard in the library.

Was it possible George had had a round of bad luck? Had he overplayed his hand? Was he in trouble?

"I'll be in the library," he said, never meeting her eyes. "I'll take tea in there."

"George," she called out as he turned to go.

"Aye?" he said over his shoulder.

One had to be delicate about these things.

"Did ye...enjoy the evenin'?"

He shrugged. "As much as any."

She forced a nervous chuckle to her lips. "Ye didn't gamble away my dowry, did ye?"

He stiffened. For one awful instant, Charlotte wondered if he'd done just that.

But in the next moment, his shoulders dropped, and he turned to her with his familiar cheeky grin. "Why? Ye have a husband lined up, do ye?"

George could always make her laugh. "Hardly." She had yet to meet a man who wasn't either intimidated or repulsed by her scientific pursuits. And unless and until she did, marriage seemed like an undesirable ambition.

"Well then..." He turned away, heading down the hall toward the library. "As a matter o' fact," he called out, "things worked out quite well. I'm out o' debt and back in the game."

She frowned as he closed the library door behind him. *Back in the game.* That didn't sound good. She was hoping his brush with financial ruin would cure his fever for cards.

Whatever business George had in the library occupied him all afternoon.

Charlotte, donning a chip straw bonnet and old half boots and tying an apron over her morning dress, spent most of the day outdoors.

From the time she'd been young, the things growing in the garden had fascinated her. She'd spent hours collecting seeds, dissecting flowers, and pollinating plants by hand.

Today was no different. She made sketches of bulging rose hips, cutting one in half to examine the interior layers. She harvested the strange curly seeds of the *Calendula officinalis*, marigold, slipping them into a paper envelope for safekeeping. She wished to study whether they would germinate if stored for one year, two years, or more. Then, feeling ambitious, she used a trowel to unearth several of the *Lilium* bulbs for study, dividing and replanting the rest.

So distracted was she that she missed her afternoon tea and had to rush into her *Narcissus jonquilla*-colored silk gown for supper. When she arrived at the table, Humphries indicated with a critical arch of his brow that, despite thoroughly washing her hands, there was still a thin rim of dirt under her nails.

She didn't care. In fact, she would just as soon dine in the garden in her boots and apron. It seemed wasteful to her to make so many changes of clothing, especially when the only other person at the table was George. And despite the talented Mrs. Abernathy and her sumptuous courses, Charlotte would have been just as happy with bread and cheese, especially since, for the first time in days, there were no guests to feed.

Despite—or perhaps because of—George's unhealthy pallor, he ate only half his supper before he laid the napkin down on the table.

"I've had a letter from Father," he said, waiting to catch her eye.

She looked up, holding her fork full of minced collops aloft. "Aye?"

He glanced at his claret. Picked up the glass. Brought it toward his mouth. Changed his mind. Put it back down.

"There's been a wee change o' plans."

"Mm?" She slipped the fork into her mouth, chewing the rich bits of beef.

"It seems they won't be comin' home for the holidays after all."

Her brows popped up. She set her fork down on the plate and swallowed the collops.

"But what about the ball?" For as long as she could remember, the de Wares had hosted a grand Christmas ball.

George raised his glass again. This time he finished off the claret.

Suddenly, Charlotte had an awful thought. "They're not expectin' us to host the Christmas ball, are they?" Her stomach tightened with dread.

"Nay."

She breathed a sigh of relief. "Then what?"

"We've been asked to spend Christmas with kin."

"What kin? Not Aunt Effie?" While Aunt Effie was a sweet old bird, she lived in a drafty estate in the Highlands. Besides, she was as dotty as a ladybug.

"Nay," he said. "'Tis a cousin...abroad."

"Abroad?" She wasn't aware they had any kin abroad. Maybe a relative from Norman times who still lived in France. But the French and Scottish weren't exactly on friendly terms at the moment. "Abroad where?"

He lifted his glass again, forgetting it was empty. When he set it back down, he stared at the stem, twisting it between his fingers.

"America."

"America!" Her shriek rang out in the dining room.

At her outburst, Humphries poked his head in to see what was amiss. Satisfied that no mayhem had ensued, he sighed and closed the door again.

"America?" she repeated in a whisper.

George scraped back his chair to reach for the decanter of claret in the middle of the table. He unstopped it and poured himself a second glass.

"What kin do we have in America?" she asked.

He sat, gazing into his glass a long while before taking another drink. "Mrs. Smith. Mrs. Eugenia Smith."

"Who?"

"She's a...distant cousin o' Mother's, a widow."

Charlotte blinked in surprise. This was the first she'd heard of cousin Eugenia.

George added, "Father thought 'twould be good for us to meet the New York branch o' the family."

"New York?"

A tingling started in her veins. Christmas in New York?

Suddenly she didn't care if Mrs. Eugenia Smith was the half-sister of her third cousin, twice removed. She'd leap at the chance to go to New York.

New York, after all, was the location of the Elgin Botanic Garden.

Since she was a young lass, when Professor David Hosack had first planted the public garden, it had been a dream of Charlotte's to see the amazing place. But she'd always considered it an unachievable dream, as likely as becoming Queen or owning an elephant.

The idea it might be possible thrilled and excited her.

"We're goin' to New York?" she asked breathlessly.

"Aye."

"Ye're serious?"

She sincerely hoped this wasn't one of George's nasty jests. That he wouldn't suddenly burst out in laughter at how gullible his wee sister was. Because if it *was* a jest, it would be too cruel for words.

"Aye." He *looked* serious. Not even a hint of humor lurked in his eyes.

"But this is wonderful!" she burst out.

"'Tis?"

"O' course, ye silly. New York is where the Elgin Botanic Garden is."

"Oh, aye," he seemed to remember. "Ye've always longed to go there, aye?"

Her eyes lit up. "And maybe we can visit Columbia College." David Hosack had once been the Professor of Botany at the esteemed college. "New York," she sighed.

"So ye *want* to go?" George acted surprised, but she was sure he was teasing her.

"O' course I want to go! Who wouldn't want to go to America?" Unable to contain her excitement, she got up from the table and began pacing. "But truly, George? We're truly goin' to New York?"

"There's a ship leavin' in three days."

"Three days!" she exclaimed, halting in her tracks. "'Tis hardly time to pack. Only three days?"

"Aye." George seemed unusually calm, considering the adventure they were about to undertake. She blamed it on his overindulgence in brandy last night. "Eight o'clock sharp on Monday mornin'."

She resumed pacing, caught up in a flurry of plans and possibilities. There was little time to prepare.

"I'll have to pack straightaway." Then she hesitated. "How many servants will we take?"

"Servants." He winced. "I don't think we'll have room for any servants. The ship's bound to be tight quarters. We'll have to manage on our own. Do ye think ye can do that?"

Charlotte nodded. Then the reality of the voyage hit her with sudden clarity. Squealing in excitement, she rushed over to George and wrapped her arms about his neck.

"Oh, Georgie, 'twill be a real adventure, won't it? Just ye and me on an ocean voyage, off to explore a new world."

Amused and annoyed by her familiarity, George pried her arms loose. "Go on now." His voice was gruff, but full of brotherly fondness. "And only pack what ye need," he called after her as she rushed from the library. "No more than three or four trunks."

That would do fine. She could stuff her gowns and hats into one trunk, her slippers, pelisses, and research books into another. That would leave two trunks for her orchids.

She had no intention of leaving them behind. Humphries and Mrs. Scott might be able to manage the house well enough while she was away. But no one could manage her collection of plants with the care and attention they required.

Fortunately, when her grandfather retired from his voyages abroad, he gave her his copy of *Directions for Bringing Over Seeds and Plants from the East-Indies and Other Distant Countries in a State of Vegetation*. She knew just how to pack her precious flowers for the journey.

It took a full day to have the special trunks built. They were three feet long, one foot wide and two feet high, with a six-inch shelf along the bottom and ventilation slots on the ends.

The next day she carefully repotted the *Orchidacaea*, wrapping each ball of roots in wet *Sphagnum palustre* moss, stringing pack-thread between each plant to stabilize it, and tucking more moss into the crevices to insulate the plants.

Then, after she tossed her clothes and shoes and fripperies into the remaining two trunks, she tucked in a few of her most precious botany volumes and several spare notebooks to record her observations.

If her brother was rather quiet, Charlotte took no special notice of it, other than to be relieved he wasn't wasting his coin at cards. She was too excited about the journey ahead to pay him much mind. Indeed, the night before they were due to embark, she was almost too excited to sleep.

CHAPTER 2

The five young surgeons stood around the pine trunk, speaking in fretful whispers.

"Are ye sure?"

"That he's goin' to be vexed? Oh, aye!"

"Nay! Are ye sure he can breathe?"

"O' course...I think."

"He'll be fine. The planks on the back side o' the crate are riddled with knotholes."

"And the *principium somniferum* ye gave him—'tis safe?"

"Safer than pure opium."

One of them sighed. "I still don't think this is a good idea."

"'Tisn't like he's given us any choice."

"Aye, that's for certain. The poor chap's not cut out for duelin'. In any case, he wouldn't have survived another year, basket-makin' with every stray strumpet that—"

"Hell and the devil!"

"Sorry. But if he doesn't stop carryin' on, he'll be dead ere Christmas."

The five young men were silent as they gazed down at the sixth, crammed into the trunk in naught but his smallclothes.

"He just looks so...helpless."

"He looks dead. Are we sure he's not dead?"

One of them lifted Travis's limp hand, feeling for his pulse. "Slow, but strong as ever," he proclaimed.

"The effects should wear off in six hours or so."

"Dash it all, he'll be furious."

"A pity we couldn't dress him properly."

"There was no time. Besides, 'tis the least o' his troubles."

"He'll live out the day. 'Tis what matters most."

They all nodded in agreement.

"Bon voyage, old boy."

They lowered the lid, intentionally busting off the latch.

A pound note insured the ship's bracket-faced chief officer asked no questions when they brought the trunk on board at the crack of dawn. And the name printed on the lid—MR. REGINALD JAMESON—assured the safe delivery of its contents.

Charlotte pulled the fur-trimmed pelisse—in a blue that matched her eyes—tighter around her. A chill breeze was coming off the sea, but she could scarcely contain her rapture as she watched the sun rise from the weather deck of *The Fortuity*. She and George had arrived early to stow their trunks. It was still hard to believe this packet ship was going to be her home for the next six weeks or so.

She expected they'd be housed in one of the eight staterooms reserved for travelers of quality, cabins that opened onto the saloon for dining.

But the captain, recognizing their distinguished family name, had instead offered one of his own three staterooms at the stern of the ship.

Though relatively lavish, the cabin was small, no more than ten feet square. A gold and scarlet Axminster rug filled the space, which also included a sturdy bed with a brocade burgundy spread, a cherry wood dressing table and armoire, a flowered porcelain wash basin, a gold-upholstered settee, and two matched chairs. Charlotte was pleased to discover the cabin was on the port side of the ship. Its four decent-sized windows would be south-facing for most of their journey. On bright days, she could open the lid of her special trunks and let her orchids drink in the sunlight.

George didn't share her enthusiasm for the journey. He seemed dour and terse this morning. She supposed he was pining over the card games he would miss.

Or the friends he was leaving behind.

Or the access to unlimited bottles of claret he'd no longer have.

Whatever it was, once they were settled in, George encouraged her to explore the vessel. Since they'd be sharing the cabin, with George using the settee for sleeping, he intended to speak to someone about hanging a curtain for privacy.

Meanwhile, she watched with fascination as the crew readied the ship to sail, dragging ropes to and fro, hauling trunks of goods, barrels of beer and water, and crates of flapping chickens and geese up the gangplank. Though she saw a dozen or so stateroom passengers file on board, *The Fortuity* was mostly a merchant vessel. According to the captain, it would deliver wool and finished cotton cloth to America and return to Britain with tobacco, raw cotton, sugar, and rice.

The sun was glinting off the gentle waves of the harbor, warming Charlotte's brow, when the last of the passengers finally boarded.

George had not returned. Perhaps he was still arranging the stateroom. It was a shame he'd miss the ship's launch.

Children with their nurses waved from the dock. A few matrons dabbed at their eyes with handkerchiefs, bidding their loved ones farewell. The captain barked out orders as broad-backed sailors weighed anchor.

Then Charlotte's eye was caught by something small and dark weaving through the people at the dock. A scruffy black dog. Full of self-importance and on a serious mission, the wee terrier sniffed along the wooden planks, likely on the trail of some unlucky rodent. It stopped to bark, and she grinned when each powerful "woof" made its feet lift off the ground.

The crew began untying the mooring line, allowing the ship to slowly ease away from the dock. The poor dog started shifting frantically back and forth, barking in panic.

Then, to the crew's consternation and Charlotte's alarm, just as the gangplank was hauled halfway in, the terrier took a daring leap over the water. While Charlotte watched with bated breath, the stubby-legged pup caught the end of the plank, scrambling its way atop the boards. It raced up the length of the gangplank, dodging the sailors' attempts to catch it, and sprang onto the deck of the ship.

Before anyone could stop the slippery rascal, the dog bolted down the midship stairs to the lower deck.

Now, even if the terrier could be retrieved, it would be too late to toss him back onto shore.

The sailors seemed to know this.

"We've got a stowaway!" one of them joked.

"Well, he'd better earn his keep."

"And he'd better stay out o' the stores."

"The stores? He'd better stay out o' the captain's rum."

There was laughter all around. Charlotte supposed they weren't too upset to have a terrier on board a ship. They were skilled mouse-hunters after all.

She couldn't help but wonder, however, if the poor thing belonged to someone who would miss it.

Then, before she could fret too much about it, she was distracted by the curious shifting under her feet. They were truly free of their mooring now and underway.

Once the sails were unfurled, the ship moved through the

harbor like a grand old dame across a ballroom, with stately elegance, swaying slightly from side to side.

Charlotte was mildly irritated that George was missing the sights. He would have enjoyed this unfamiliar waterside view of the royal burgh they knew and loved. The shore drifted past, its banks populated by storehouses, piers, and dozens of sailing vessels of all shapes and sizes.

Nearly an hour passed before *The Fortuity* left the protected harbor at Leith to venture into the open sea. More sails were unfurled. The water grew rougher. And what had been a cool breeze became a chilling wind that tangled her hair and buffeted her cheeks.

Gathering her pelisse about her, she made her way toward the stairs that led to the lower deck. She clung to the rail so she wouldn't lose her footing as the ship tilted. A crewman helped her descend the shallow steps.

She expected George would be in their stateroom, either hanging the privacy curtain or sleeping off another late night of drinking.

But he wasn't there. And no curtain had been hung. He hadn't even moved the settee. Where could he have gone?

She waited for him in the cabin, using the time to record her *Orchidacaea* observations, a task made difficult by the listing of the ship. She theorized that their growth while aboard the ship would be erratic. They'd been uprooted from the environment to which they were accustomed, after all.

Rather like Charlotte herself.

When she finished and George still wasn't back, she began searching for him. She scoured the entire main deck. She inquired at the maproom, the boatswain's cabin, and the carpenter's cabin. She even peered in at the galley, where the cook was preparing a mouthwatering pork roast.

She took a quick inventory of the weather deck above, where, now that they were in the open sea, no one but the ship's crew had the fortitude and sea legs to stride easily from bow to stern. Young lads climbed into the rigging like monkeys and trimmed the sails with expert skill, while Charlotte had to cling to whatever railing or post she could reach for balance.

George wasn't there.

He certainly wasn't swimming in the bilge water below decks.

So unless he'd stumbled upon a card game in one of the other passenger's cabins, there was only one place he could be. The hold.

Normally, passengers like Charlotte would never venture into the hold. The goods stored there were the responsibility of the captain until the ship arrived at port. And some of those goods were quite valuable. Until they reached America, they were his property, and the hold was his domain.

But curious Charlotte seldom let rules prevent her.

George was missing. She had to locate him.

If she got caught, she would simply plead ignorance. There were advantages to being perceived to be a featherbrained female.

Finding the door unguarded, she crept into the forbidden interior, securing the door behind her.

The hold was dim, lit by two small portholes. It took a moment for her eyes to adjust to the dark. Pallets, boxes, casks, and trunks were stacked ceiling-high, secured to the bulkheads with rope. Bags of grain slouched in one corner. Bottles shivered against each other in divided crates.

As the ship labored through the waves, the wood creaked, and the waves slapped against the bulkheads. The odors of brine, oil, and hemp lingered in the stale air of the close quarters.

A quick assessment told her George wasn't here.

But she wasn't alone in the hold. Sitting beside one of the crates, staring up at her with big black eyes, was the intrepid stowaway terrier.

She had to smile. The wicked imp looked none the worse for his risky flight. She crouched down to take a closer look.

"Good mornin', wee one," she murmured.

The pup came to his feet. But he didn't wag his tail. Instead, he regarded her with suspicion.

"Who do ye belong to, eh?" She clucked her tongue. "Someone's bound to miss a handsome fellow like ye."

Sensing she was no threat, the dog sank onto his hindquarters again. Then he lowered farther to rest his head on his paws.

Charlotte pursed her lips in empathy. She couldn't just leave the sad creature here in the hold. It seemed a clean enough animal. It was neither mangy nor starving. It wasn't a stray. It clearly belonged to someone.

Perhaps she'd keep the pup in her cabin. She could save morsels of food from her plate to feed it. And at night it could snuggle at the foot of her bed.

"How would ye like to come with me?" she asked, reaching out for him.

He lifted his head and began growling at Charlotte.

She prudently withdrew her hands, promising, "I won't hurt ye, lad. I'll only keep ye safe till we can find your proper home."

She wondered if he even *had* a proper home anymore. The captain certainly wouldn't be turning the ship around to return him. And if he'd left family behind in Edinburgh, she doubted the owners would pay for the dog's passage back from America.

On the other hand, perhaps he belonged to someone on board.

"Come with me," she said, reaching out again. "Maybe we can find your owner."

He didn't growl this time. But he stood his ground, refusing to budge, staring at her in somber stubbornness.

She sighed. Then she had an idea. "Hey, wee fellow, how would ye like a nice bit o' roast pork?"

Perhaps she could lure him away with the promise of a meal.

As if he understood, he licked his chops. But when she stood up, trying to coax him to come with her, he laid his head back down in regret.

She glanced at the trunk beside which the terrier was stationed. He seemed to be standing guard over it.

She narrowed her eyes at the name burned into the large pine box.

MR. REGINALD JAMESON.

The name was unfamiliar to her. And she knew most of the important families in Edinburgh.

MR. REGINALD JAMESON.

That was it. No residence. No further shipping information.

Then she calculated the size of the crate. Her eyes widened.

She'd heard tales of dogs visiting their master's graves, sitting there for days without food or water, waiting for the master to return.

Was the pup's owner dead?

Good heavens! Was Mr. Reginald Jameson's dead body in that trunk?

She gasped in horror.

Which startled a sharp bark out of the dog.

Which startled a foul word out of Charlotte.

"Shh!" she cautioned herself and the dog, wondering if she could whisk the beast away before he started making enough fuss to...wake the dead.

The terrier started pawing at the crate and whining.

Charlotte grimaced. Now what was she to do?

She wanted to get out of there with all haste. But not without the pup.

If the sailors discovered the dog had no owner—at least not one who was living—they might just toss him overboard.

She couldn't let that happen.

"Come on, lad," she murmured, eager to get as far away from Mr. Reginald Jameson as possible. "I'm afraid your master's not comin' home. I fear he's gone to heaven." Even as she said the words, she wasn't so sure. After all, what kind of cad would die and leave such an adorable wee pet behind to fend for itself?

The dog scraped at the trunk again and gave two curt barks.

And then the trunk budged.

CHAPTER 3

Travis Jameson couldn't open his eyes. His lids were too heavy. His tongue felt thick in his mouth. And his limbs ached as if someone had tied them in a knot.

In the distance, as if he were dreaming it, he heard Campbell bark.

Damn it, he had to wake up.

He was breathing, thank God, though the air felt close, stagnant. He could vaguely sense his heart pumping in his chest. But something was making him lethargic, paralyzing him.

Had he been drugged?

He tried to remember.

But it was all too much effort.

It was so much easier to drift off on a cloud of numb surrender.

Campbell was whining now, nagging Travis to take him for a walk.

Travis knew too well the consequences of ignoring Campbell's demands. He'd had to clean up more than one mess in the house.

He tried to rouse himself. And failed.

Then he heard a muffled feminine voice.

Gradually, like an image under the lens of a microscope, wisps of memory came slowly into focus.

Sir Wyndham. Travis had been caught with Sir Wyndham's wife. Now he remembered.

Sir Wyndham had returned early from his London trip to discover his wife half-naked in their bed and Travis in his bedroom. Things had gone rapidly from bad to worse.

Lady Wyndham, of course, could not defend Travis. Nor would Travis allow her to try.

There had been angry words. Accusations. And finally, a challenge. A duel with pistols at dawn.

Travis had had no choice but to accept. To do anything less would have stained Lady Wyndham's honor.

When his friends found out, they dragged Travis to The White Hart to spend what everyone was sure would be his last night on earth at the bottom of a tankard.

But then what had happened?

It was all a fog.

Campbell barked again. This time, Travis shook the cobwebs from his brain and banged his head against something hard. He managed to pry open his eyelids. But it didn't matter much. It was still as dark as night. Maybe it still *was* night.

Where was he?

He tried to move. Half of his body felt numb, nerveless. The other half tingled with the painful recovery of sensation.

In the next instant, three things happened.

He discovered he was unable to move more than a few inches in any direction, trapped in some kind of wooden enclosure.

The awful fear that it might be a coffin brought him fully alert.

And panic made him surge upward to burst out of his prison, wrenching the lid half off its hinges.

He blinked, shielding his eyes against the sudden light with his arm.

GLYNNIS CAMPBELL

He was in a ship's hold.

Campbell was skittering happily before him, his tail wagging furiously.

And beyond Campbell stood the most beautiful lass Travis had ever seen.

Unfortunately, her lovely features were distorted by an expression of pure terror.

That expression could mean only one thing. The woman was about to scream.

Travis did what he had to do. As her lips formed a shocked "O," he lunged out of the box, seized the back of her head, and clapped his other hand over her mouth.

His actions were utterly ungentlemanly. Brutal. Barbaric.

But they were a necessary evil. Like cauterizing a wound.

Until Travis could figure out what had happened—how he'd gotten here and why he'd been put in a box in the hold of a ship—he was sure that drawing attention to his predicament couldn't be a good thing.

The woman was too stunned for the moment to struggle against him. But that wouldn't last forever.

And though he'd temporarily subdued her, his dog was not so easy to silence.

Campbell began barking. With delight. Or excitement. Or rage. Travis wasn't sure which.

But if he kept it up, the blasted terrier was going to bring the entire ship's crew down on them.

"Campbell!" he hissed. "Be quiet!"

As usual, the stubborn dog ignored him.

"Campbell!" he whispered fiercely.

Still the cursed beast defied him.

From the corner of his eye, Travis saw the lass lowering her mortified gaze.

It was then Travis realized he was bare-chested, dressed in naught but his smallclothes.

And he heard the sound of approaching footsteps.

He acted on instinct.

Releasing the lass, he snatched up Campbell in one hand.

Then, holding the pup strategically in front of his scantily clad *genitalia,* he straightened to face with courage whatever consequences were about to arrive.

If Charlotte weren't still reeling with shock, she might have fallen into a fit of laughter. The man was actually trying to look dignified, despite his obvious dearth of clothing and his hilariously clever attempt to cover that fact. With a dog.

But he'd startled the dickens out of her, springing out of that trunk like a ghoulish Jack-in-the-box.

And when he'd lunged toward her, seizing her head in his hands, her life had flashed before her eyes.

Did he mean to steal her breath? Snap her neck? And drag her to hell?

In the next blink of an eye, she realized three things.

One—he wasn't dead, not even a little.

Two—he didn't intend to hurt her.

And three—he was just as confused as she was.

Four things, she amended. For someone freshly sprung from a coffin, he was about as handsome a corpse as she'd ever seen.

And she was fairly sure—once he'd let her go and whisked up the terrier—he'd have a reasonable explanation for his behavior.

But as the burly chief officer breached the door of the hold, demanding to know what was going on, the Jack-in-the-box was struck speechless.

At the man's lack of an explanation, the chief officer ground out, "We don't abide stowaways on this ship."

Charlotte took one look at the humiliated black terrier and blurted out, "He's not a stowaway, officer. He belongs to me."

She meant to snatch the wee pup away at that point and hold him protectively against her bosom. But she dared not remove him from his current occupation.

Both men turned to her, baffled.

"I meant to keep him in my cabin," she explained.

The chief officer glowered.

"I don't know how he got out," she lied.

The naked man frowned.

"But I assure ye 'twon't happen again," she promised.

The two men were still looking at her with perplexed glares.

She bit her lip. She had to convince them.

"I'll feed him scraps from the table. He won't make a peep, I promise. And at night he can curl up next to—"

The naked man cleared his throat.

The chief officer straightened. "Now see here, Miss..."

Glancing back and forth between the men, she abruptly realized her mistake. The stowaway wasn't the dog. It was the man.

"Oh." Her face grew hot. *"Oh."*

By then, of course, she felt it was too late to withdraw her offer. To do so would have been rude.

Thinking quickly to cover her error, she said, "Once the privacy curtain is installed, o' course." Then, remembering the best defense was a good offense, she turned to the officer, crossly crossing her arms. "Where *is* that curtain anyway?" she demanded. "I requested it hours ago."

While the officer gaped like a trout, Travis had to bite his lip to keep from grinning.

The lass was quick of wit. That was certain. Faced with a humiliating situation, she'd managed to think on her feet and even rock the officer back on his heels.

If only Travis had been able to think that quickly when he'd been caught with Mrs. Wyndham's unmentionables about her ankles, he might not have suffered his current fate.

But he'd been too concerned about the compromised state of Mrs. Wyndham's health to string together a plausible excuse for his presence in her bedroom. Which was how he'd ended up in the ludicrous position of agreeing to duel her husband in order to defend her honor.

Travis realized now that his friends must have drugged him and stowed him on the ship out of desperation, to save him from certain death by dueling pistol.

Still, no matter what the consequences, he had never allowed a woman to bear the brunt of impropriety, even when it meant shouldering blame that didn't belong to him. He wasn't about to start now.

"That won't be necessary, Miss," he said, covering her mistake. "Campbell and I will stay in the hold. When we reach the next port," he told the officer, "I'll disembark. And I'll pay for my passage. I give ye my word."

How he'd do that, he wasn't sure. It appeared his mates had left him neither clothing nor coin. But he had patients in several towns. Surely one of them would be willing to temporarily cover his debt.

"The next port?" the officer groused. *"The next port?"*

"Aye. Where are we bound? London? Southampton?" He hoped it wasn't too far. He hated to inconvenience his patients. And he did intend to return to Edinburgh eventually. He'd somehow make things right with Lord Wyndham, once the man's bluster blew over.

The officer's scowl deepened.

The lass replied with unadulterated cheer, "New York!"

He blinked. "I beg your pardon?" Surely he'd heard wrong.

The officer spoke between clenched teeth. "We're bound for the States."

"The States?" he said in disbelief. "The United States?"

"Some of us are anyway," the officer said in black tones of threat.

Bloody hell! Had his friends actually meant to send him to America? Or had they just stowed him on the next available ship?

The officer narrowed his eyes. "Ye might still be able to swim to Calais if I toss ye overboard now."

"Nay!" the lass cried. "Ye'll do no such thing. I...I meant what I said. Mr. Jameson and his travelin' companion are welcome to stay in my cabin."

Travis was too stunned to realize the lass had called him by name. He was too shaken to even thank her for her mercy.

He couldn't go to America. All his friends were in Edinburgh. Hell, his patients were in Scotland. It could be a year or more by the time he earned enough to pay for return passage.

Maybe he *would* be better off trying to swim for shore.

"If ye'll be so kind as to hang that curtain..." the lass prompted the officer. "We'll also require one o' those sleepin' hammocks. And perhaps ye can send someone to bring him proper clothes."

The officer's scowl deepened as his face purpled. He wasn't accustomed to receiving orders from a woman. If Travis didn't intervene, the lass might end up tossed overboard along with him.

"What if I work for my passage?" he offered. "I've got some doctorin' skills."

"We don't need a doctor," the officer scoffed. "We've got a cook. And he's got a knife."

Travis winced. The state of medicine aboard a ship was appalling. "Then I'll work at whate'er ye need."

"There," the lass decided. "'Tis settled." She arched a brow at the officer and added pointedly, "Unless ye'd rather explain to the captain how a stowaway managed to slip on board...on your watch."

The officer straightened. He knew when he was beaten.

"There's no need to trouble the captain," he grumbled with a slight bow of his head. Then he glared at Travis. He might have capitulated to the lass's request. But that wouldn't stop him from tormenting his new slave of a stowaway at every opportunity. "Ye'll report to me in an hour."

Travis nodded. The officer gave him one last scathing perusal, shook his head, and strode away.

Finally, Travis remembered his manners.

"Thank ye, Miss..."

"Charlotte de Ware."

He blinked. Not the Edinburgh de Wares? Theirs was an old landed family who'd been in Scotland for centuries.

"Pleased to make your acquaintance, Miss de Ware," he said with a respectful dip of his head. "I'm—"

"Mr. Reginald Jameson?" she supplied. At his puzzled frown, she smiled and added, "It says so on your trunk."

Continuing to clutch Campbell against his nether regions, he turned carefully away and returned the half-broken lid to its proper position. There it was in block letters. MR. REGINALD JAMESON. His uncle's name.

Reginald Jameson lived in New York. Which meant Travis's friends had indeed meant to send him to America. They must have known Sir Wyndham would comb every inch of Scotland to find him. And they believed he'd be better off in the hands of his eccentric and enterprising uncle than facing off against a jealous husband. He hoped they were right.

As they stood conversing like casual acquaintances—Charlotte and the mostly naked man before her—it was all she could do to maintain her equilibrium. Not only were her limbs adjusting to the motions of the ship. Her sensibilities were being pulled to and fro by the sight of the handsome stowaway before her.

He was definitely not a gentleman, despite his good manners. His dark hair was longer than was fashionable and unruly. His angular jaw was bristled. And his physique was far from the fleshy, pale ideal of the idle rich. He looked instead like a laborer, trim and fit.

What was it he'd said? That he had some doctoring skills? Glancing at his well-muscled arms, she guessed he wasn't a physician of prestige. He must be a surgeon then. Most surgeons she'd seen were barely a notch above a butcher.

She gulped. The enormity of what she'd offered to this perfect stranger was beginning to sink in.

What would George say? How would he feel, having to share his half of the cabin with a stowaway of questionable character? Not to mention the man's protective mongrel?

Hoping to learn more about her cabin mate, she tried to make light conversation. "So tell me, Mr. Reginald Jameson, how did ye come to stow yourself away on a ship?"

"Travis, Miss," the man said.

"I beg your pardon?"

"My name is *Travis* Jameson. Reginald is my uncle."

"I see."

She didn't see at all. Indeed, she was trying *not* to see. It was difficult to think while her vision was dominated by the sight of a bare-chested, bare-legged man.

"So ye climbed into his trunk and..."

"'Twas not by choice, I assure ye. I believe my friends enclosed me in there—"

"Your friends?" she asked in disbelief. "What kind of friends would impress ye into service?"

It was common for captains of the Royal Navy to drag drunken men aboard their ships and sail away, forcing them to become sailors. She'd never heard of anyone dragging a man aboard a merchant vessel.

"'Tis a complicated tale," he admitted. "But I think they

meant well. They intended for me to be delivered into my uncle's safe hands."

His answers only invited more questions. Why hadn't the man's friends simply paid for his passage? Why had they sent him all the way to America? Why had they left Campbell behind, forcing the poor wee dog to leap aboard at the last moment? And why had they left Mr. Jameson in his unmentionables?

Before she could ask any of these questions, a crewman returned with a hammock and a bundle of clothing. The garments were the worst sort—a wrinkled linen shirt and a stained blue jacket, short and sloppy sailor's trousers, threadbare stockings, and a pair of worn leather shoes.

But he seemed glad of any clothing at all.

And Charlotte was glad for an excuse to depart.

"I'll take Campbell to the cabin." She held out her arms for the dog.

But the man held him fast. "I'm grateful for your offer, Miss. Truly I am. But I won't stay in your cabin. 'Twould tarnish your reputation. Campbell and me, we'll be fine here in the hold."

She furrowed her brow. The hold was dark and cold. Even her *Orchidacaea* wouldn't survive six weeks here.

"'Tis a very long journey, sir."

"This will do." By his satisfied expression as he glanced around the hold, one would have thought he was perusing a grand manor house. "I'll hang the hammock here," he said, indicating a pair of beams, "and let the sea rock me gently to sleep."

She had to smile at that. The man was clearly a romantic.

And indeed, part of her was relieved. Convincing George of the merits of showing charity to a common stowaway—not to mention his scruffy companion—would have been a challenge.

"If ye're certain..."

"I am, Miss," he said, inclining his head. "And I thank ye for your kindness."

With a blush and a quick bob, she left.

She took one last tour of the deck, searching for George, to no avail.

By the time she entered her stateroom, the privacy curtain had been hung. It was not very attractive. It hung from the beam, subdividing the cabin like a sail. In fact, it may have *been* a sail.

She lifted the corner to peer in at the other side. Her brother wasn't there.

She supposed it was useless to be cross with him. After all, George would turn up eventually. In the meantime, she'd unpack her trunks and settle in for the journey.

She had filled the armoire with her clothing and just slipped the last of her books onto the captain's already crowded shelves when seven bells were rung for dinner.

The captain set an elegant table, under the circumstances, with porcelain, silver, and crystal. There were ten other privileged guests in all, six single men and two with wives. But they managed to sit comfortably around the great mahogany table that dominated the saloon.

There were introductions, sumptuous food, and frothy conversation. But Charlotte had difficulty enjoying it, since George had conspicuously refused the captain's invitation to dinner. Indeed, she neglected mentioning her brother to anyone, for fear of drawing attention to his unforgivable slight.

At the end of the meal, Charlotte remembered Campbell. She secreted away part of her thick slice of roast pork and a buttered roll in a cloth napkin, which she smuggled into the hold.

Campbell was there by himself, sitting beside the wood trunk. He regarded her with quiet dignity, much like his master, as if to say he was perfectly fine living here in the dim, dank, dark of the hold.

He did perk up, however, when she laid out the feast she'd

brought. The starving thing wolfed down the meal with such eagerness, she feared he might eat the napkin.

When she retrieved the napkin and turned to go, Mr. Jameson was just arriving.

Startled to find her there, he nearly dropped his parcel. A napkin full of bread.

"Well, Campbell," she said with a grin, "aren't ye a lucky dog? Now ye'll have *two* dinners."

Mr. Jameson grinned back.

And Charlotte's heart nearly stopped.

He'd washed his face. He'd pulled his overlong hair back into a neat tail. And his broad smile displayed teeth as white as a *Dendrobium crumenatum* orchid.

His clothes might be ragged and rumpled. Too tight in some places. Too loose in others. But he somehow managed to look as distinguished as a duke. And as handsome as a rake.

She'd just opened her mouth to ask him what tasks he'd been set to when the chief officer's voice growled out from the hatch above.

"Mr. Jameson!"

"Aye, sir!" he called back, giving her a sheepish shrug.

She took the rest of the bread for Campbell.

"Go on," she said with a wink. "I'll see his belly is full."

Travis had never worked so hard in his life. The price of stowing away on a vessel was apparently steep.

He spent an hour scrubbing the brass fixtures in the maproom. He stitched ripped sails for another hour. In the galley, he helped cut up vegetables for the crew's evening stew. Then the chief officer sent him topside to swab the deck. By the time the crew gathered at the mess table for their afternoon break, his palms were raw, stinging from the seawater.

The rest of the men were pleasant enough, though a rough

lot. They were a motley crew of salt-toughened seadogs and fresh-faced lads, ruddy Scots and dark-skinned foreigners. They offered Travis a tankard of grog and swapped tales of their adventures while docked in Edinburgh.

"What a prime night I had," a Scotsman declared. "There's naught finer than Edinburgh cherry, am I right, lads?"

Several of the men cheered.

"Edinburgh?" an islander scoffed. "Ah, but you have not been to my homeland. I tell you, nothing compares to the ladies of Jamaica."

Most of the men issued friendly boos of protest.

"Wait, lads!" a third chimed in. "Ezra may be right. I've been to Jamaica. And I've ne'er sampled sweeter quim than that of Ezra's ma."

The crew guffawed at that. Even Ezra had to laugh.

One of the younger lads bragged, "I rogered a different doxy every night last week."

"Every night? Is that so?" a stout Highlander replied, adding as an aside to the rest of the crew, "With his wee purse, they must have been three-penny uprights."

Everyone roared with laughter.

A grizzled graybeard barked out, "As long as ye didn't bring the clap back with ye."

A man with ginger-colored hair answered for the lad. "'Tis all right, McGee. The ladies all assured him they were virgins."

More laughter made the rounds.

"Besides," the redhead added, "we've got our own nimgimmer on board now, isn't that right, Doc?" He turned to Travis.

News apparently traveled fast on board a ship. Though Travis wasn't a nimgimmer, the slang for a specialist in venereal disease, he might need to become one if the crew's boasts were at all true.

"Is that right? Have we got us a Sawbones?"

Travis grimaced. He hated that term. He'd stitched up gashes, cauterized wounds, and removed tumors. But he'd not once sawed off a limb. "Aye, I'm a surgeon." And just to be sure the nickname wouldn't stick, he added, "Ye can call me Jameson."

"Wait." The boastful lad's eyes widened. "I know ye. Ye were at The White Hart last night, aye? *Travis* Jameson?"

Travis's hand stiffened on his tankard. He nodded carefully.

"They say ye're a buck o' the first head," the lad marveled, "cuckoldin' half the lords o' Scotland!"

The men looked at him in shocked reverence.

"Is it true?" the redhead asked. "Are ye a fancy man?"

Before he could deny it, the others chimed in.

"A scapegrace."

"And a scoundrel."

"A rascal."

"The worst o' the riff raff."

"He's one of *us,* lads!"

The crew burst out in laughter and clapped Travis on the back. By then, it was too late to change their minds. Like everyone else of his acquaintance, they'd decided he was a philanderer. It seemed pointless to argue with them. And indeed, it served his interests—and the interests of his patients—to let them believe that fiction.

But apparently, the lad had learned more at The White Hart than just about Travis's reputation.

"Ye stowed away 'cause o' the duel, didn't ye?" he cried. He turned to the others, telling the story in excited tones, "One o' the cuckolds challenged Mr. Jameson to pistols at dawn this morn!"

Travis frowned. He was sure he'd be labeled a coward for running away from a duel. A caitiff. And a cur. And that was going to make the rest of the ship's journey even more miserable.

But the sailors lived in a different world. A world where it was more respected to be cunning than brave.

"Clever lad!" one of them said, punching him in the shoulder. "He'll ne'er find ye in America."

"And ye'll get a crack at a whole new bevy o' doves!"

"Here's to the lasses of America!" someone yelled, raising a tankard. "And beware to the poor sods who call them wife!"

Everyone laughed and cheered, taking a swig.

What else could Travis do but lift his tankard and drain it?

CHAPTER 4

Charlotte's cheeks were aflame, and her ears were burning. She knew her habit of listening at doors was wrong. But she convinced herself she was doing important investigation. After all, if Mr. Jameson was truly a scoundrel, she should reconsider her acquaintance with him.

What she heard confirmed her worst fears. Not only was he an unapologetic roué, he was a coward who had run away from a fight. And apparently, he'd lied to her about it. Charlotte could think of nothing more despicable.

Thank heavens, she couldn't decipher much of what the sailors were saying. But she was sure most of it was filthy.

Before she could be subjected to any more disappointing revelations, she turned on her heel and repaired to her stateroom again.

She was quite finished with Mr. Jameson. He'd shown his true colors. She would have naught more to do with him.

Of course, there was still the matter of the man's terrier. She couldn't abandon Campbell. It wasn't right to blame an innocent pup for the sins of his master. So she'd continue to bring him food.

But she vowed she'd not utter another word to Mr. Jameson.

Unfortunately, her promise was tested a few hours later. The chief officer, evidently unaware of Mr. Jameson's scandalous reputation, saw fit to allow the rogue to serve at supper.

Charlotte was already dismayed by the fact she still hadn't located her brother. She wondered if he'd drunk himself into a stupor somewhere. But it was doubly upsetting to have to face the undeniably charming Travis Jameson for the first time since learning of his disgraceful character.

Determined to pay him no heed, she nonetheless found her glance straying to him as he poured Madeira for the diners, offered up a basket of soft rolls, and dished out the salmon-gundy with surprising care and skill.

Once, when the silver-haired matron at the table, Lady Forbes, addressed Charlotte, she'd been so distracted by the way Mr. Jameson's fingers caressed the stem of her glass as he refilled it that she had to have the question repeated.

"I wondered if this was your first ocean voyage, Miss de Ware," Lady Forbes said.

"Oh. Aye."

Charlotte smiled, and then she couldn't think of anything else to add, creating an awkward silence, at which point the matron turned to the young lady across the table. "And you, Lady Adams?"

Charlotte glanced at Lady Adams.

The woman looked as if she'd seen a ghost. She quickly lowered her gaze and murmured, "I've never seen...never been on an ocean voyage."

Charlotte narrowed her eyes. What was troubling Lady Adams? The young woman's fingers trembled as she reached for her Madeira. She took a generous swallow, as if she meant to steady her nerves.

"Well, 'tis *my* fourth voyage," the elder woman announced, "and I can tell you there's naught to fret about, my dear."

But Charlotte didn't think it was the voyage that worried Lady Adams. And she observed, as the conversation continued blithely on, that the woman's fingers tightened on her glass whenever Mr. Jameson neared the table. Charlotte began to suspect Lady Adams might be acquainted with the stowaway.

Her suspicions were all but confirmed when she glanced up to see Mr. Jameson catching Lady Adams' eye and giving her an almost imperceptible nod.

That gesture could mean only one thing. Mr. Jameson *did* know Lady Adams. And there could be only one way a titled lady and a notorious rake like Travis could have crossed paths.

The nervous Lady Adams must have availed herself of Mr. Jameson's charms. She was upset, clearly afraid the scoundrel would reveal their acquaintance to her husband.

Charlotte, disgusted and perturbed, spared a glance at Lord Adams. He seemed a decent enough fellow and not uncomely. He continued to fork salmon-gundy into his mouth, completely oblivious to the drama unfolding around him.

By the time the sweetened flummery was served to finish the meal, Lady Adams seemed reassured that Mr. Jameson wouldn't expose her secret. She'd even begun to laugh and jest with Lady Forbes.

Charlotte vowed to forget about Mr. Jameson and his licentious indiscretions. She had more pressing concerns, after all. Concerns like visiting Elgin Garden. Keeping her orchids alive. And finding her brother.

She toyed with her flummery, having lost her appetite.

The captain leaned toward her to murmur, "I trust the accommodations are to your likin', Miss?"

"Oh, aye," she said. "Ye've been quite generous, Captain."

"'Tis an honor," he confided, motioning to Mr. Jameson to come refill his glass, "bein' entrusted to see the daughter o' Lord Charles de Ware to America."

She smiled, scraping a spoonful of flummery from her bowl.

Something struck her as odd about his statement. He'd made no mention of George, the *son* of Lord Charles. Was it just an oversight? Or was the captain subtly pointing out George's absence from the table?

"I fear I must apologize on my brother George's behalf," she said as Travis poured the captain's Madeira. "'Tis the most curious thing. But I've not seen him since we left port." She gave a little laugh and slipped the spoon into her mouth. The flummery was sickeningly sweet.

The captain chortled as if she'd made a jest.

She blinked, choking down the bite of flummery.

Then he drew his brows together in puzzlement. "Your brother?"

"Aye," she said. "He went to speak to the chief officer, and I haven't seen him since."

"Your brother," the captain clarified.

At the sound of the captain's consternation, the rest of the diners grew silent.

Humiliated, Charlotte felt the need to explain to everyone. "George is not normally so unsociable. I fear he may feel ill or...or perhaps lost his way on the ship." She didn't want to say what she really feared—that he'd gone off to someone's cabin and gambled away his coin or lost himself at the bottom of a tankard of grog.

"But, Miss," the captain said gently, "he's not on the ship. He only purchased passage for one."

Charlotte froze. What was he talking about? Of course George was on the ship. The captain must be mistaken.

And yet even as she had that thought, she realized it could be true.

George had been acting strange all morn, quiet and out of sorts.

He'd never returned to the stateroom.

He'd never moved the settee.

He'd never hung the curtain.

Perhaps he'd never even made the request to the chief officer.

All at once, she couldn't speak. Couldn't breathe. The flummery she'd just swallowed sank like a stone. Fear coiled in her belly. The faces around the table swam before her eyes.

Was it true? Had George bought only one ticket?

Was she alone?

All by herself in the midst of the vast, roiling ocean?

Abandoned and cast adrift on unfamiliar seas?

Suddenly she felt sick. The blood left her face. Sweat broke out on her brow. And she felt her stomach lurch in rebellion.

"Come with me," Mr. Jameson said sharply, banging the bottle down on the table as he seized Charlotte by the elbow.

If she'd had a shred of strength left in her, she would have resisted. But he would brook no argument. While everyone at the table gasped at the liberties he was taking, he scraped back her chair and hauled her to her feet.

"Here now!" the captain protested.

"She's ill," Travis called over his shoulder.

He half-dragged, half-carried her up the stairs to the weather deck, where the cold, fresh air felt like a slap across her face. She still felt nauseated, but at least the immediate urge to empty her stomach was gone.

"There," he said, securing her hands on the railing. "Better?"

She nodded.

She only felt better by degrees. But at least she didn't feel as if her knees might buckle beneath her.

"Keep your eyes on the horizon," he directed. "'Twill help ye keep your bearin's."

Charlotte stared out across the indigo water. At the flecks of white foam that floated atop the waves. And the orange-hued clouds that clung to the horizon below the darkening twilight sky.

She wasn't sure she would ever regain her bearings.

What had happened? What had George done? Why had he sent her off alone on this ship?

She shivered as the wind teased the bottle green silk of her gown.

Mr. Jameson quickly tore off his jacket. Not satisfied to simply hand her the garment, he placed it upon her shoulders, then turned her toward him to straighten the jacket and fasten the top button.

"Thank ye," she whispered, grateful for the warmth of the garment enveloping her.

It was shocking how quickly she'd been reduced to seeking refuge in the arms of the very scapegrace she'd hoped to avoid.

Yet his eyes as he gazed down at her were full of genuine empathy and concern.

Suddenly it felt like this man she'd barely met was her only friend in the world.

It was no wonder, she thought, the handsome rake was able to talk so many lasses out of their unmentionables.

Travis regretted having to strong-arm Miss de Ware to the weather deck. But he knew if he'd waited one more instant, the poor lass would have cast up her accounts all across the captain's dining table.

Sometimes, when attempting an unpleasant but necessary task, like setting a bone or removing a splinter, expeditiousness was best.

He was just as relieved for the breath of fresh air anyway. Seeing one of his former patients on the arm of her husband in the intimate quarters of the saloon had unsettled him. He wondered if he'd leaped from the frying pan into the fire. On board a ship, there was no escaping a jealous spouse.

Her anxious manner certainly didn't help things. She looked like she might blurt out a damning confession at any moment.

Fortunately, he was able to catch her eye and give her a nod to assure her of his discretion. He meant to feign ignorance. No secret would be spilled from his lips. As far as anyone knew, they had never met.

Lady Adams seemed to trust him after that. He felt he could be certain of her silence on the matter.

As far as his current patient, Miss de Ware would be easier to cure than Lady Adams had been. She was suffering from shock and seasickness. Lingering on deck a while would cure her seasickness. As for her shock…

"Why?" she asked, gazing up at him with eyes as wide and blue as the evening sea. "Why would George send me alone to America?"

Why indeed? He couldn't say. In his view, a man would have to be mad to abandon his sister among the sort of riff raff that inhabited a packet ship.

He might not be able to solve her predicament. But he could bloody well offer her his protection.

"That I don't know, Miss. But ye've no cause for worry. I'll watch o'er ye. 'Tis the least I can do to repay ye for your kindness." He placed reassuring palms lightly on her shoulders. "Ye have my word. I vow I'll defend ye and see ye safely to port."

"Ye will?" Despite her dire situation, she lifted a brow, and an involuntary giggle erupted from her, startling him. "And who will defend me from *ye?*"

Her remark set him back on his heels. He released her like a hot coal. "What do ye mean?"

She seemed to regret her accusation almost at once. "I'm sorry, Mr. Jameson. 'Tis a kind offer. But I fear your reputation as a villain precedes ye."

He frowned. She'd known him less than a day. How could she already have formed an opinion about him?

Then he remembered the crew. Perhaps one of the loose-lipped sailors had warned Miss de Ware about trafficking with a scoundrel like him.

"I must protest, Miss de Ware. I assure ye my reputation is largely unfounded."

"Is it?"

Her eyes dipped to his mouth, as if judging whether lies fell from his lips. Then, though he was sure she wasn't aware of it, she wet her lips with the tip of her tongue.

If she'd known how inviting a gesture that was, she never would have made it. Especially not toward a man she considered a villain.

But something about the way she was staring at his mouth and the languid drift of her gaze back up to his eyes made him see her—not as a patient and not as an innocent he'd just vowed to protect—but as a woman.

A beautiful woman.

A desirable woman.

For the first time in his life, he almost wished he *were* a rake. In that moment, with the sea breeze gently blowing her dark curls, her dreamy eyes fixed on his, her delicate shoulders dwarfed beneath the oversized sailor's coat, he wanted naught more than to plant a long, lingering kiss on her alluring mouth.

"A Christmas gift," she murmured.

"I beg your pardon?" For one mad moment, Travis thought she might have read his mind.

"George said 'twas like a Christmas gift, goin' to New York."

Travis frowned. It appeared they *would* arrive just before Christmas. "Aye?"

"Maybe he couldn't afford the passage for two," she said hopefully. "Maybe he was too ashamed to tell me." She tucked the corner of her tempting lip under her teeth. "He knew how much I wanted to see Elgin."

"Elgin?" he said, surprised at the way his heart fell. He

suddenly wondered if she would let Elgin kiss that bonnie mouth.

"George promised me we'd go."

"And will this Elgin watch o'er ye once ye're in New York?" Travis might never avail himself of her charms. But he was still concerned for her welfare.

"What?" She was gaping at him in confusion.

"Is he an honorable gentleman?"

"Who?"

"Elgin."

For the first time since they'd left the captain's table, Charlotte's face dissolved into a grin of genuine amusement. "Not who. What. Elgin Botanic Garden."

His brows came together. He knew that name.

"David Hosack's garden?" he asked.

She gasped in wonder. "Ye know it?"

"I've heard of it." Every medical student he knew aspired to be like David Hosack. A physician, a professor of natural history, and an expert botanist, Hosack had famously treated the American statesman Alexander Hamilton after his fatal duel. With Elgin Botanic Garden, Hosack was helping to determine the usefulness of native plants, contributing to the field of medicine.

"George promised to take me there," she said, her eyes alight. Then, as if a cloud passed across her face, they dimmed. She realized her brother's promises were empty now.

"I'll take ye to Elgin," he blurted out.

"What?"

He shrugged. "Why not? 'Twould be of interest to me as well."

"'Twould?"

He nodded.

If he'd stopped to think for one instant, he would never have made such a rash promise. The lass was not his responsibility.

She probably didn't even want to be seen with a man of his questionable virtue. Besides, Travis had much bigger problems of his own to solve. He also didn't have a pence to his name.

But he couldn't bear to see the disappointment in her face.

Surgeons were supposed to fix people, damn it.

And Miss de Ware desperately needed his help.

"I'd consider it an honor," he told her.

She rewarded him with a bright smile and a soft cry of glee. And when she impulsively reached for his hand, clasping it gratefully between her own, he hardly noticed the pain as she squeezed the rubbed-raw flesh of his palm.

It was a failing of Charlotte's—in addition to her reckless sense of curiosity—that she was prone to acting on impulse.

She should never have accepted Mr. Jameson's offer of accompanying her to the garden. But once her dreams of going to Elgin seemed crushed, all she'd seen was a dashing hero offering to come to her rescue. So relieved and delighted was she by his gesture that she completely forgot about his past.

His scandalous reputation.

His sinfully wanton behavior.

His adulterous dalliances.

And now she'd put herself in the position of holding his hand.

Not that it was unpleasant. His flesh was warm, and there was a nimble strength in his fingers. But now that she'd clasped his hand, she wasn't sure how to gracefully *un*clasp it.

One side of his mouth curved up in a smile. His eyes sparkled like dark crystals. A tendril of his chestnut hair had come loose and hung with rakish charm over his brow. Merciful heavens. The man was as handsome as Lucifer himself.

'Twas little wonder his affections were in demand.

But of course, she wouldn't hold him to his promise. Once

they reached New York, she'd release him from his obligation, which he'd obviously made in haste. She was sure her mother's cousin Eugenia would be glad to accompany her to the garden.

Meanwhile, she shouldn't remain in the company of such a man. She should stop staring into those glittering, dangerous eyes. And she absolutely must release his hand.

She told herself she would.

In another moment.

When a convenient opportunity arose.

"Ahoy!" one of the crewmen shouted. "What's goin' on there?"

Charlotte gasped. But Mr. Jameson gently extracted his hand and took a smooth step backward, salvaging her honor.

"Miss de Ware required a bit o' fresh air," he called back. "I'm makin' certain she doesn't tumble overboard."

The watchman waved to acknowledge his reply and turned away.

"Thank ye," Charlotte whispered, glad he'd made excuses for her.

He gave her a polite nod.

Then she smirked. A man like Mr. Jameson was probably accustomed to such subterfuge. He was likely an expert at slipping out of a lady's embrace and climbing out of a mistress's window.

"Do ye feel well enough to return to the saloon?" he asked.

She furrowed her brow. "Oh, I couldn't." She didn't think she could endure the double humiliation. First, her confusion regarding her brother. And second, having left the table so abruptly.

"I can take a quick peek and see if they've finished," he offered.

"Would ye?"

"Wait here a moment. And hold fast to the railin'."

Charlotte did cling to the railing, but not because she feared tumbling overboard. Her heart was racing, and she felt dizzy from her encounter with the charming Mr. Jameson.

The evening sky had now turned a deep purple, as dark as the markings on an *Oncidium pulchellum*. But unlike the flower's markings, which directed insects to the pollen-covered stamen, the cloud-covered heavens offered no direction.

Charlotte too felt as if she traveled under a starless sky, without guidance or direction. Would George have been so willing to send her off alone if he'd known in whose hands she'd end up?

Surely not, she decided. Yet a part of her was almost glad George wasn't on board. It might be wicked and reckless of her, but she was rather glad of Mr. Jameson's company.

He returned after a moment. "'Tis all clear," he said with a wink.

"Oh!" She suddenly remembered the wee stowaway. "I forgot to save some salmon-gundy for Campbell."

"I'll give him a bite o' my dinner."

"Ye haven't dined yet?"

"Nay, the crew eats after the officers."

"That hardly seems fair. The crew labors twice as hard as the officers."

"True enough. But sometimes," he confided with a lift of his brow, "life isn't fair."

She realized then how selfish she'd been, blubbering because her brother had sent her to New York on her own. At least she had a seat at the captain's table. And family with whom to spend Christmas in New York. And return passage to Scotland.

Poor Mr. Jameson had been stowed away against his wishes. He was forced to do hard labor lest he be tossed overboard. And he'd arrive in America with nary a cent.

"Shall we?" he said, offering his arm.

For a roué, he had very good manners. He helped her down the steps and accompanied her to her stateroom.

Then, in typical physician fashion, he lowered his brows and advised, "If ye feel a twinge o' seasickness again, ring for an officer to prop open your windows. The fresh air should settle your constitution."

"Aye, sir," she said with a smile, giving him a mock salute.

He grinned back and gave her a slight bow.

She had just entered the stateroom and closed the door behind her when she remembered his coat. She swiftly opened the door again.

"Pssst!" she hissed, "Mr. Jameson!"

He turned.

"Ye forgot your coat."

She'd begun to unbutton the garment when she saw his eyes widen. She blushed, realizing what she'd said and what it looked like. Without a word, he strode quickly to the cabin. She swiftly removed the coat and handed it over.

A trace of a grin touched his lips as he shook his head and left with prudent haste.

Securing the door behind her, she leaned back against it, sighing at her foolishness. Hopefully, no one had witnessed their exchange. If being in the company of the scandalous Mr. Jameson hadn't already ruined her reputation, she might just manage to do it herself.

CHAPTER 5

Eight bells had sounded when Charlotte blew out the candle in her stateroom and climbed under the covers of the large feather bed. Lying in the dark, peering out the window at the endless black ocean, she felt vulnerable and insignificant.

She'd been uprooted from her comfortable home. Enclosed in a wee, dark, wooden box. And sent on a journey to a strange new world.

Just like her orchids.

She couldn't be sure whether either of them would flounder or thrive. She had to try as best she could—for her flowers and herself—to maintain a semblance of order, a sense of normalcy.

Mr. Jameson was threatening that. He was not a normal part of her life at all. Like the waves rocking the ship, his presence left her unsteady and off-kilter. He was unpredictable, dangerous, and distracting. A man like him could make her forget her priorities and neglect her duties. He could make her forget who she was.

And yet there was something exhilarating about being in his presence. Something life-giving. And attracting. An energy emanated from him, as potent as the buzzing of a bee, tempting the tightly closed bud of her sheltered heart to blossom.

She exhaled into her pillow, unsure whether it was a sigh of dread or relief. If she wished to survive this journey, she would have to confront her inexplicable attraction to Mr. Jameson and decide whether he was a companion plant or a parasite.

As it turned out in the end, she needn't have worried so much. She actually didn't encounter Mr. Jameson much in the daily schedule she set for herself.

Her botany studies kept her busy in her stateroom most morns. The trunk George had brought aboard—the trunk he claimed contained his clothes—he'd thoughtfully filled instead with her books. So there was plenty to keep her entertained.

She left the orchid boxes open during the day to let the leaves soak up the southern sunlight. She took detailed notes and measurements, observing that the plants seemed to have gone into a sort of growth stasis. A few blooms dropped off, which was not unexpected, considering the shock they'd undergone.

She always stopped by the hold at midday to give Campbell a good scratching and to bring him a wee bite of dinner. But Mr. Jameson was never there. She supposed the chief officer kept him busy elsewhere on the ship.

On rainy days, she remained in her cabin, reading or sketching. She'd started making her own illustrations of her orchids, diagramming the various parts according to Linnaeus's designations. It was a challenging task, considering the variations in the flowers. In some, the *rostellum* was nearly impossible to locate, deep within the flower. In others, the size differential between the lateral *sepal* and the *labellum* was so minor as to be indistinguishable.

On sunny afternoons, she strolled above deck, enjoying the temperate breeze ruffling her muslin skirts and wafting through her curls. She squinted up at the sapphire blue skies across which stout ships of white cloud sometimes sailed. She gazed down at dark teal waves tipped with pale foam.

Still, she rarely encountered Mr. Jameson. Whatever deck she occupied, he was assigned work elsewhere. It seemed almost as if the captain and chief officer conspired to keep them apart.

Perhaps that was for the best. After all, once they arrived in New York, they would likely never see each other again.

She'd decided unequivocally that she would release Mr. Jameson from his promise to take her to Elgin. Coming to terms with the fact she was alone on this journey, she was determined to buck up and face her fate with courage.

She learned to bathe in a small tub of lukewarm rainwater. To fall asleep in the cradle of the sea. To use a bucket of ocean water for a chamberpot. Even to enjoy a tankard of grog.

There was no reason she couldn't employ this newfound independence to find her own way to Elgin.

It wasn't until a fortnight into the voyage that she found her resolve tested, when the chief officer assigned Mr. Jameson to the saloon again to serve supper. Apparently, it was an assignment not to the chief officer's liking. He despised the stowaway and made no bones about saying so. But the regular server was suffering from some illness, and no other crewman possessed the finesse to serve the captain's refined guests.

When she entered the saloon and saw Mr. Jameson standing with his hands formally clasped behind him, she felt her heart leap unexpectedly. She beamed at him. He winked at her. And then she remembered her place and the other diners. The chief officer gave her a scowl, and she glanced away, making her giddy way to the table.

She'd forgotten just how attractive Travis Jameson was. How his mahogany eyes twinkled. How that lock of dark hair fell with lusty allure over his brow. How his lips curved at the corners with sly humor.

But seeing him now, she would have sworn he was even more handsome than before. A fortnight spent in the warmth of the sun and the invigorating spray of the ocean, hauling rope and swabbing decks, had weathered his fair skin and toughened his muscles. He looked vibrant and refreshed. Ignoring him proved to be a Herculean task.

She hardly tasted her food. She barely recalled what was served. And she almost forgot to save a bite for Campbell.

After supper, Lady Adams, the woman with the questionable past with Mr. Jameson, delayed Charlotte's departure, requesting a word with her in private. What she could want, Charlotte didn't know. She hoped Lady Adams wasn't going to launch into some sort of jealous tirade. Charlotte might enjoy the friendship of the stowaway. But she certainly had no designs upon him. Who would be foolish enough to encourage a liaison with a roué like Mr. Jameson?

Lady Adams would, she decided. Even with a husband of her own. She'd struck up some sort of relationship with the infamous rake. It followed that she might attempt to warn Charlotte away from a man she perceived as her property.

Nonetheless, there was no way to politely refuse the woman. Secreting the napkin full of Campbell's food among her skirts, Charlotte obliged Lady Adams, inviting her into her stateroom.

The lady gazed around the cabin in wonder, exclaiming at the elegance of the furnishings, puzzled by the dividing curtain that Charlotte hadn't bothered to have removed, eyeing with curiosity the books, notes, and botanist tools scattered atop the hastily made bed.

"'Tis a lovely cabin," she said softly.

Charlotte smiled, unsure what to say. She was eager for the lady to get on with whatever stern warning she wished to issue so she could take Campbell his dinner.

"May I?" Lady Adams inquired, indicating the chair.

"Please." Charlotte's shoulders sank as she surrendered the napkin to a table and sat across from Lady Adams. Apparently, the conversation was going to last long enough to warrant chairs.

"If I may be so bold as to inquire," the woman said in a voice that was anything but bold, "how long have ye known Mr. Jameson?"

"Mr. Jameson?" It was as she feared. They were going to discuss Travis. "Not long at all. I met him on the ship."

Lady Adams gave her a sympathetic, disbelieving smile. Then she leaned forward in confidence. "Oh, Miss, ye don't have to conceal anythin' from me. Ye see, I believe we may have somethin' in common."

Charlotte's mouth fell open. Now she truly didn't know what to say. If Lady Adams was referring to her adulterous relationship with Mr. Jameson, they had absolutely nothing in common.

"'Tis naught to be ashamed of," Lady Adams said sweetly.

Charlotte could only stare at the woman. Naught to be ashamed of? She wondered what *Lord* Adams would have to say about that.

"'Tis the very thing Mr. Jameson has been determined to prove," Lady Adams said.

Charlotte's jaw tightened. It was, was it? 'Twas a challenging theory, she supposed, to prove there was naught wrong with adultery.

By Perdition, she was beginning to despise Mr. Jameson. He'd obviously pulled the wool over this naïve woman's eyes. As for Charlotte, he wouldn't find her so easy to gull.

Lady Adams continued. "I just wish to give ye my best wishes, Miss. What he did for me was nothin' short of a miracle. I'm sure he'll do the same for ye."

Charlotte was stunned speechless. She felt her cheeks turn rosy at the lady's frank speech.

Then Lady Adams pressed tentative fingertips to Charlotte's forearm. "Most of all, I want to assure ye, ye need not worry for your reputation. Mr. Jameson is completely trustworthy and thoroughly discreet."

"How nice," Charlotte said, smiling through clenched teeth.

If he was so discreet, then how had Charlotte figured out their relationship long before Lady Adams' confession?

"Well," Lady Adams said, at a loss as to what more she could offer in the way of conversation, "thank ye for your hospitality." She rose, prompting Charlotte to rise as well, and gazed meaningfully into Charlotte's eyes. "Good luck with...with Mr. Jameson and...and..." She gestured to the array of botany materials, which were clearly beyond her understanding. "Your...pursuits."

Once she was finally gone, Charlotte snatched up the napkin of food and stomped out toward the hold, infuriated with the vile Travis Jameson and ready to give him the sharp side of her tongue.

But when she arrived, Campbell was by himself. He perked up when she came in with his food and began madly wagging his tail.

"Here ye go, lad," she said, crouching down to scratch him behind the ear. "Ye're a good pup, aren't ye? Nothin' like your villainous master." She hand-fed him a bite of roast chicken. "Ye'd ne'er lead a lady astray." He wolfed it down, and she gave him another. "Or cuckold a woman's husband." He made quick work of that bite as well, and she placed the next on the flat of her palm. "And then try to claim 'tis naught to be ashamed of." He slurped up the bite, tickling her palm with his tongue.

Then she had to laugh at herself. Campbell was a dog. They weren't the most discriminating of creatures. The wee black terrier would likely mate with any bonnie pup that crossed his path and see naught wrong with it.

It seemed Mr. Jameson *did* have something in common with Campbell after all. They were both dogs. And Charlotte couldn't decide which of them had less scruples.

For days the chief officer had kept Travis busy—repairing rope, polishing brass, cleaning portholes, and endlessly swabbing the deck with seawater to keep the boards from mildewing.

When Travis wasn't doing menial chores, he did minor surgeries. He'd removed a splinter from a young lad's thumb and clipped a fish hook out of a crewman's forearm. He'd suggested an extra serving of gingerbread to Lord Adams, who tended to feel queasy when the seas got rough. He'd even recommended the chief officer use goose fat as a salve for his blistered heel.

Campbell had fared well enough in the hold, being a good sport and pretending to enjoy his daily ration of lobscouse and hardtack.

But after a fortnight, Travis was convinced he could rule out ship's mate from his list of possible occupations. His complexion had grown unfashionably swarthy from long days spent in the sun. His muscles, which had protested at first, had finally given up the fight, and he could keep up with any of the seasoned crew. His palms were callused, and his fingers were stiff from hauling rope. Like it or not, he was becoming a seaworthy laborer who no longer possessed the refined and sensitive hands of a physician.

His shipmates were good enough company, with a talent for spinning yarns, but they lacked the intellect of his fellow surgeons. He missed conversation about the latest surgical techniques, the development of tumor removal, and notes from the lectures at the University of Edinburgh.

Worse, the crew was unable to let go of the notion that Travis was a "buck of the first head," the most wicked of rogues. So they nagged him for tales of his great exploits. As always, he claimed he was not one to kiss and tell, leaving them to wonder how unspeakably vile his acts of debauchery must be.

It didn't escape his notice that after the watchman had discovered Travis lending assistance to Miss de Ware on the weather deck, the chief officer had made sure that opportunity didn't arise again.

He couldn't blame the man. With the way the crew had painted Travis, he was not the sort of man with which a proper young lady should fraternize.

Still, it staggered the imagination how few times he even glimpsed the lovely Miss Charlotte. The ship wasn't that big.

So it was a surprise when, after seventeen days at sea, Travis was finally granted an opportunity to see her.

The crewman who normally served at supper had had a severe flare-up of gout, for which Travis prescribed rest and staying away from sweetened rum. It then fell to Travis to serve the meal.

He had to admit it was a relief to trade his bucket of seawater for a bottle of Madeira, even if he wasn't allowed to drink it himself. He could at last be reminded of the civilized man he'd once been and brush up on his gentler manners. He could also steal glances at the lovely Miss de Ware at supper.

She seemed to be blossoming in the fresh sea air.

Unlike some of the passengers the crew referred to as "live lumber," who claimed to be hopelessly bored by the long voyage, despairing of ever touching land again, she took to the ocean like she'd been born to it. He heard her mention her seafaring grandfather at dinner, so perhaps it was true.

And though she never addressed Travis directly, all evening she'd given him secret smiles that set his heart racing.

Too soon, supper was over. By the time Travis finished clearing the table and washing the dishes, the diners had already retired to their staterooms. Someone had left a piece of roast chicken on their plate, so he'd stolen the morsel for Campbell. The lucky dog would eat well tonight, better than Travis.

The rest of the crew would be gathering soon for their own dinner. Travis decided to feed Campbell before he joined them for their ubiquitous lobscouse.

When he threw open the door of the hold, he was so startled to see an intruder in what he'd grown accustomed to think of as his quarters that he almost dropped Campbell's treat.

Then he saw who it was.

"Miss de Ware," he said with pleasure.

She seemed just as startled as he was. At first. Then she shot to her feet with a frown and demanded, "What are *ye* doin' here?"

Taken aback by her hostile tone, he answered, "I...live here."

Realizing she was the intruder, she nonetheless lifted her chin to say, "I was just bringin' Campbell his dinner. I'll be goin' now."

He didn't want her to leave. He'd forgotten how much he enjoyed her company. Even when she was in a high dudgeon, as she seemed to be now.

"I'm sure Campbell's glad of a visitor. He likes ye, ye know."

She was flustered by his compliment and passed it off with a shrug. "He only likes me because I give him what he wants."

He grinned. "Dogs are not so different from humans, I suspect."

Her eyes went wide with astonishment and outrage. "I don't know what ye mean. I have nothin' ye want."

He would beg to differ with her. She seemed to possess a lot of what he admired in a lass. A kind nature. A brilliant mind. An indomitable spirit.

"I only mean that we're all creatures driven by our desires," he clarified.

That seemed to make her even more livid. "I assure ye, Mr.

Jameson, I am *not* driven by my desires." She lowered her voice to a hiss to add, "Ye will not make a wanton of me as ye did Mrs. Adams."

He recoiled in shock. "What?"

Even she seemed to sense she'd overstepped the bounds of politeness. She clapped a hand over her mouth.

"What about Mrs. Adams?" he demanded, narrowing his eyes. He wouldn't let anyone slander a lady's character. Not even Miss Charlotte de Ware.

"I'll say no more," she declared, snatching up her skirts to elbow her way past him.

He stopped her, seizing her arm.

She gasped. "Unhand me, villain!"

"I won't let ye drag a good woman's name through the mud," he said.

"Oh aye," she bit out, trying to tug free, "because what happened between ye is naught to be ashamed of, right?"

He frowned. That was true. "Right."

"Let go o' me!" she barked.

He had no choice then but to do as she asked.

"Ye're despicable," she seethed, sidling past.

That hurt and enraged him. He turned on her with all the force of his frustration.

"I'm despicable? Is that so?" He shook his head. He was anything but despicable.

"I've heard the tales," she fired back. "I know all about ye."

"Indeed? And what have ye heard?"

"That ye're a scoundrel and a rake. A scapegrace and a ne'er-do-well. A rogue and a rascal. A churl and a rake."

"Ye said that already."

"What?"

"A rake. Ye said that already."

"Ye're *twice* a rake."

"Is that so? And what proof do ye have?"

"I've heard it with my own ears."

He clucked his tongue in disappointment. "And I thought ye had more between those ears than stuffin'."

She gasped at the insult. Her mouth formed a great "O" for outrage. Then she clamped her lips in an angry line and closed her eyes to smoldering slits.

When she lost the capacity for words, she gave him a punitive shove. Her actions made Campbell join in the argument, barking in protest as his two best friends in the world sulked in silent but powerful fury.

"If that's how ye feel," he snarled, "then I won't trouble ye with my presence again."

"Fine."

"Fine."

Out of ammunition, Travis fired what he considered a final, futile shot across the bow. "And ye needn't come to the hold again. I'll be feedin' Campbell from now on."

For one instant, she looked hurt. But she recovered quickly with a threat. "Ye know, he probably won't touch the bilge rat stew ye've been eatin'."

"Better that than the hummin'bird's tongues ye've been feedin' him."

They were both too proud to take back their impetuous words.

She growled once, and then bit out, "Good night, sir."

She slammed the door with great force as she exited, making the candle in the hold's lantern gutter out. And Travis was left in the dark with Campbell, whose morose whimpers echoed the hollow pulse of his own sad heart.

It had taken Charlotte half the night to fall asleep. She'd tossed and turned in the soft feather mattress as if it were a bed of nails. Finally she'd managed to stop thinking about the despicable Mr. Jameson when she closed her eyes.

But she woke in an instant when some great force tossed her out of the bed and onto the rug. When she shook the stars from her head and tried to rise, the cabin reeled sideways, and she tumbled onto the wooden planks.

Wind screamed through the gaps of the windows like a keening widow. The books slid off the shelves, dropping onto the deck with a banging like cannonballs. Outside her door, she heard men shouting.

What was happening?

As if gravity had taken a holiday, the furniture shifted, slamming into the bulkheads, first one way, then the other.

Fighting paralyzing fear, Charlotte crawled across the sloping floor and battled her way toward the door.

The chaos was no better when she managed to open the door of the cabin. The lanterns in the saloon swayed wildly, sending jagged shadows across the deckhead and illuminating the panicked faces of the other passengers.

Her heart seized. She wondered if *The Fortuity* was capsizing.

The captain scrambled down the steps to their deck. His face was stern, and his hair was windblown.

"Hold fast!" he cried. "'Tis a nor'easter! Keep to your cabins! We're goin' to batten down the hatches and ride her out!"

With that, he climbed back up, closing and sealing the passage with an iron grate and a tarpaulin. But instead of making Charlotte feel safe, she felt as if she'd been enclosed in a coffin. She was sure the ship would either be blown apart or knocked keel-side-up. And she would end up at the bottom of the sea.

The passengers dutifully followed the captain's orders, staggering back to their cabins and securing the doors.

As for the crew, they were likely battling the storm from the weather deck, striking the sails and heading into the wind. It seemed a perilous place where one stray gale or rogue wave could sweep a man off the deck to his death.

She chewed at her lip.

Mr. Jameson was probably out there.

Which meant Campbell was alone in the hold.

There were trunks and barrels in the hold, butts and crates that could harm a wee terrier. Besides, the poor pup must be terrified.

Ignoring the warnings of the other passengers, she closed her cabin door behind her and zigzagged across the saloon. At some point, she'd ripped her lawn chemise, and it slipped off of her shoulder as she clung to whatever solid handholds she could find. In the passage leading to the hold, she banged her hip on the bulkhead when the ship rocked violently sideways. But somehow she dragged herself to the hold door, tearing her thumbnail on the brass latch as she lugged the door open.

Two frightened eyes shone out at her as Campbell cowered beside Travis's trunk. By some miracle, the lantern was still alight. But as she feared, the contents of the hold were a mess. Crates had come loose from their ropes, and a heavy barrel strained at its tether, tipping and threatening to break free. Parcels hanging on hooks from the deckhead swung like cathedral bells.

"'Tis all right, Campbell!" she shouted. "That's a good lad. Stay there."

But just as she took a step toward him, the ship hit a particularly rough trough, dropping with a sharp and sudden jerk. The deck disappeared abruptly under her feet, sending her tripping across the hold. Her ankle twisted, and a jagged agony coursed like hot lightning up her leg.

Campbell gave a loud yelp of pain.

Ignoring her injury, she clawed her way toward him.

When she reached the pup, he licked her hands and tried to get up. But his back legs were trapped under a wooden crate that had fallen onto its side.

While the wind roared and the wood of the ship creaked a dire warning, Charlotte gritted her teeth against the throbbing in her ankle as she found her footing. She slipped her fingers under the edge of the crate and lifted it up with all her might.

It shifted a few inches, just enough for Campbell to crawl free. Then, as she let the crate slam back down on the deck, the ship wrenched sideways again.

The last thing she saw was a lantern swinging toward her head.

CHAPTER 6

Travis had carved bullets from soldiers injured in battle. He'd removed goiters from sickly noblemen. He'd once sewn up a seven-inch slash made by a gentleman's sword. And he'd set bones broken in carriage accidents.

But naught had unnerved him more than breaking into the hold after the storm and lifting his lantern to find Campbell standing vigil over Miss de Ware. She lay pale and silent on the deck, surrounded by a sea of splintered wood and shattered glass, A trickle of blood marred her brow.

His heart dropped into his stomach. Despair threatened to paralyze his limbs.

But he shoved his emotions down. There was no time for them. He had to think like a physician.

Disregarding his own safety, he knelt beside her in the debris, planting the lantern on the deck by her bare shoulder.

He pressed his fingers against her throat, cursing the calluses that had lessened the sensitivity of his fingertips. Her skin felt clammy. But she had a strong pulse.

He bent down to her, lowering his cheek toward her parted lips. She was still breathing.

Then he lifted her curls carefully away from the gash in her forehead. The cut looked minor, and the blood had clotted. But the knot there indicated a heavy impact. That was probably what had knocked her unconscious.

He needed to rouse her. Current practice suggested that concussion could be prevented by keeping the patient awake.

First, however, he had to make sure there were no other injuries.

Starting at the midline of her skull, he felt for cracks or swelling, moving his fingers outward, and carefully lifting her head to examine the back side. There was a knot there too, where she had hit the deck. But it was dry. The skin hadn't been broken.

He felt the vertebrae at the back of her neck. They seemed in place.

Her clavicle was intact. He swiftly examined each arm from shoulder to wrist—*humerus, ulna, radius*—but found no breaks or swelling.

He ran his fingers gingerly along each of her ribs, a simple task through the thin lawn of her chemise. They appeared to be unharmed.

He flipped her chemise up with brusque efficiency to check her lower limbs. Cradling her left heel in one hand, he gently lifted her leg. The flesh was bruised. But the *femur, patella, tibia,* and *fibula* appeared straight.

Lowering her limb, he moved to her right leg. He saw the injury at once. Her ankle was swollen. There was no way to tell if it was broken until she was conscious.

He covered her limbs against for modesty and slipped her torn chemise back up over her shoulder. He'd learned long ago that the flailing a person did to conceal their body during an examination caused more harm than good.

Then he lightly patted her cheek.

"Miss de Ware," he called softly.

Her eyes twitched.

"Miss de Ware, wake up."

She furrowed her brow.

"Wake up, Miss de Ware."

She gasped in a quick breath, and she blinked. "Campbell!"

To his surprise, the dog woofed back.

Before he could caution Miss de Ware against sudden movement, she pushed up to her elbows, muttering to herself, "Campbell. Campbell's hurt."

Travis frowned. *Was* he? Before he could glance at the dog, she continued rattling on.

"Oh!" she exclaimed. "Mr. Jameson. What happened?" She pressed fingertips to her head, glancing at the blood on her fingers with minimal concern. "Has the storm passed? Are we safe? Where's Campbell? A crate fell on him and—" She tried to get up.

"Miss de Ware!" he interrupted, clutching her shoulder. "Ye've been injured."

"I'm fine," she insisted. "But poor Campbell..."

Travis supposed he wasn't going to get any cooperation from Miss de Ware until he looked after the terrier.

"Promise me ye'll stay put," he said, "and I'll see to Campbell."

"But I'm fine."

He pinched the hem of her chemise between his fingers. Sometimes a single action could say more than a mouthful of words. He flipped back the bottom of her gown, just enough to expose her ankle. "Ye're not fine."

She caught her breath, and her brows rose. "Oh."

"But if ye insist I look after the dog first..."

"I do," she said as he covered her ankle again. "A crate fell on him."

He smirked. The selfless lass cared more about a tough old terrier than she did herself.

"Can ye fix him?" she asked, worry wrinkling her brow.

"Let's see."

Campbell *was* injured. Though the dog put on a brave face, his back leg had been damaged. The skin hadn't been punctured, but the leg was swollen, probably cracked. Travis wasn't sure it could be repaired.

"Is it broken?" she asked.

"Aye."

"But ye can make it better, aye?"

"'Tisn't the same thing, treatin' a dog and a human."

"But ye can do it?"

He hated to dash her hopes. "If 'tis a simple break, perhaps. I can immobilize the limb to let it heal and hope for the best."

"Good." Then, in case he had any reservations about his skills as a surgeon, she added, "I know ye can do it."

She had more faith than he did. But then he'd learned to be a cynic when it came to medicine. Too many treatments failed. Too many remedies were based on tradition rather than science. He'd learned to keep his expectations low.

Now that Charlotte had seen her damaged ankle, swollen to double its normal size, she began to feel it. It throbbed with every pulse of her heart, and when she tested it, a sharp twinge warned her to keep it still.

She also grew aware of her state of undress. Not only was her frail lawn chemise ripped. It was also indecently sheer.

But propriety was the least of her worries.

At least the ship hadn't capsized. And now that Mr. Jameson was safe and whole before her, tending to her and Campbell, she regretted her verbal fisticuffs with him earlier. He might be a gifted libertine. But he was also a gifted surgeon.

"How are the rest o' the crew?" she asked as Mr. Jameson cleared out a spot on the deck to sit cross-legged.

"No one was lost," he said.

Charlotte breathed a sigh of relief. "And the ship?"

"She needs minor repairs. But we'll know more at daybreak."

He picked up Campbell and set the dog carefully on his lap. Leaning the animal against his inner thigh, he turned him so that his injured leg was uppermost.

Then, he picked among the shards of the broken lantern until he found two pieces of the smooth-edged wood frame.

"What are ye doin'?" she asked.

"Makin' a splint. I'll put these on either side o' his leg and wrap it to keep the bone straight."

"'Tis what I do to my *Orchidicaea*," she marveled, "to keep them growin' straight."

"Exactly," he said, measuring the wood against Campbell's leg. "These should do," he said. "Now I need a bandage."

She didn't hesitate. "Here," she said, offering him the hem of her chemise. "Ye can tear this."

He frowned at the delicate embroidery. "'Tis too fine for Campbell."

"Nonsense. 'Tis ruined anyway."

"Are ye certain?"

It was on the tip of her tongue to tell him she was sure it wasn't the first lady's chemise he'd torn asunder. But considering his heroics in the storm, she bit back the retort and nodded.

Unfortunately, when he clenched his fists in the fine lawn and wrenched them apart, the garment split, not in a neat few inches along the bottom, but up the front by nearly half a yard.

They both gasped at his faux pas. But then his look of horror suddenly struck Charlotte as hilarious. She burst into laughter. And the more mortified he looked, the funnier it seemed.

"My apologies," he said, which made her giggle even more.

Campbell barked, as if he wished to join in the merriment.

Somehow he managed to tear a modest four-inch strip of cloth from the bottom to wrap neatly around the splints. Though Campbell jerked once or twice in pain, he remained calm and trusting.

When Mr. Jameson placed him gently on his feet again, the pup shook off the trauma of his ordeal and limped off on his new limb to sit beside Charlotte.

"Now your turn," he said.

Distracted by Campbell's procedure, Charlotte had had little time to think about her own injury. But now she shivered in trepidation.

"Cold?" he asked in concern.

"Scared," she replied.

"May I?" he asked, indicating her ankle.

She bit her lip and nodded.

His fingers were gentle as he probed the swollen flesh there and turned her foot this way and that. But it still hurt badly enough to draw a few hisses between her teeth.

"'Tis as I thought," he said, resting her heel in his hand, "a sprain, not a break. I'll wrap it, and ye'll have to stay off of it a while. But it should heal with no complications."

She sighed, relieved. "I suppose ye'll need more o' my chemise?"

"Regrettably. But I'll fetch ye decent clothes from your stateroom and bring them to ye in the hold."

She chuckled. "'Twill doubtless be the first time ye helped *dress* a lass rather than *undressin'* her, aye?"

She'd thought her comment was lightly amusing, given his reputation was no secret. But he seemed to see no humor in it.

His face was grim as he cautiously tore a second four-inch strip from the bottom of her chemise. "'Tisn't the truth, ye know, what they say." He narrowed his eyes at her ankle as he slowly wound the strip of cloth around it. "But I don't expect ye to believe me." He overlapped the fabric, checking to make sure it wasn't too tight. "'Tis an unfounded rumor that's unfortunately grown legs." He tucked in the edges and declared her as well as he could make her for now.

He left then to fetch her a new gown. She remained in the dark with Campbell, forced to reconsider her opinion of the rakish Mr. Jameson. To be honest, she thought, scratching Campbell behind the ears, the stowaway *didn't* behave at all like a scapegrace. He'd been appalled at tearing her garment, and he was fetching her clothing to save her from embarrassment.

It was possible the crew had exaggerated his sexual exploits. But what about Lady Adams? What reason would she have to lie?

When he returned, it was in breathless haste.

"Will ye be all right to dress?" he asked, handing her her sarsnet gown of pale green, one blue slipper, and an oar.

"Aye."

"I'm needed in the galley. I'll leave the lantern here," he said, hanging it on a hook in the deckhead. "Take care. Don't put weight on that leg. Use the oar as a crutch. And don't even think o' climbin' any steps."

He turned to go, then turned back. "Would ye mind keepin' Campbell in your cabin, just for the night? The splinters are treacherous here."

She nodded. After he was gone, she dressed as quickly as she could, given the circumstances. She'd follow Mr. Jameson's instructions as much as possible. But there was no way she wasn't going to investigate the storm damage. Someone might need her help. And she wanted to see what had happened to her orchids.

In Mr. Jameson's absence, she made a unilateral decision. Campbell would stay in her stateroom until his leg healed. There were too many obstacles in the hold that could do harm, not only splinters, but barrels that could crush a wee pup.

Besides, it was a dark and gloomy place, not fit for a bright-eyed terrier. Mr. Jameson would just have to contend with those arrangements, for she didn't intend to ask his permission.

The two of them limped across the shadowy saloon unobserved. But when she entered her stateroom, it was pitch black. She'd have to wait until dawn to examine the plants and see how much damage they'd sustained. For now, she was just grateful the windows hadn't broken in the storm. The rug was dry, so no rogue wave had washed away her orchids.

Suddenly she heard a loud uproar from outside her door. A cacophony of men's voices. And the scrambling of feet across the saloon.

The hubbub probably had naught to do with her. But Charlotte's curiosity got the best of her.

"Stay here, Campbell," she said, setting him gently in the middle of the big feather bed. "I'll be right back."

Using the oar, she half-limped, half-hopped toward the galley, where she heard an argument raging.

The door was partly open, and the interior was lit by several lanterns. She peered through the narrow opening. Her eyes widened as she witnessed a horrifying scene.

The chief officer was seated atop a squat barrel. His impossibly crooked right arm was stretched across a chopping block. Several crewmen restrained him. Someone offered him a bottle, and he gulped down several swallows, then grimaced. His face was red, and he was sweating profusely. A crewman shoved a short, thick piece of rope between the officer's teeth. Every few moments he groaned with suffering as he bit down on the rope, kicking his feet against the greasy deck of the galley.

From behind the rope, the chief officer yelled, "Do it quick!" as spittle flew from his mouth.

The cook stepped in front of him, brandishing an enormous cleaver.

"Nay!" bellowed Mr. Jameson. "Put that away, for the love o' Christ!"

Charlotte flinched.

The cook hesitated.

The chief officer screamed again, banging his boot heels against the wood.

"Out o' my way!" the cook shouted.

"Ye bloody butcher!" Mr. Jameson cried, seizing the cook's wrist. "I can fix it! At least let me try!"

They snarled at each other, at an impasse, while the chief officer writhed in pain.

"Fine," the cook decided, wrenching out of Mr. Jameson's grasp. Then he shook the cleaver at the stowaway. "But if ye fail, I'll be usin' this to lop your head from your shoulders."

Charlotte gulped. She was sure she didn't want to see whatever was about to happen. And she was just as sure she couldn't tear her eyes away.

"I'll need ye to hold him steady," Mr. Jameson said. "'Twill hurt like the devil."

The crewmen put their backs into it, Two young lads clung to the officer's legs to be sure he wouldn't slide off onto the slick deck.

"Hold his elbow in place," Mr. Jameson directed. He prodded the man's lower arm repeatedly until he found the spot he sought, a process that made the poor man whimper in anguish. Then he clamped the man's wrist firmly in both hands. "Ready?"

"Aye," the crew replied, bracing themselves.

Mr. Jameson pulled with all his strength, steadily, while the chief officer screamed in agony. After a moment, Mr. Jameson seemed satisfied and released his wrist. "There."

The chief officer slumped in exhaustion on the barrel. He spat the rope from his mouth, breathing heavily.

"Well?" one of the crewmen asked.

The officer scowled. Then he glanced down at his arm. "'Tis straight now, isn't it?" he said in amazement.

"As a rudder," another shipmate said.

"'Tis still broken," Mr. Jameson warned. "But if we splint ye well, and ye don't use it for a bit, ye'll be back to boxin' the Jesuit and gettin' cockroaches in no time."

The men laughed in relief, all except the cook, who probably felt cheated out of a meaty bone to flavor his stew.

While Mr. Jameson fashioned a splint for the chief officer, the rest of the crew dispersed. Quickly, before she could get caught, Charlotte hobbled back to her stateroom.

Campbell, overwhelmed from all the excitement, had fallen asleep where she left him.

Charlotte, just as weary, curled up beside him in her clothes.

But she couldn't drift off so easily. Her brain was spinning with everything that had happened in the last day.

Beginning with her embarrassing discussion with Lady Adams.

Her wretched quarrel with Mr. Jameson.

The destructive and terrifying impact of the storm.

The stowaway's heroism in the face of danger. And his considerable skill as a surgeon.

Her opinion of Mr. Travis Jameson had been vastly changed. No longer able to paint him in broad strokes as a villain, she had to admit he was bright and brave and kind.

An honorable man.

A brilliant physician.

A loyal shipmate.

Whatever wicked secrets lurked in his history, he had shown Charlotte naught but gentlemanly consideration and care.

He deserved her utmost respect.

She vowed she would never utter another unkind word to Mr. Jameson.

Indeed, she fully intended to forgive him the indiscretions of his past.

Many voyagers traveled to America to make a new beginning, to embark upon a new life. And so it must be for Mr. Jameson. She'd allow him to start with a clean slate, to become a changed man.

This time when she stroked Campbell's soft fur and closed her eyes, she was filled with new purpose. Her spirit at peace, she finally drifted off to slumber.

That peace was interrupted just before dawn, when she was awakened by Campbell's soft whimpering. She cracked open one eye and saw he'd managed to clamber down from the bed and was scratching at the door.

"What is it, lad?" she croaked.

Campbell continued to whine until Charlotte at last capitulated, rising with the sun to open the door for him.

Before she could catch him, he ran off.

"Where the devil are ye goin'?"

Neglecting her orchids for once, she worked her foot into her one blue slipper, grabbed the oar, and limped off after the runaway terrier. She feared he might leap off the ship and prayed he wouldn't take the steps to another deck where she couldn't follow.

ChAPTER 7

ravis was dead tired. He'd spent the first half of the
night fighting the storm and the second half repairing
its damage. By virtue of the fact he had saved the chief
officer's arm, the man had told him to take the day off and sleep
for as long as he liked.

But his dog had other plans. By the time the sun started to
peer through his porthole, Campbell came scratching and
whining at the hold door.

Travis rolled out of the hammock and stumbled to the door,
cursing as his bare foot caught a stray wood splinter among the
wreckage.

He extracted the sliver, and then opened the door.

His scruffy canine patient wagged his tail in greeting.
Thankfully, it looked like his splint had held. But Campbell
didn't rush in to the hold. He simply waited expectantly at the
door.

"What?" Travis snapped, running a weary hand through his
tangled hair.

Then he noticed his second patient hobbling toward him
with the aid of an oar, wearing her soft green gown and one
blue shoe.

Travis straightened and cleared his throat, smoothing his rumpled slops.

"Miss de Ware."

"Ye must call me Charlotte," she said, surprising him. "Please."

"Charlotte," he repeated. Her name was as lovely as she was. She still had a bit of crusted blood on her brow. But her color was much better today. And she seemed to have mastered the oar as a crutch. Temporarily distracted by his role as a physician, he almost forgot his manners. "And ye—ye must call me Travis, o' course."

"Travis."

He realized she was the first person in a long while who'd called him that. To his friends, he was Jameson. To his patients, Mr. Jameson. And the ship's crew seemed determined to address him as Sawbones, despite his demonstrated distaste for amputation.

He decided he rather liked the sound of his name on her lips.

"How are ye feelin'?" he asked.

"Remarkably well." Her blue eyes sparkled like the sun-tipped ocean. "But I'm afraid this wee lad missed ye terribly."

Travis shook his head at the dog. "Foolish, faithful pup. Ye'd rather languish in the dank hold with me when ye could spend the night on a soft feather bed?"

"I fear he prizes loyalty over luxury and won't stay where he's put as long as his master isn't there," she said, clucking her tongue.

Travis furrowed his brow. He hated to inconvenience Miss de Ware—Charlotte, he corrected—by making her keep the dog in her quarters. But he'd need to thoroughly sweep the splinters of wood and glass from the deck of the hold before it was safe to let Campbell return.

Before he could tell her he'd start on the task straightaway, she added, "And so I believe ye should share the stateroom with us."

She might have knocked him over with a feather. Dumbfounded, all he could manage was, "I beg your pardon?"

"A curtain is already hung in the cabin," she said, "so ye needn't worry about privacy. Ye can sleep on the settee or hang your hammock from the deckhead. Campbell will have a safe place to stay while his injury heals. And the poor pup won't be hobblin' all o'er the ship, tryin' to find his master. So...are ye agreed?"

She made it sound like a practical solution. Almost. Until he thought about the consequences.

"Absolutely not," he decided.

"What? Why?"

"Ye said it yourself," he said. "A man o' my reputation—"

"Piffle! Ye said the rumors weren't true. And I believe ye."

Travis had learned long ago that the crisis of a life-threatening illness—or in this case, a life-threatening storm—made a person feel helpless. And when patients felt vulnerable, they were kind, forgiving, generous. Sometimes *too* generous.

So it seemed with Charlotte. She'd apparently forgotten their disagreement and forgiven him for his sins.

Her words and her trust affected him more than he expected. But he still couldn't let her hasty, heartfelt offer compromise her own reputation.

"*Ye* may believe me," he told her, "but no one else does."

"I don't care," she declared with a cocky tilt of her chin. "My father is Sir Charles de Ware. Nobody would dare question the reputation of a de Ware."

He smiled and shook his head. Her confidence was engaging and amusing. He wondered if the esteemed and no doubt protective Sir Charles de Ware would find it so.

"I insist," she insisted. "And if ye won't agree, then I'll have the chief officer hang an extra hammock in the hold, and I'll join ye there."

A laugh burst out of him. The lass was certainly a bossy minx.

In the end, she won the argument. Somehow, the way she explained it to the captain made him agree to her demands. The chief officer made no protest, mostly because Travis had literally become what he jokingly referred to as his right-hand man. The other passengers, who'd received medical attention from Travis for their bruises and abrasions, restricted their criticism to speculative looks. And whatever conjectures the crew made regarding Charlotte's morals, they were careful not to voice them aloud.

Charlotte's stateroom was luxurious indeed. The cabin was spacious, bright, and airy, with plenty of windows. Of course, her belongings were still strewn all over the deck, victims of the storm. Books littered the floor like stepping stones. Gowns in summery colors flowed out of upended trunks like spent blossoms. But the most surprising thing was the spill of earth and moss from one of the overturned wooden boxes.

"Your orchids?" he guessed, gesturing toward the flowers sprinkled among the dirt.

"Oh no!" she cried, rushing over to them.

"Ye brought them with ye?"

"Aye." She carefully righted the wooden box and began scraping up the dirt, trying to salvage the plants. "'Tis my life's work."

He raised his brows in wonder. "Ye're a botanist?"

"Aye."

"That's why ye wanted to go to Elgin," he realized.

He'd assumed Charlotte merely liked orchids for their beauty. But he should have guessed her true interest when she referred to them by their scientific name.

A curious excitement filled his veins. He'd found a kindred

spirit. To discover Charlotte was a woman of science was enticing. It was a rare person who took an interest in science. But even rarer was a scientist who was female.

The surprising Miss Charlotte de Ware was becoming more and more fascinating by the day.

"What can I do to help?" he asked.

"Naught, really. I'll just have to pack them again and hope the roots and rhizomes haven't been too damaged." She sighed, adding, "But my research is ruined."

He knew how she felt. Of course, when one of his subjects was damaged, it ruined more than just his research.

"Please," she said, "make yourself at home. This will take me a while."

He also recognized, though she was too polite to say so, that she didn't want him poking his nose—or his clumsy fingers—into her research. He understood perfectly. He felt the same way. Research was a solitary pursuit.

The dividing curtain was a sail that stretched from bulkhead to bulkhead and deckhead to deck. On his side of the stateroom was a settee, a dressing table, an overturned chair, a bucket under the table, a wash basin, and two empty trunks. One glance at the short, spindle-legged, silk-upholstered settee convinced him to hang a hammock for sleeping in his half of the cabin. He scrounged up a few rags to toss into one of the trunks for Campbell.

When he was done arranging his quarters, he quietly slipped over to her side. Charlotte was seated on her hindquarters on the deck with a box in front of her and her injured ankle protruding from her gown. She seemed intently focused on arranging the moss-packed plants into their correct spaces in the box, making notations in a notebook beside her.

While she worked, he returned her furniture to its proper place and began restoring the library shelves, arranging the books by subject as best he could.

He was impressed by her collection. She had an enormous tome by Antoine Laurent de Jussieu called *Genera Plantarum*, on the classification of plants. A smaller book by John Ellis gave *Directions for Bringing Over Seeds and Plants, from The East-Indies and Other Distant Countries in a State of Vegetation.* He opened it to discover several illustrations that looked exactly like the trunk Charlotte was repacking. There was also a small, very recent publication, a report on various crops by an organization called the Caledonian Horticultural Society.

Most impressive of all were her two volumes by a scientist whose name he recognized, Carl Linnaeus. He'd only ever seen Linnaeus's important work on taxonomy when one of his patients smuggled it to him from the university library.

These were translations from the original Latin, and it appeared she had only the volumes related to botany. But they were still awe-inspiring to him as he sat on the rug beside the bookshelves, with Campbell dozing beside him, and carefully leafed through the pages.

Linnaeus had been the first to establish scientific terms to classify organisms based on their characteristics, by order, genus, and species. It was this type of classification that had helped Travis identify similar diseases in order to predict their behavior.

As he skimmed the pages, he learned that Linneaus classified plants by a sexual system of organization. A plant's class was distinguished by its stamen or male organ, and the order by its pistil or female organ. He emitted a startled cough, wondering what kind of audacious science the young lass was practicing.

Then his eye was caught by an intriguing passage about leaves serving *as bridal beds which the Creator has so gloriously arranged, adorned with such noble bed curtains, and perfumed with so many soft scents that the bridegroom and his bride might there celebrate their nuptials with so much the greater solemnity.*

Travis raised his brows. It seemed Miss Charlotte de Ware wasn't quite as innocent as she seemed.

He glanced over at her as she took meticulous measurements of the plants, recording her findings in a dog-eared notebook. Her unabashed candor actually pleased him. A true scientist had to discard modesty, after all, to look at nature with an unbiased eye.

He closed the book and picked up another—one devoted solely to orchid taxonomy, *Genera Orchidacearum,* by a botanist called Olof Swartz. When he set it on his lap, the book fell open to an illustration.

For one instant, his eyes widened. It appeared to be an anatomy drawing—one he might find useful in his own field of study—of the female reproductive organs.

But it wasn't. And when he realized that, he became even more intrigued.

It was the diagram of an orchid.

He was astounded by the similarity. The botanist must have been as well, for Swartz gave the orchids sexual characteristics, even boldly labeling the outer petals of the flower *labellum.*

Indeed, Travis was so captivated by observing the parallels between the anatomy with which he was familiar and the flower's structure, he didn't notice that Charlotte had finished her work and was standing over him.

"Fascinatin', isn't it?"

He slammed the book shut, waking Campbell.

She gave a little laugh. "Go on," she said. "Ye can read it if ye like." Then, realizing he might be a common surgeon who couldn't read, she added, "Or look at the pictures anyway."

It bothered him that Charlotte assumed he was uneducated. Which was silly, of course. He was accustomed to being underestimated. And it had never bothered him before.

Besides, what reason did she have to think otherwise? He'd been thrown into a crate as a nameless stowaway. The crew called him Sawbones and spread rumors about his debauchery. Most of the medicine Charlotte had seen him employ on the ship relied on skill, practice, and common sense, not book reading.

But he didn't want her to believe he was illiterate. He wanted her to know exactly who he was. As foolish as it might be, he wanted to earn her respect.

So he opened the book again.

"The lateral sepals," he asked, pointing to the petals in the drawing, "are there always two? Or are the variances due to a split in the *labellum*?"

Her eyes lit up. "Come," she said, taking his hand. "Let me show ye."

Half an hour later, he might not have been able to recite back to her all the scientific names of the two dozen orchids of the collection she'd shown him. But he could tell her every subtle hue that gleamed from her pair of beautiful blue irises.

How long had it been, he wondered, since he'd seen a woman through a man's eyes and not a surgeon's? Since he'd looked at a female with anything but clinical interest?

For the last year, he'd been so deeply engaged in his research that women had become mere subjects of study. His natural empathy had been cured early when he began to occasionally lose a patient. Eventually, out of necessity, he'd forced himself to maintain a safe detachment. Aloofness. Distance.

With Charlotte, distance seemed impossible.

Indeed, sitting here so close to her, he was tempted to trespass the mere inches between them and press a soft kiss to her flushed cheek.

But she suddenly exclaimed, "Upon my soul! I've been gushin' like a leaky boat for the last half hour, haven't I? I feared I've bored ye half to death."

"Not at all."

"'Tis just so pleasant to talk to someone who understands—or at least convincingly *feigns* to understand—my passion." She gave him a saucy wink. "But enough about my studies. I fear I've quite monopolized the conversation." She hobbled to her chair. "What about ye? How did ye come to be interested in medicine?"

He started to answer, and then noticed her bandages looked a bit snug. He dragged one of the small trunks over. "If ye elevate the sprain, 'twill keep the swellin' down. May I?"

"O' course." She smiled. "Ye know, for an alleged rogue, ye seem inordinately polite."

He gently cupped the back of her bandaged heel and rested it on top of the trunk.

Then he settled back down on the rug. Campbell limped up to him, and Travis scooped the dog up in his arms, giving him a quick scratch and settling him onto his lap.

"I lost my mother five years ago to a virulent cancer," he told her. "I suppose that's why I wanted to study medicine."

"I'm sorry." She looked sincere. "Did ye attend Edinburgh?"

All the best physicians—those with the wherewithal—attended the University of Edinburgh. Travis had neither the funds nor the social standing for higher education.

"Nay, I taught myself."

"Ah. Like me."

Travis frowned. He'd never thought of that. But he supposed it must be true. For a man, attending university was a matter of wealth and position. For a woman, it was an impossibility.

"I had friends at university who lent me their books," he confided.

"I had a father who indulged me," she said.

"When ye're determined, ye find a way."

"So true," she agreed. "Is your specialty cancer then?"

287

"Aye."

"What type o' cancer?"

He hesitated, not sure how much he wanted to divulge. Then he looked into Charlotte's eyes. The lass was genuinely curious and interested. Though she looked like a wide-eyed, innocent lass, there was a maturity about her that inspired him to be honest with her.

"The same kind that killed my mother," he said. "Cancer o' the uterus."

Her blank pause made him think she either didn't understand the term or believed, as most did, that it was a disease of prostitutes and women of loose morals. Neither assumption was true.

"'Tis a wretched disease," she said without judgment.

He nodded.

"And are ye makin' any progress?" she asked.

Her response made him want to grab her and kiss her. No one ever asked him that. Not even his friends. They only scoffed at his relentless drive to find a cure.

Instead of kissing her, he replied, "Some. But there are... challenges."

"What kind o' challenges?"

"'Tis a disease no one understands. Not even my fellow surgeons." He frowned. "They all think 'tis a...a..." He tried to think of a polite term she would understand.

"A venereal disease, aye? 'Tis the accepted wisdom."

"Aye, exactly. But 'tisn't true," he eagerly insisted. "The disease is an anomaly o' nature, not a failure o' morality. Accordin' to my research, it has naught to do with vice. *Or* virtue. There's no sexual transmission. None detectable at least. It behaves like any other cancer."

He was speaking more frankly with her than he ever had with another person. It was thrilling.

"And ye're determined to prove it," she said.

"I *have* to. Woman are growin' ill. They're dyin'. But they're sufferin' in silence. All because they're too ashamed to seek treatment."

"Like your mother?"

"Aye."

"But ye've found a way to cure them?"

He gave her a discouraged frown. "Not always. But I can treat them. Those women with the courage to come forward anyway."

Charlotte gave a little gasp. Then she furrowed her brow and narrowed her eyes as if she solved a difficult puzzle. "Women like Lady Adams?"

He recoiled with a blink. How had she guessed? He opened his mouth, ready to issue a stern denial. His reputation and his patients' safety depended upon protecting their identities, after all.

"She tried to tell me," Charlotte realized as the memory of her conversation with Lady Adams began to flood her mind. "But I didn't understand."

"She told ye?"

How Charlotte could have so misunderstood the sweet lady's words, she didn't know. But she was mortified to think of how rude she'd been.

"I think she believed I was one o' your patients." She gave Travis a sheepish smile. "She said what ye'd done for her was a miracle. She told me 'twas naught to be ashamed of. And she wanted to assure me o' your discretion."

He nodded. "Lady Adams is a kind soul. One o' my successes. But please say naught to anyone about it. If her husband were to find out..."

"He'd never understand," Charlotte finished, shaking her head. "He'd think his wife had been unfaithful."

"Right. Any man would." He idly pet Campbell's head. "Even the treatments have to be done in secret."

Charlotte's brain was whirling with enlightenment, alive with curiosity. And now that she was able to connect all the facts, she began to wonder about the conclusions she'd drawn.

"Why, Mr. Jameson," she accused, "I'm beginnin' to suspect ye aren't a philanderer at all."

He barked out a self-mocking laugh. "Are ye disappointed?"

"But ye let everyone believe that. The ship's crew. Me. Your mates in Edinburgh. That man who challenged ye to a duel."

"What else was I to do? 'Tis better they imagine I'm *swivin'* all the lasses of Edinburgh than performin' controversial medical procedures on them. Besides, I'd rather take on the guise of a villain than cast shame upon ill and innocent lasses."

It was the most noble thing Charlotte had ever heard. Here was a surgeon who cared so much for his suffering patients that he would stake his own honor and reputation on improving their health.

Her heart swelled until a lump lodged in her throat. Her eyes filled with adoring tears. And then Charlotte did what her father claimed she did best. Acted on impulse.

With a soft, admiring sigh, she leaned down from her chair, placed her hands on either side of his head, and planted a kiss on the good doctor's mouth.

How she expected him to respond, she didn't know. She hadn't thought that far ahead.

What he did was kiss her back.

Capturing her shoulders in his hands, he inclined his head and slanted his mouth over hers. Pressing tenderly at her lips. Again and again.

A faint moan escaped her.

A light growl escaped him.

His lips were warm and slightly wind-chapped. But she could sense desire and hunger on them, An answering vibration coiled within her ears, filling her head with intoxicating need.

Like a bee sampling an orchid, his tongue slipped out to taste her lips. She responded, blossoming beneath his touch, opening to allow him access.

Their tongues met and danced together until she thought she would faint from the intoxication of the nectar he offered.

And then the jealous sea slapped the ship, making it lurch and jarring them apart.

But as she gazed breathlessly into his smoldering eyes, her own eyes glimmered with the birth of lust and the promise of many more kisses to come.

As it turned out, Campbell found sleeping in Charlotte's big feather bed far more comfortable than where he was supposed to bed down.

Eventually, so did his master.

The crew and other passengers grew accustomed to seeing Travis carry her onto the various decks. And she grew accustomed to having him carry her, even after her ankle had admittedly healed.

By day, Travis helped her catalog the progress of her orchids, which helped erase the heartbreak of losing eight of them in the storm. In return, she helped him reconstruct his research notes, since his notebooks had been left behind in Scotland.

By night, since they were both creatures of science, they let their inquisitive natures lead them to experimentation.

Of course, being in polite company, they were discreet about their activities, and, being knowledgeable scientists, they were cautious about their intimacy.

But they managed to conduct a series of amorous experiments that left them breathless with the thrill of discovery.

They completed a thorough exploration of the art of kissing.

They determined the effect of touch on the various surface areas of the body.

Travis assisted her in experiencing the ultimate blossoming of her bud of desire. And Charlotte carefully indulged her own curiosity regarding the mysterious workings of human pollination.

Time passed in a blur of pleasure and enlightenment.

Not in Charlotte's wildest dreams had she imagined she'd fall for a stowaway who had a reputation as a rake.

Never had she thought, among a motley crew of sailors bound for America, she would find a man with whom she had so much in common.

And little did she know that in the span of just six weeks, she'd grow to love an ordinary surgeon so deeply and completely.

CHAPTER 8

Charlotte stared out across the still, gray sea from the weather deck, toward the buildings in the distance. The dull sky was the color of iron, and the clouds hung low on the horizon, as dismal as her mood.

While the other passengers chattered excitedly about finally seeing the last of the seemingly endless and temperamental ocean, Charlotte counted the minutes left with dread.

There weren't enough of them.

In less than an hour, by the captain's reckoning, they'd dock at the port of New York.

Life aboard *The Fortuity* had been an incredible adventure. One Charlotte wished could last forever. Because she couldn't bear to think of leaving Mr. Travis Jameson.

Her throat clogged with unspent tears of sorrow and frustration, for there was naught to be done.

Charlotte was expected to spend Christmas with her mother's cousin.

Travis needed to work his way back to Scotland, which might take years.

Even if, by some miracle, they managed to find their way to each other in Edinburgh, they would never be allowed to marry. He was a common surgeon with a reputation as a scoundrel. She was a gentleman's daughter, expected to uphold the family honor.

Even the arrival of Campbell, hopping merrily up beside her at the railing—his splint long-gone but his gait forever changed—couldn't cheer her on this glum day.

Travis dipped his mop in the bucket of seawater and swabbed the weather deck for the last time since the journey's beginning.

Campbell, who had free run of the ship now, limped across the planks to join Charlotte at the railing. She picked him up, placing a sweet kiss atop his furry black head.

Travis's heart cracked. The sight of the two of them together made his eyes burn with unshed tears.

He'd never felt so devastated. How would he live without Charlotte?

She was beautiful. Brilliant. One of a kind.

But as much as he'd miss the incomparable lass, he feared Campbell would miss her more, for there would be no way to explain to a wee pup why his best friend in the world had abandoned him.

All the breath deserted him. There was no use denying it. Travis had fallen incontrovertibly in love with Charlotte. The disease of love was incurable. And he was sure he would die of it.

Since there was no remedy, the best he could hope for was to treat the symptoms, keep the patient out of pain as much as possible, and give him something to look forward to.

With that in mind, he took one last swab at the deck, poured the remaining saltwater overboard, parked his mop and bucket, and strode across the weather deck toward the woman he adored.

"Elgin," he said by way of greeting.

"Elgin?"

Her false-bright smile belied the sorrow in her eyes. She'd been thinking about their departure as well.

"Elgin," he confirmed. "In a fortnight."

She bit her lip, as if afraid to hope, for fear that hope would be dashed.

"Say ye'll meet me there," he said with reckless confidence.

"But...how?"

"Ye mean to go there with your kin, aye?"

"Aye."

He took her by the shoulders and gave her a grim look. "I'm sure I can find my way. Saturday, two weeks hence. I'll meet ye there. I swear."

She gulped as she met his gaze. There were so many variables, so many unknowns, that the odds of success were impossible to calculate. But he could tell she wanted to believe him.

"Promise me," he insisted.

On the verge of tears, she compressed her lips and nodded.

They stood together at the railing in silent sorrow then—Charlotte, Travis, and Campbell—staring at the approaching city, until Travis was needed to furl the sails and man the capstan.

When they reached the dock, he remained on the ship, holding tight to Campbell, unable to say a formal farewell to the woman who was taking his heart with her. He watched while the sailors unloaded her trunks and ducked away as she briefly perused the ship, searching for one last glimpse of him.

Soon the bustle on the docks distracted her, and she was lost in a sea of people. Only then did he disembark.

The captain, impressed by Travis's seamanship, and the chief officer, thankful for his medical services, immediately forgave Travis his debt for the journey.

Now all Travis had to do was find his Uncle Reginald, start earning return passage, and discover the location of Elgin Botanic Garden.

"Miss Charlotte de Ware?"

The pinch-mouthed woman who spoke Charlotte's name had a severe look about her. Her black hair was streaked with the same gray as her narrowed eyes and the fur of her pelisse.

"Aye, ma'am?" Charlotte was having enough trouble keeping up a happy countenance appropriate to meeting one's kin. The fact that Mrs. Eugenia Smith looked as if she'd just sucked on a lime only made things worse. She had none of the softness of Charlotte's mother, whose twinkly blue eyes and sweet smile could charm a diehard curmudgeon.

"All these..." Mrs. Smith said, indicating Charlotte's trunks with the end of her walking cane. "They're yours?"

"Aye."

"No, this won't do at all." She spoke to a tall, lathy man beside her. "She may keep two of them, no more."

Charlotte was stunned.

The man nodded and began loading her trunk of clothing onto a waiting carriage.

"Wait!" Charlotte cried.

She quickly surmised from Mrs. Smith's hostile expression that there would be no compromise on the number of trunks.

"Please," Charlotte said, pointing to the two trunks of orchids. "Take these."

What she would do without a change of clothing, she didn't know. But her collection of *Orchidicaea* was irreplaceable.

"And please," she added, "take care with them."

He ignored her second request, but at least he didn't overturn the boxes when he hoisted them onto the back of the carriage.

Charlotte, determined to earn the stern woman's favor, gave her a polite smile and asked, "How am I to address ye, ma'am?"

"Rarely," she said with a scowl of disapproval. "But when you must, you may call me Mrs. Smith."

Charlotte blinked. Perhaps things were done differently in America. But in Scotland, a cousin was met with great affection. A kiss on the cheek. Or at least an affectionate clasp of the hand.

Instead, Mrs. Smith actually poked Charlotte's shoulder with the end of her cane. "Turn around. Let me look at you."

Charlotte was too shocked to respond.

"Turn," the woman repeated, "around."

Charlotte did as she was bid and was appalled when the woman stuck her cane between Charlotte's ankles, lifting her gown up several inches.

"You aren't lame, are you?"

Charlotte flushed. "Nay." She wasn't anymore, thanks to Travis's good care.

Mrs. Smith then scowled into her eyes and said, "And you aren't with child?"

Too stunned to speak, Charlotte shook her head.

"You'll do," Mrs. Smith decided.

Charlotte had never been so mortified. She'd hoped that spending the holiday with kin in America would take her mind off her broken heart. But now she felt like she didn't have a friend in the world.

Once Charlotte's trunks were loaded atop the carriage, the man helped Mrs. Smith into the carriage. But when Charlotte tried to follow her, the woman's cane blocked her way.

"You'll ride on top, with James."

Charlotte's eyes widened. But before she could sputter out a reply, James lifted her up by the waist onto the driver's bench on top of the carriage.

She was still speechless when James sat down beside her,

picking up the reins and clucking to the pair of horses to urge them forward.

So upset was Charlotte that she couldn't even enjoy the sights of the city as they traveled down the cobbled streets of New York. The horses clopped past block buildings crowded shoulder to shoulder. Huddled in her pelisse, she shivered, but not from the cold. Dread found its frigid way into her heart. It felt almost like Mrs. Smith was treating her like...

Mustering up her courage, she asked James, "What did Mrs. Smith tell ye about me?"

"You?" he replied. "Not much. Only that you came from Scotland. And your contract is for five years."

Charlotte's knuckles went white where she gripped the edge of the bench. She felt sick. Betrayed. Unable to breathe.

George hadn't sent her to spend Christmas with kin.

He'd sold her as a bloody indentured servant.

It took less than a week for Travis to find his uncle.

It seemed America had looked kindly upon the eccentric Reginald Jameson. *Professor* Reginald Jameson, he corrected. The man's keen interest in natural history had led to a position at Columbia College, where he'd become an esteemed scholar and a well-respected member of New York society.

Once Travis mentioned Reginald's name, he'd been welcomed into the college—and his uncle's household—with open arms.

Travis could not have been more delighted. Americans apparently didn't draw the same distinctions between surgeons and physicians. A man was judged by his talents and his intellect, not by his birthright.

Once he spoke to his uncle about his research into uterine cancer, the professor quickly found him colleagues with whom he could discuss and debate his findings. He learned about a groundbreaking surgery done in America a year ago by Ephraim

McDowell, a former student of the University of Edinburgh, in which a cyst was successfully removed from the uterus of a patient.

Within another week, his uncle, impressed by his lively interest, dedication, and meticulous notes, secured a place for Travis among the medical students at Columbia.

He couldn't wait to share his good fortune with Charlotte.

Saturday finally came, the day they were to meet at Elgin Botanic Garden. He got there at the crack of dawn, though he knew it would probably be hours before Charlotte arrived.

Even Campbell seemed to sense his excitement as they ambled along the paths of young saplings. The wee terrier romped about, wagging his tail, and even barking a few times as Travis softly whistled a chanty he'd learned aboard *The Fortuity*.

Midday came and went. Travis's heart leaped every time he saw a dark-haired woman in a fur-lined pelisse stroll past. But it was never Charlotte.

It was the middle of the afternoon when Travis shared the bread, cheese, and apple he'd brought with Campbell. The terrier's enthusiasm had waned. After taking one last bite of cheese from Travis's fingers, he circled and settled on the grass for a nap.

Travis watched the sun go down and the stars come out before he finally accepted that Charlotte was not going to show up.

She'd probably come to her senses, living in a fine house with her mother's cousin. Now that she'd returned to the bosom of her family, she'd probably realized she had no business trafficking with a common surgeon, especially one with a reputation like his.

She was right. He wasn't good enough for Miss Charlotte de Ware. He'd been fooling himself, thinking otherwise.

But it was with a sad sort of irony that he realized he had *become* good enough for her. Leaving his reputation behind in

Scotland, he'd become a new man in America. A man of respect. Of social standing. And eventually, of wealth and property.

Still, she had made her choice. Indeed, he expected her mother's cousin was tempting Charlotte with all sorts of eligible dandies who'd been born with prestige and titles. It made him feel ill. But it didn't surprise him.

He hoped one of them would take her to see Elgin eventually. It had been her dream, after all.

With a heavy heart, he scooped up Campbell, tucking the terrier under his coat, and trudged home.

Charlotte wept silently into her work-chapped hands. She perched on the edge of the straw-stuffed pallet in the tiny room that had become her place of refuge. The stars outside her window doubled in her tear-filled eyes as she thought about the hero she'd never see again.

She wondered if he'd gone to Elgin today. Waited for her. Left when she didn't show up.

He'd never find her. No one would ever find her. She was invisible now. Untraceable. A servant without a last name. Without a family.

She dabbed at her eyes with her apron. She needn't have worried about losing her gowns, as it turned out. She'd been given the castoff clothing from the previous servant. A servant, Mrs. Smith was irritated to inform her, had died before her contract was up.

Charlotte's only joy was tending to her *Orchidicaea*. She no longer had time to keep scientific records on their growth. Mrs. Smith kept her employed from dawn to dusk. But she watered them carefully and let them take turns absorbing the sunlight that seeped through her small southern window.

She wondered if they would last as long as her term of indenture.

Sometimes she wondered if *she* would last through her indenture.

She fell asleep that night, dreaming about leaving her tiny room forever and finding her way to Elgin Botanic Garden.

She awoke the next morn—and every morn for the next two weeks—to begin again her regular daily chores of helping the lady to dress, serving meals, and completing the endless tasks that kept a manse of such enormous proportions clean.

The de Ware family home was just as large. But they had an entire staff to manage it. Their servants were provided with comfortable rooms and decent food. They were paid a salary. They didn't have to live on table scraps and castoff clothing. And they didn't have to labor for five years to earn their freedom. Four years, eleven months, and three days, she corrected.

Just before breakfast, while Charlotte was violently polishing the silver and staring at the falling snow, imagining the revenge she'd exact on her brother, if and when she finished her prison sentence, Mrs. Smith called her aside.

It was Christmas Day. Mrs. Smith had a parcel wrapped in brown paper.

How Charlotte could have overlooked the date, she didn't know. After all, she'd been decking the mantles with evergreen boughs, hanging mistletoe, and placing ornaments on the gigantic fir tree in the middle of the salon for a week.

Perhaps she had blocked it from her mind, knowing it would only remind her of the Christmas she was missing with her family.

"As you know, I'm having guests for supper this evening."

"Aye, ma'am."

Mrs. Smith had told her that when Mr. Smith was alive, he'd financially backed exploratory expeditions all over the world. Every Christmas, he sponsored a supper for his beneficiaries, mostly so he could hear tales of their findings. She had continued that tradition, though she admitted her donations were not quite so foolishly generous.

"This is for you," Mrs. Smith said, handing her the package.

Charlotte blushed at the unexpected gift, for she hadn't gotten anything for Mrs. Smith.

"I want you to wear it this evening," she explained, taking the edge off of Charlotte's embarrassment. She looked at Charlotte's frayed apron with scorn. "I can't have you wearing that filthy thing."

An apron. It was a new apron. Of course.

"Thank ye, ma'am."

Charlotte donned the new garment, which was as white as the snow outside. She resumed her duties, trying her best to keep it clean.

To her surprise, as the hour advanced, Charlotte began to look forward to the supper. Mrs. Smith hadn't received guests in all the time she'd been there. It would be pleasant to see new faces. And if the guests brought tales of adventure from all over the world, it might prove an entertaining evening indeed.

She was reminded of the exciting tales she'd heard from her grandfather when she was a young lass. Though she was certain half of them were invented, every orchid he'd brought to her had come with its own origin story.

Suddenly feeling impulsive and inspired by the festive spirit of Christmas, Charlotte hurried to her room. Perhaps Mrs. Smith's guests would be impressed by her collection of exotic blooms.

She'd just finished tucking the last orchid among the sprigs of holly on the table when the first guests arrived.

Travis wasn't stubborn about many things. But he refused to leave Campbell alone on Christmas.

He wasn't particularly keen on going to a withered old widow's supper anyway. Wearing an ascot and tails and trudging through the sludgy snow wasn't his idea of an enjoyable evening.

But Uncle Reginald had insisted. He said the host family had historically given generous contributions to several professors at the college, funding their research. It would serve Travis well to befriend those kinds of benefactors.

So Travis had surrendered. But he'd insisted, if he had to go, then so would Campbell.

To his credit, Campbell had been an absolute gentleman all day. He hadn't barked at the neighbor's cat. He hadn't brought a dead mouse into the house. And he'd scratched at the back door when he needed to relieve himself. Every time.

So the three of them bundled up for the snow and traveled across town to the oversized gray stone mansion that dominated the block.

Reginald rapped the heavy brass knocker three times. A man in crisp livery answered the door. He lowered a brow in disapproval as he saw Campbell tucked into Travis's coat.

"May we?" Reginald prompted with a growl. "It's damned cold outside."

The man, startled, opened the door wide.

The entryway teemed with guests carrying on lively conversations. They were slowly inching their way into the drawing room, where Travis could hear a string quartet playing Christmas songs.

Reginald went in first, handing the man his hat and greatcoat and greeting a fellow professor he recognized.

Travis was just stomping the snow from his boots when Campbell let out a sharp bark and leaped out of his arms. The terrier slipped through the door, past the servant, and into the crowd.

"Campbell!"

Before Travis could stop the bloody beast, Campbell began squirreling his way between the guests' legs, causing more than

303

a few feminine shrieks. His snuffled his way madly around the entryway, hot on the trail of some invisible prey. Then he bolted into the drawing room.

Reginald shook his head, glowering at Travis.

Travis muttered a curse under his breath, along with a prayer that the hostess didn't own a cat. This was the last time he'd trust Campbell's good behavior.

Somehow Travis managed to squeeze his way through the milling guests in the entryway and the drawing room. For a moment, he lost sight of the wretched animal. Then he heard a few startlingly dissonant violin notes and knew Campbell was to blame.

Finally Travis spotted the dog sniffing intently along the edge of the room. Stealing up on the runaway, he was able to corner him by the fireplace.

With a crow of triumph, he swept the mischievous mutt into his arms. As he held tightly to Campbell, fighting the dog's efforts to squirm free, his eye was caught by the greenery gracing the mantel.

Tucked into the traditional evergreen bough was a trio of exotic yellow blooms with maroon markings.

A curious frisson of recognition shivered through him.

"Oncidium altissimum," he murmured. Why he remembered that, he didn't know.

He turned toward the quartet of musicians playing "God Rest You Merry Gentlemen." On a table beside the cellist, slipped into a vase full of ivy, was a cream-colored orchid with brown spots.

The music seemed to fade as the strange humming in his ears grew louder.

He peered into the adjoining dining room, where the table was set for dinner. Amidst the linen, china, crystal, and silver, strewn among the garlands of holly, were more orchids of yellow, lavender, and white.

Campbell started bucking wildly against his grip, and Travis frowned down at the dog, commanding him to be still.

Then he lifted his eyes again. Behind the dining table, in a servant's apron, looking as pale as a *Vanilla planifolia,* stood the most beautiful flower of all.

Charlotte.

His heart slowed.

The music disappeared.

Time stopped.

Then Charlotte dropped the pitcher she was holding. It shattered on the marble floor, bringing instant silence to the room.

Taking advantage of Travis's loosened grip, Campbell wriggled free and bolted across the dining room. His tail wagging madly, he jumped up on Charlotte, nearly knocking her over in his enthusiasm.

Travis too forgot his manners.

Still in his snow-covered greatcoat, he charged across the room.

Swept Charlotte into his arms.

And vowed he'd never let her go.

EPILOGUE

Travis purchased her indenture that very night, of course.

Charlotte said it was the best Christmas gift she'd ever received.

He insisted he'd done it for Campbell, since the wretched mutt wouldn't let him rest until he fetched her home.

Since Travis was forced to use an advance on his wages from the college to fund her freedom, his uncle offered to let the two of them live at his house until the debt was paid.

Reginald instantly adored Charlotte—almost as much as Campbell did. He fawned over her and bragged about her scientific proficiency until the botany department at Columbia finally agreed to let her serve as an assistant to one of the professors.

Just after the New Year, Travis took her to Elgin Botanic Garden, helping her realize her dream. Unfortunately, the plants were completely covered in snow. But he vowed to take her there every month so she could observe their growth.

Meanwhile, Charlotte's orchids continued to thrive in their new environment, lined up along the south-facing windows of Uncle Reginald's house.

She sent word to her parents, assuring them she was safe and happy and letting them know that she planned to be married in the spring to a promising American physician.

Rather than sending back a letter, the de Wares arrived in person, traveling aboard a packet ship very similar to *The Fortuity*. They claimed they had no intention of missing their daughter's wedding.

They brought a sober and remorseful George as well, whom they said was there to fulfill a debt of honor by serving out Charlotte's period of indenture for Miss Eugenia Smith.

Travis and Charlotte spared her parents the awkward details of how they'd met and fallen in love. There was no mention of stowing away or sharing a cabin. America was a place of new beginnings and social equality, and they decided their relationship should be no exception.

The wedding was lovely, modest, and uniquely American as well. The bride's bouquet was naturally comprised of orchids, and she delightedly recited the scientific names of each one to guests who commented on their curious beauty. When the priest grew suddenly dizzy and overheated, it was the groom who interrupted the ceremony, making him sit with his head between his knees while he applied a compress of ice in a napkin to the back of his neck.

The reception was peppered with lively conversations about research projects, maritime travel, botanic and medical discoveries, and the nation's still young democracy.

Though they didn't know it yet, before the following year, the newly wedded couple would give birth to an intrepid lass named Mary, who would grow up to marry her own world explorer, a Mr. Lawrence Hardwicke.

Lawrence and Mary, in turn, would become the proud parents of a daring artist name Mathilda, who would one day set forth from civilized New York on an adventure as a mail order bride in the wild frontier of the West. There she would find a love—as all the generations of her legendary family had—as true as the North Star, as eternal as time, and more precious than gold.

More books from the California Legends series:
Native Gold
Native Wolf
Native Hawk

ԸHANK YOU FOR
READING MY BOOK!

Did you enjoy it? If so, I hope you'll post a review to let others know! There's no greater gift you can give an author than spreading your love of her books.

It's truly a pleasure and a privilege to be able to share my stories with you. Knowing that my words have made you laugh, sigh, or touched a secret place in your heart is what keeps the wind beneath my wings. I hope you enjoyed our brief journey together, and may ALL of your adventures have happy endings!

If you'd like to keep in touch, feel free to sign up for my monthly e-newsletter at www.glynnis.net, and you'll be the first to find out about my new releases, special discounts, prizes, promotions, and more!

If you want to keep up with my daily escapades:
Friend me at facebook.com/GlynnisCampbell
Like my Page at bit.ly/GlynnisCampbellFBPage
Follow me at twitter.com/GlynnisCampbell
And if you're a super fan, join facebook.com/GCReadersClan

ABOUT The AUThOR

I'm a *USA Today* bestselling author of swashbuckling action-adventure historical romances, mostly set in Scotland, with over a dozen award-winning books published in six languages.

But before my role as a medieval matchmaker, I sang in *The Pinups,* an all-girl band on CBS Records, and provided voices for the MTV animated series *The Maxx,* Blizzard's *Diablo* and *Starcraft* video games, and *Star Wars* audiobooks.

I'm the wife of a rock star (if you want to know which one, contact me) and the mother of two young adults. I do my best writing on cruise ships, in Scottish castles, on my husband's tour bus, and at home in my sunny southern California garden.

I love transporting readers to a place where the bold heroes have endearing flaws, the women are stronger than they look, the land is lush and untamed, and chivalry is alive and well!

I'm always delighted to hear from my readers, so please feel free to email me at glynnis@glynnis.net. And if you're a super-fan who would like to join my inner circle, sign up at http://www.facebook.com/GCReadersClan, where you'll get glimpses behind the scenes, sneak peeks of works-in-progress, and extra special surprises.